ROYAL IN TROUBLE

It took several long moments for the ear-splitting clamor to sort itself out into shouts and curses, the sound of mighty horns bellowing, the shrieks of panicked animals, and the hoarse cries of wounded warriors.

Her head ringing, Diligence gaped in disbelief at the roil of bright shapes that twisted and lunged just beyond the wagon. A second ago there had been nothing but rain between her and the sloping walls of the basin. Now armored warriors were everywhere, their battling shapes blotting out the gray sky, filling the empty hollow like a mad tide from edge to edge.

"Where—" She lifted her arm to shield her face as a pair of elaborately costumed combatants—the nearer clad in overlapping plates of jet and scarlet, his opponent a shimmer of gold mail dressed with green—came together in a fierce clash of arms directly outside her window. She flinched back as two mounted warriors reared high on massive steeds. A quartet of hooves shod with spike-edged metal slashed the air inches from her nose. . .

Might and Magic

Book One: The Dreamwright

Geary Gravel

A Del Rey® Book

BALLANTINE BOOKS • NEW YORK

A Del Rey® Book
Published by Ballantine Books

Copyright © 1995 by Bill Fawcett & Associates

"Might & Magic" is a registered trademark of New World Computing.

Library of Congress Catalog Card Number: 94-94646

ISBN 0-345-38292-7

Manufactured in the United States of America

First Edition: February 1995

10 9 8 7 6 5 4 3 2 1

This book is dedicated
with gratitude and admiration to JACK VANCE, whose expertly wrought dreams have for many years demonstrated
the incredible power and beauty inherent in words.

ONE

NEATNESS REWARDED

Hitch was rinsing out his breakfast bowl when the stonecrush attacked the camp.

He had waited patiently for the marchmaster to settle his bulk against a mossy log for his customary early-morning nap before sneaking out of the clearing. Any nod the older man gave to the virtues of cleanliness was confined to carelessly swabbing out his own bowl with the coarse cloth over his elbow, and he expected his pack-man to follow suit without complaint. Hitch had already been beaten twice for disobedience on the journey. It had occurred to him that if he kept on at that rate, he would be black and blue by the time they reached Waterside. So he sat with arms clasped around his knees, his grummidge-smeared bowl on the grass at his side, and watched one of the travelers mend a tear in her backsack while he waited.

Finally his master's snores began to growl through the crisp autumn air. A quick look around assured Hitch that the others were occupied with their usual pastimes: the silent woman at her mending, the bug-eyed twins bickering over a game of dig-the-ditch, the fat salver teasing the pointers with a scrap of grayish meat, and so forth. Hitch tugged on his ill-fitting boots, rose with a grimace for his pinched toes, and slipped unnoticed from the clearing.

The rank brown grass was stiff with last night's heavy frost. It crunched underfoot as he made his way with care through the iron thicket that sprawled over the incline to the south side of the campsite. Once clear of the brambles, he sauntered down to the shallow creek that tripped and gurgled some fifty yards below.

A small garrison of spitfrogs puffed out their cheeks and aimed tiny streams of greenish water at his ankles, before abandoning their posts with a chorus of plopping sounds.

Shafts of amber-golden sunlight slanted down from a break in the clouds. Hitch paused at the edge of the creek to admire the tawny mist smoking above the water's surface. It might not be an exceptional day, he told himself, but it was going to be a good one.

He was kneeling down to splash water into his bowl when he heard the first terrified scream. The polished surface of the gourd slipped from his fingers and he lunged after it with an oath, wetting one leg to the crotch in icy water. He retrieved the implement and crouched frozen at the riverbank, listening. After a brief silence, the scream was followed by a welter of shouts and heavy crashing sounds.

Hitch mounted the gentle slope to the edge of the thornbrake. The ground beneath him was shaking convulsively, as if trees were being felled nearby. Tucking his bowl into his backsack, he crept slowly up through the thicket, halting just inside the outermost lattice of pronged branches.

Something huge bobbed and capered in the clearing.

Hitch had a glimpse of curved black horns and pale, wrinkled skin. He shrank back among the brambles, chest heaving, his eyes squeezed shut and his callused palms jammed tight against his ears. He could still hear the awful sounds above the rapid pounding of his pulse. After a while, the noises changed in character and volume. Finally they stopped altogether.

Hitch counted silently to five hundred. He dropped his

hands and opened his eyes. The clearing was still. He took a gulp of air and crawled out of the thicket. Scratches covered his thin face and hands, and little bits of rusty thorn festooned his loose trousers and jacket. A spot of blood welled from his lower lip where he had closed his teeth hard without thinking.

The other members of the marchmaster's party had fared far worse.

The stonecrush was the heaviest of the mountain hobs, and the one with the biggest feet. Hitch had only ever seen one once—and that time from a distance—when he was out picking berries with the greatfather of his village. With its grayish pink hide the color of lichenous boulders, it was adept at camouflage, often stalking its prey in absolute silence for hours before falling on it and stamping it to jelly.

The boy's jaw hung loose as he surveyed the clearing. The creature had accomplished its goals in a remarkably short span of time. The hummock of rock that had occupied the heart of the campsite was level ground now, while the flattened grass about it bore a dapple of dark stains.

The stonecrush habitually consumed its victims and their varied accoutrements whole, disdaining only artifacts of worked metal and glass, dyed fabric, and cured animal hides. According to the greatfather, the hob also had an eye for decorative patterns, a somewhat unexpected attribute for so massive a beast. Shreds of clothing and the remains of half a dozen leather backsacks had been arrayed in a ragged arc at the wood's edge. Belts, ankle totes, and haulstraps lay just inside the half circle like a mound of slaughtered serpents. In front of them stood seven pairs of boots, their scuffed toes pointing neatly inward toward Hitch.

The boy gave a low whistle, skirting a shallow crater left by the hob's right foot in the softened earth near the clearing's edge. I could take a bath in that, he thought, and rinse out my bowl besides, if I cared to wait for rain. Moving to the display of set-asides, he began trying on boots. He located two that fit him moderately well and discarded his own sole-worn pair with a sigh of relief. Newly shod, he took a few moments to stride up and down the clearing in an unsuccessful search for the marchmaster's jewel-headed walking stick. He clicked his tongue and gazed off into the trees, trying to recall if the greatfather had said anything about the stonecrush's propensity for eating gemstones . . .

Hitch gathered the backsacks together and sat down cross-legged on a clean patch of grass. He opened them one by one in his lap, trying to match them in his mind with their former owners as he combed through personal oddments in search of useful items. One sack, which he recognized as the property of the obese and foulmouthed salver from Tenhundersten, was filled with a surprising assortment of delicate lace undergarments. Hitch examined each one critically before saving out three pairs of the finest. The tatwork was of excellent quality; perhaps they could be bartered for food or lodging on his way to the city.

The little man whose mottled coloring had proclaimed him a native of the Upper Steppes had carried a waxy packet of preserved eels and a yellow incisor the size of a child's fist mounted on a hoop or collar of silver filigree. Trophy? Talisman? Hitch tossed the packet over his shoulder and added the tooth to his pile. Salted eels made his gorge rise, but luck was one thing he could always use in abundance—though the Steppeman's recent experience might suggest it was not an infallible aid.

The sack belonging to the gaunt, gray-faced woman who never spoke turned out to contain a flagon of bloodred wine and a loaf of oatbread the length of his forearm. Under a leather flap in the bottom of the bag he found a handful of hard little objects, like clusters of sharp spikes, wrapped in a wad of burlap. He almost threw them into the grass, then returned them to their hiding place with a shrug.

The other sacks yielded a quantity of provisions, a well-thumbed three-volume guide to common hobs and flickers, and a wicked-looking finger knife, which he strapped to his left hand.

The gray-faced woman's backsack was the largest and most intact of the lot. Hitch transferred the contents of his own small sack, then added the items gleaned from his late comrades. He eyed the bulging container pensively. Would a stranger be sorting through *his* belongings someday, choosing and rejecting his treasures according to the needs of the moment?

From the serpents' tangle of intertwined leather, Hitch chose a slender belt of figured gray encrusted with a frieze of tiny red gems. He wound it twice around his waist and rose to his feet.

He hoisted the swollen sack and balanced it expertly on one hip, adjusting the straps and rings that would bind it to his back. As he was fiddling with a stubborn catch, a gleam of crystal caught his eye from the woolly undergrowth at the clearing's far edge. He settled the pack and went to investigate.

Hitch snaked his arm into the wiry tangle and drew forth the marchmaster's walking stick. He hefted it into the air with a cry of delight, admiring it in the wan sunlight. The stick had first caught his attention two weeks earlier, at the start of the journey. The gnarled, three-foot length resembled an upside-down root with its tapered foot and splayed, fibrous cap. A bluish gemstone the size of a rockfruit was clasped in the twisty cage, as if the root had happened upon the jewel during its sojourn beneath the ground and resolved to capture it. Hitch drove the pointed end of the staff into the soft earth and struck an imperious pose, every inch the wily marchmaster as he shaded his eyes toward the wall of dark trees on the other side of the ruined campsite.

The only problem was that he had no idea which way to march.

Most hobs were as fond of the taste of bark and parchment as they were of flesh and bone, and the stonecrush had apparently gulped down the marchmaster's ivory map case along with its owner. To make matters worse, Hitch had seen no sign of the group's trio of pointers in the clearing's meticulous devastation. It was possible that the stonecrush had devoured them as well, sour-smelling pelts and all. More likely the agile creatures had made their escape while the great hob was occupied with their larger companions, and were even now running their frenzied circles somewhere deep in the surrounding wood.

Hitch pulled the walking stick from the ground and lowered himself to a hump of rock that had managed to survive the hob's footwork. How many more days had the marchmaster promised them before they reached the city— thirty? Forty? He looked up at the pale morning sun just topping the trees, and tried to recall where he had seen it yesterday at this time. As he sat pondering, a faint rhythmic noise reached his ears from the heavy growth of forest to his right. He held his breath, listening as the sounds grew louder. Something quite large was making its way toward the clearing without bothering to seek out the easiest path through the close-set trees. Gooseflesh prickled along his forearms. He glanced at the walking stick: perhaps the recent diner had suddenly felt the need for a toothpick.

Hitch heaved to his feet. Choosing a path that seemed to fall directly opposite the source of the disturbance, he plunged between the nearest pair of tree trunks and disappeared into the forest.

TWO

MESSAGE FROM MOTHER

Being made to wait sometimes had its advantages.

Diligence had used the long half hour spent sitting outside the door to the High Study to attack her problem logically and from several fronts, as she had been taught. After thirty minutes, she had narrowed down the probable reasons behind her father's summons to two, with the second decidedly more likely than the first.

It was possible that the overcook and her humorless staff had finally succeeded in unraveling the tangled trail that led to the perpetrator of last octant's memorable fiasco in the Southwestern Dining Hall. Possible—but only barely—with the incriminating batch of noxious chemicals still safely buried six feet beneath the summer spice garden. Diligence allowed herself a small grin and shook her head. Far more likely that one of the hallboys had spied her sneaking table scraps to the alter pens again last night. Sumpas had been roving the lower passages till well after moonrise, and it would be just like the runny-nosed little wretch to go scurrying off to his master with a highly embroidered account of Diligence's disobedience.

She sat with her legs drawn up beneath her on the ancient livewood bench and weighed her options. At the moment, the exact nature of her fate seemed dependent on a pair of linked variables: the degree of her father's ire over whichever of the two incidents had been reported to him,

7

and the amount of time he'd been able to devote to the choice of a suitable punishment. Diligence gnawed the knuckle of her right thumb. Fortunately for her, there had been a lot going on lately—almost constant traffic to and from the Hub over the last two weeks, not to mention the drought and the firestorms—which suggested that he would have had limited attention to focus on the misdeed of a wayward child.

Or so she hoped.

Diligence tucked her head down between her shoulders and hugged her arms around her waist with a mournful sigh. Truly she had no desire to spend one of the few weeks they had left in the South cleaning out the forward stables with a crumb brush like the last time.

There was a rustle of leaves and a creak of hinges as the door to the study opened. A tall man in a gray skullcap stepped partway into the hall. Diligence recognized Neek, a gaunt, unsmiling fellow who had lately arrived from the Hub to join her father's staff. "Harvest's Daughter," the man intoned formally, bowing his long head low. "He will see you now." Diligence rolled her eyes and walked past him into the dimly lit study, careful to keep her own head bowed low and to simulate such meekness as she could muster. A young scrivener stood yawning just inside the doorway, a talking board in one nail-bitten hand and a clutch of awls and colored styluses in the other.

Eyes down, she made her way across the circular chamber and climbed into the wicker chair that hung suspended from the ceiling opposite her father's desk. A small throat-clearing sound from somewhere in the room reminded her to unfold her legs and plant her bare feet flat on the mossy carpet. When she finally raised her eyes, she was startled and a bit dismayed to find old Pomponderant standing straight as a prayer oak in his purple robes behind her father's chair. The presence of her tutor was an unexpected factor, and all but confirmed that her infraction had not been taken lightly.

The large man seated behind the desk shared his daughter's wheat-blond curls and fair complexion. He followed her gaze. "Ah, Pomponderant," he said over his shoulder, as if becoming aware of the old man's presence for the first time. "Pleasant morning, is it not?"

The scholar gave a twitchy shrug. "A matter of perspective," he replied. "Those who take their pleasure in a warm sun and a brisk wind, with a tang of appleberries in the air, might safely employ such an appellation."

"Just so." The big man nodded judiciously. "A mudcreep, on the other hand, would no doubt shudder in its bog, cursing whatever unkind fate had ordained so atrocious a beginning to its day." He squinted across the room at the gray figure loitering by the door. "Neek!"

"King?" The tall man stepped smartly forward.

"Neek, you have my leave to contemplate the outer surface of my study door for several minutes."

The Hubman stood swaying uncertainly on the figured carpet, his narrow brow furrowed. "King, I do not—"

"Exit the chamber," the king elaborated. "And take the scribbler with you. I will summon you both when your further assistance becomes necessary."

Neek gave a curt bow and turned to go, a pink flush creeping upward out of his tight gray collar. The young scrivener followed listlessly, pens and board in hand.

Worse and worse, Diligence thought. Her father's private remonstrations were usually far more severe than his public ones.

The king folded his hands across his ample waist and regarded his offspring where she hung like a captive bird from the ceiling. "And how do you find the morning, Daughter?"

"Very well, Father." She summoned a shaky smile. "As

I am no mudcreep, its attributes strike me as pleasant in the extreme."

"Mmm. More to the point, I suppose: How did you find the night?"

"Also quite pleasant." She tried to keep the stammer out of her voice. "I slept straight through till well after sunup." Here it comes, she told herself. The table scraps for sure. She scanned the cluttered surface of the desk for a crumb brush. Damn runny-nose Sumpas!

"Your father, unfortunately, was not permitted that luxury," the king remarked. "I was awakened a good hour before dawn by the arrival of a message from your mother at the Forward Gate."

Diligence straightened abruptly in the pendant chair, causing it to swing slightly from side to side. "My *mother*?" It felt as if the room were spinning madly about her.

The king lifted a small leather sack from the desktop and weighed it in his hand. "The messenger was a creature in the semblance of a man made of glass. It waited patiently while we roused a scribe, then delivered its message three times in a loud and brittle voice. After that it would answer no queries, standing motionless outside the gate until the sun's first rays fell upon its transparent skull, at which instant it collapsed into a pool of smoking liquid."

"I captured a dram of the stuff," Pomponderant confided with satisfaction. He brought a slender vial from within his robes. "After suitable analysis, I shall consign it to a sealed chamber in my quarters and watch it with my eye device. Perhaps a glass infant will emerge by moonlight."

Diligence was staring raptly at the wall to her father's left, trying to construct the strange scene in her mind. "What was the message?" she asked at last.

It was her father's turn to gaze off into emptiness.

"As you are no doubt aware, the Wheel has lately been

beset by various troubles of the land and sky: storms of flaming air here in the south, with drought still plaguing the Herders just behind us, and vast stretches of restless earth awaiting us in the north. Three months past, the kings gathered in the Hub and a scrying was performed with cold fire and goats. The results were inconclusive." He passed the sack from palm to palm as he spoke. "The Keepers concocted a disturbing theory, that we who Turn have allowed ourselves to fall out of step with the Wheel and thus assured its imminent destruction. They justified their fears with yards of scrolls near black with calculation. Their proposed remedy was a correction in the form of a Wheel-wide quarter-turn advance, to be initiated as soon as possible."

"An advance?" Diligence looked blankly around the chamber. "You mean leave the South? So soon? The harvest isn't nearly finished here."

"Nor are the eastern crops yet ready for our scythes." Her father dismissed the proposal with a wave of his hand. "Fool's brabble. There were heated arguments, and it was finally resolved that the imbalance must go deeper than a simple forward movement could repair. It was decided that we should consult the Dreamwright for an answer to our puzzle. At the will of the kings, an envoy was dispatched to the Unseen Wall, there to entreat the aid of Amonwelle, who names the Dreamwright as kin. This morning her reply was delivered by the man of glass." The king took in a deep breath and raised his blond-stubbled chin toward the door. "Neek!"

There was a creak and a rustle. A moment later the Hubman stood before the king, the young scrivener blinking at his side. Diligence noted that the boy's eyes looked puffy and remembered that he had been turned out of bed before dawn.

The king set down the little leather sack and gestured to the scrivener's talking board. "Tell it."

The boy had to clear his throat twice before he could begin. Even then he was hard-pressed to keep the quaver from his voice.

"Convey greetings," he read, "from Amonwelle of the Rooted to the Folk of the Turning Land and to its Kings. The Dreamwright my brother does agree to your request for consultation, upon the delivery of these few tokens of friendship: that sword of El called Manscythe, that was misplaced in the Battle of the Stolen Air; nine new buds from a tine tree; seven alters in good health; and fourteen yeofolk with adequate provision." The boy paused for a gulp of air, and Diligence allowed her glance to stray to Neek. The Hubman wore a sneer of distaste, which he took no pains to conceal.

"In addition," the scrivener continued, "for my own trouble, a small boon is requested. That Amonwelle's daughter Madawyn accompany these trifles for a visit to her mother's land, the duration of such to be determined by we two." The message went on to specify the date and the circumstances of the audience with the Dreamwright. Finally the boy lowered the board and fell silent.

"Madawyn," Diligence breathed. "No one's called me that since I was a baby." There was a strange churning coldness in her belly as she searched her father's troubled face. "I thought I was to stay among the Turning Folk until my twenty-first birthday. That's four long years from now and more."

The king heaved a sigh. "It is true the birthpact stipulated that your first two-score years were to be spent here on the Wheel. Still, the request was not unexpected. Your mother has ever been a mercurial creature, constructed of equal parts caprice and impatience. No doubt she has grown restless for your company and welcomes any opportunity to hasten your arrival. Certain factions among the Keepers and their supporters in the other Advancements have already put forth the notion that we send an alter in your stead." He flicked a sour glance at Neek. "In truth, I would gladly do so, were your mother not certain to uncover the ruse in an eyeblink—and nullify the agreement in another."

Pomponderant stirred in the shadows at the king's back. "To say nothing of the consequences should Amonwelle take offense at so coarse a deception, and dispatch a brace of whirlwinds to devastate a portion of the Wheel in reprisal." The old man considered. "Or summon up an army of glass men to seal off the northern trade routes."

The Hubman snorted. "You magnify her capabilities," Neek declared. "The Standing Folk are people, for all their strangeness, who mix their blood with ours in accordance with ancient treaties. To allow your daughter to embark upon this perilous journey merely to satisfy a woman's whim smacks of frailness."

The room seemed to echo with silence as the king half rose to his feet behind the great desk. Neek quailed back a step, and even Diligence shrank from the expression on her father's ruddy face, wishing her chair were resting firmly on the floor, instead of hung from the ceiling like a bunch of peppers.

"Have a care, you gray little man," the king said in a low, dangerous voice.

"Memories grow short in the Hub," Pomponderant observed from his place in the shadows, "if you have forgotten the fate of the Effulgency during the Battle of the Stolen Air, when twice ten hundred candlemen were felled at the will of Amonwelle."

"I had heard a somewhat lesser figure," Neek said stiffly. "At any rate, there has never been a treaty between the candlemen and the Unseen Wall, whereas we—"

"Out," said the king. Diligence watched her father's fingers dig into the brocaded arms of his chair as he slowly reseated himself.

The Hubman lifted his pointed chin defiantly. "If I may be permitted—"

"*Out!*" Everyone jumped when the king's knotted fist struck the desktop. When the door had creaked shut behind Neek and the trembling scrivener, he returned his attention to his daughter.

"Diligence. Daughter. It is true there may be some peril in this undertaking." His eyes measured her gravely. "Yet I have noted a certain restlessness in your manner this past year, and I sense that a trek outside the Wheel may not contradict your own desires at this time, for all its swerve and stray." He nodded behind him. "Pomponderant has coincidentally announced his own intention to depart the Turning Lands. Should you choose to do this thing for your people, he has expressed his willingness to accompany you halfway round the Wheel and beyond till your paths diverge."

Diligence looked at her old tutor with surprise. Pomponderant leaving? "Of course I'll go," she said. "Of course."

Her father inclined his head in gratitude. "As your mother well knows, El's sword Manscythe reposes in the kings' storehouse in the Hub. It has already been sent for." He lifted the small leather sack again and unpuckered its mouth. "It may take some time to locate the requisite number of tine buds. The trees no longer flourish as they once did in these parts. At any rate, we anticipate your departure in four weeks' time, in order for your party to arrive at the meeting place at the agreed-upon date."

"Yes, Father." Diligence clambered down from the swinging chair, her head crowded with thoughts. What had begun as a summons to judgment had ended as a door creaking open onto a whole new world. As she turned to leave the room, her father cleared his throat. "One more item, Daughter. Cook will no doubt wish to prepare a great feast in honor of your leavetaking. Perhaps you might spend one of your remaining weeks assisting her staff in the sorting and labeling of the several thousand herb casks stored in the undercellar." He gave a small cough. "It seems a mysterious blight has ruined the summer spice garden and rendered its contents quite inedible . . ."

THREE

A BIRD ON THE SILL

Hitch crouched behind the rocks at the top of the hill and looked down. Below him was a tiny valley and at the center of the valley sat a small cottage. He had been watching the cottage faithfully for two days, absent only to search for food in the surrounding wood or to relieve himself in the bushes.

It was a tidy-looking house, round like a pumpkin and built of curved staves plastered with yellow mud, with a combed thatch of whipgrass for its roof.

Hitch examined it warily. He had heard of abandoned houses that were later occupied by hobs, who built nothing for themselves. The creatures kept up appearances for as long as they were able, sometimes succeeding in luring in unsuspecting travelers, whom they pounced upon and tore to bits with their long arms and slashing teeth.

The first night that he had come upon it, the little house had glowed with a cheery light, the circles of its windows warm orange against the blue-black of dusk. By daylight, nothing stirred: no one going in, no one coming out. On the second night, the cottage had stood dark, and Hitch's fears that he had stumbled upon a hob-house returned. Perhaps the previous night's fire had been burning in the hearth when the owner met his doom, and had simply taken a while to go out.

On the morning of the third day, something had changed. The front door was open.

Hitch sat behind his rock at the top of the hill and stared down as the hours of morning passed, with nothing moving below but a small gray bird that paused now and then in its wheeling flight above the valley to drop down out of sight behind the cottage. From time to time his stomach reminded him how long it had been since he'd had a true meal. For the past few days he had been reduced to foraging for berries and sugarbark. He shivered in the wind that roamed down from the distant peaks. His chilled bones encouraged reminiscence as well, numbering the ages that had passed since he had sat with warm walls around him. His stomach grumbled and he licked his lips. He was starting to long for the salted eels he had discarded weeks ago at the clearing by the iron thicket.

Hitch looked up at the cloudless sky. The gray bird soared beneath a bright noonday sun. It was common knowledge that sensible hobs shunned the open sunlight. He narrowed his eyes and looked down the valley. If he planned to venture closer, this would be the time to do it. Gathering up his backsack and his walking stick, he crept out from behind the rock.

He came quickly down the grassy slope, wishing for more cover on the unadorned ground. He stole forward silently, keeping to the blind side of the cottage, where stacked wood obscured the view from the windows. Finally he crept up alongside the yawning doorway.

It was dark inside. He considered rapping on the door with the foot of the jeweled walking stick, but could not bring himself to break the silence. Heart thudding, he sucked in his breath and stepped over the threshold, swinging his head rapidly from side to side to spy out anything waiting to spring at him from the shadows.

There was a little kitchen hung with dried herbs and a

sitting room with a cold fireplace. Hitch moved around slowly, squinting and testing the air. He could discern no odor of hob dung.

There was a doorway near the chimney. In the back he found a small bedroom that shared the fireplace from the other side. An old woman lay on a low pallet against the outward-curving wall. At first he thought she was dead, but when he stepped closer a floorboard creaked and she made a fitful noise, white fingers fluttering on the blanket at her breast. The room smelled of sickness. Her brow was beaded with sweat and her eyes rolled sightlessly in her head as he stood staring down. She was breathing in little gasps.

The shutters were drawn wide on the window above the pallet, and as he watched, a bird landed in it with a quiet flurry of gray wings. The woman seemed to grow calmer at the sound of its claws on the wooden sill. Her eyes drifted shut. When she opened them again she was looking at Hitch. He bent down as she lifted her chin, lips trembling as if she wanted to speak. "Roots and barley in the cupboard," she whispered. "Water in the well behind the house. Why not make us a soup?"

He found a black iron pot hung on a chain inside the fireplace. He brought in a log and some kindling and started a small blaze going, then chopped up the roots along with some dried pepperstalk from the kitchen, mixing in a handful of berries he had brought with him out of the forest. The soup smelled richly aromatic after his beggar's fare. He got his gourd bowl out of his backsack and divided the meal, bringing the old woman her portion in the small white pottery vessel figured with blue fishes that he had found on the hearth. She was too weak to feed herself, so he propped her head up with his backsack and gave her sips out of a wooden ladle.

That night he slept on the hearth, a cloak of dark green

wool he had taken from a peg by the front door as his blanket. In the morning the old woman seemed much improved, though still terribly weak. He unshuttered the window over the pallet to let the pale golden sun stream into the little bedroom. Then he warmed some water in the fireplace and helped her to wash herself.

Talking seemed to hurt her throat, but she asked him his name and where he was from, and he told her that he had been wandering in the woods for many days, hopelessly lost since the massacre of his party. The old woman had never heard of Waterside, but was able to describe in detail a small pass lying to the east of her valley that would take him swiftly through the mountains. Beyond the peaks lay a lake and a narrow stretch of forest, which opened out onto a wide plain where caravans of traders sometimes passed. The telling made her sleepy, and she nodded off in the midst of his thanks.

Winter was getting closer and the nights were chill. Hitch brought in more logs to stack by the fireplace, then busied himself with other chores. It was late morning and he was chopping herbs in the kitchen for their noon meal when he heard the skritch of claws on wood coming from the bedroom. When he looked in, he saw that the gray bird had returned. It watched him fearlessly with a bright black eye, tilting its head to follow him as he crossed the floor to the old woman's pallet.

"Shall I shoo it away?" he asked.

She shook her head with a smile. "She'll be gone soon enough," she said in her leaf-rustle whisper. The old woman lifted her hand, thin as a claw itself and ridged with blue veins. "Only stay by my side a little while and hold my hand," she asked him. "I might float away on the breeze, as small and light as I am, and I'm not ready for that—not just yet." Truly she looked frail and fleshless, but her grip was firm when he took her hand. The bird flew off when he settled down next to the pallet—not as if he had startled it, but as if it had somewhere else to be. Soon the old woman was tossing on the thin straw, her eyes roving in their sockets as she murmured words in a voice too soft for Hitch to make out. Her pale brow grew shiny with sweat and he feared the fever had come back.

Time dragged by in the tiny room while the frail figure stretched and muttered. Hitch had begun to doze himself when suddenly the bird was back at the window. Again the dry sound of its feet on the sill seemed to draw the old woman out of her dreams. Her breath slowed and she released his hand with a sigh. He went to get her some mint tea, and when he returned the window was empty. The old woman was smiling, her long hair massed around her face like a gray cloud on the straw pillow. "Such beauty on the land," she gasped as he helped her raise the tea bowl to her lips. "Sugarbarks afire with color, and the wind holding his breath; everything waiting, waiting for winter . . ."

He felt her forehead, barely able to make out her words as she raved on in her husky whisper about the valley and the forest that surrounded it, the clear, chill taste of the air above the mountain peaks. But her skin was cool and he found no trace of fever.

She had become clearheaded again by nightfall, and told him fragmented tales of her girlhood and her later years in a land far from this one. "And then, when my good Jova died," she croaked, "I knew it was time to yank my roots and follow the green moth again."

Hitch had been playing with a twist of brown grass in his hands, his eyes on the floor as he listened to her stories. Now he raised his head and looked around the room in puzzlement. "Moth? You saw a moth?"

She gave a silent chuckle. "I mean I was curious. I mean it was time to take a chance and maybe find out something new." When he crawled off to sleep on the hearth that evening, he found himself looking forward to the morning and to more stories of distant lands.

His host's strength seemed to be slowly returning. She was awake early the next day, and they spent an hour talking before Hitch went outside to gather kindling and dig up certain autumn roots from the small vegetable garden by the well.

When he entered the bedroom just before noon, he was not surprised to find the gray bird there ahead of him. The black eye followed him as the old woman beckoned him to her side. "Will you hold my hand?" She raised her thin arm with a look of anticipation. He took her bony fingers in his own and settled down next to the pallet. The bird watched for a few moments, then spread its wings and glided from the sill.

Again the woman seemed to slip into a fevered dream, and again the trance dissolved upon the return of the bird an hour or so later. They spent the afternoon in quiet conversation, with Hitch evoking much merriment from the old woman when he displayed the lace undergarments he had taken from the fat salver's pack back at the clearing. She taught him a bawdy traveling song she had learned as a young woman, and he went to his bed on the hearth with the melody still skirling through his head.

But the following morning she was much weaker. Hitch saw how the flesh drew tight across the bones of her face and knew that her recovery had been a false one. He stayed by her side during the morning, and when midday came and the bird appeared, he held out his hand to her without being asked. She eyed it longingly, and started to reach out to him, but then she curled her fingers up on her breast beneath the ragged quilt and turned her face away.

"Is there anything you want?" he asked.

She made a small motion with her head, as if she were too overcome with despair or pain to reply. But a moment later she did speak, and her voice was steady and free of any sadness. "I want an end to this fire in my throat," she told him. "I want to follow my green moth and see where it takes me. And I want you to have my thanks." She flicked her clouded eyes to the visitor that still waited in the window. "Remember now: gray and not very large, with a band of white just so across the underside of the wings. Not many in the south, I judge, but in the east and north she'll know you . . ." Her voice trailed off into a dry wheeze. She breathed unsteadily for a few moments, then began again. "If you can, drag what's left to the high place you watched from: behind the rocks where the little ones can get at it easily. Winter's nearly here and it's not been a good summer for them."

Hitch had never told the old woman about his days spent crouched behind the rocks. His own people used fire to bid farewell to their dead, and the idea of placing her corpse up there in the open air for scavengers to find repelled him. He was silent for a while; then he told her he would do as she asked. When the bird flapped away a few moments later, her eyes began their mad roving as before, then slowly drifted shut. They did not open again, nor did the bird return that day. In the afternoon, he carried her frail remains up the slope and laid them out as she had requested. That evening he brought the green cloak into the bedroom and curled up on the floor with it next to her empty pallet. It took him a long while to fall asleep.

He was lying there the next morning when he heard a dry sound at the window and knew the bird was on the sill. He opened his eyes and looked up at it, his mind cloudy with dreams. The bird cocked its small head at him, the black eye bright. He was still half-asleep, and as his own eyes drifted shut again he heard the flurry of its wings.

Suddenly cool wind blew in his face. His whole body

seemed to twist and turn in empty air. He looked around him in astonishment as the little cottage fell away beneath him. He soared up and out and over the land, gray wings flashing in the sunlight of the new day. Filled with a joy that ached in his chest, he circled the valley, dipping low after a while over the place where he had laid out the old woman's body. He hung there for a few quick heartbeats only, then mounted the growing winds and rose higher and higher toward the distant peaks, the whole world with its bright forests and hidden dells spreading out green and blue and orange like a map unrolling. Time fell behind him and he gloried in his flight. The sun was starting its decline when he finally began his descent back to the valley and the cottage.

Something caught his eye as he spiraled lazily down toward the grassy slopes. A thread of dusky movement snaked up from the broad river that ran bordered by evergreens to the west of the valley. He stooped above it on the wind, watching as the thread became a ribbon of dark figures, moving with a crafty, skulking gait that set his small heart pounding. He dropped farther down for a closer look, and saw that they wore helmets constructed of shards of bone taken from the skulls of men or animals, and that they carried strange weapons. In the middle of the line, a tall, boxlike device crafted from black wood swayed on poles set on the hunched shoulders of four of the skulkers. He dipped low enough to see that a single figure rode swaying in the shadows inside the covered chair.

Their path was taking them in the direction of the valley. Alarm tingling in his small body, he darted back toward the little cottage and the unshuttered window.

Hitch opened his eyes to find himself still curled up on the floor by the pallet. There was a scrape of claws against wood and a flutter of wings. He sat for a few moments, blinking stupidly at the jumble of images in his mind, not sure what to believe. Then he remembered the black line of skulking figures, the bone helmets and the curved weapons.

He threw the green cloak over his shoulders and gathered up his backsack. A hard roundness jogged against his lower back. He had planned to take the white bowl with the painted fishes to help him remember her. Now he removed it from his sack and set it gently on the hearth.

The jewel-headed walking stick leaned where he had left it by the front door. He snatched it up and sprinted out of the cottage, went several yards up the slope of the hill, and turned around in his tracks. Hurrying back into the tiny bedroom, he pulled the shutters in and latched them tight above the empty pallet.

He climbed the hill at a brisk pace and left the valley, heading toward the pass she had told him about, the winding pathway he had seen for himself as he rode the wind high in the golden sky. As he made his way through the bright-leafed trees, he thought several times to catch a glimpse of gray wings flashing up above, but the sky was growing dark with the onset of evening, and it might have been a trick of the light and the shadows.

He looked back over his shoulder when he reached the pass. He could see nothing of the valley in the gathering darkness.

No doubt they had found their way to the cottage by now. Hitch adjusted his pack and walked on, a thin, determined smile on his lips. Whatever their purpose, they would find no one at home in the little house—only a cold hearth and a bedroom with a shuttered window.

FOUR

THE PATH OF FIRE

The moon was up and the choir-wolves were howling again outside the circle of wagons. Diligence lay on the soft bed and listened to the changing chords of their eerily beautiful song.

She had been averaging four or five hours of sleep a night since their departure from the Wheel twelve days ago. Up till then, her whole life had been spent in the ceaseless, ordered migration of the Turning Folk, and it was difficult to adjust to a new rhythm—or to the complete lack of any rhythm. For a child of the Wheel, it felt utterly strange to be striking out on a path that actually led away from all that was familiar. When she went to her bed at night in the wagon set aside for her use, she imagined herself lashed to a forward-thrusting line that took her farther from her homeland and brought her deeper into the unknown with each day that passed.

In truth the line was more meandering than thrusting. The great Northeastern Gate through which they had departed opened out onto a land dotted with bogs and silt-bottomed streams. The recent earth tremors plaguing the Eastern and Northern Cantles had cleaved open yawning fissures in what solid ground there had been, forcing the small caravan to choose its trail carefully.

Her fellow travelers were an oddly assorted group, forty-three in number, including the yeofolk and the alters. Aside

25

from Diligence, the caravan was made up of old Pomponderant, who would be continuing with them for a short while yet outside the Wheel, till the interests of the Society took him elsewhere; a taciturn Hubwoman named Nury, representing the eight kings; Breitling, a cartographer from the Lower Steppes who doubled as marchmaster; Welleck, his wagoneer; the requested seven alters and an alterman, along with fourteen yeofolk and their two handlers; a cook; twelve soldiers, gallant in their sable uniforms marked with the stylized sickle of the Harvesters; and the same yawning scrivener who had recited the message from Amonwelle in her father's High Study.

Diligence turned onto her side and pounded her silken pillow into a more serviceable shape as the wolves embarked on a new melody. The soldiers had tried to silence them the first few nights they had serenaded the caravan, but finally abandoned the effort as a waste of time. The choir-wolves were wraithlike in their ability to melt into the wilderness when threatened, emerging one by one after a brief hiatus to blend their isolated voices into a sonorous instrument of great power. The ear-stopples that the marchmaster had offered to each of the travelers had given Diligence a sense of being walled off from the world that she had found highly unpleasant, and she had declined to wear them after the first night, determined instead to utilize one of her tutor's mental disciplines to filter out the unwanted noise.

She found herself wondering again about Pomponderant's reasons for deserting the Wheel. He had been her teacher for the last seven years, and she had known all along that he might pack up and leave at any time. Like all members of the Society, he was allowed to come and go as he pleased in most civilized lands, that fellowship's ceaseless quest for knowledge being widely recognized as an undertaking of considerable importance. But why now? When she had questioned him after the meeting with her father, he had replied only that he had certain business in the East, and that no one would be well served if he opened his mouth any wider about it. She had expected little more. In the years that Pomponderant had turned with the Harvesters in her father's employ, he had managed to instill in his eager pupil his own fierce love of learning, while revealing almost nothing about his inner motivations and deeply held beliefs.

Her head raised up from the pillow as sudden silence descended on the small encampment with the effect of a clap of thunder. The lack of noise came as a jolt after the constant multitoned wailing, and she had to search her memory to see if there really had been a thunderclap, or any other great sound preceding the abrupt cessation of the wolves' song. The silence persisted. Cautiously, she descended from her bunk and moved to the divided door at the end of the long car. She opened the upper half and peered out.

The air was very cold. No one else was moving in the space inside the huddled vehicles, though she made out the black silhouettes of two guards standing watch on opposite sides of the camp. She was ducking back into the wagon when a hint of unexpected motion in the darkness caught her attention. She looked up.

A bright golden light was moving with measured slowness high above, like a distant torch being carried against the star-speckled blackness of the heavens. At first Diligence thought it was an errant flicker, dropping out of the night to investigate the wagons, and her hands flew up automatically to shield the top of her head. Like most people, she had been exposed since early childhood to stories of the flicker's supposed longing to make its nests in human hair, and to many a frightening tale of unwary girls and boys whose heads had been singed to the bare scalp. She lowered her arms sheepishly. They were only foolish tales—

and anyway, the golden light was much too high in the air
to signify one of those small creatures. As she tracked it,
she gradually became aware of a far-off whining sound,
like a choir-pup who had not yet tuned his voice to match
the pack's. Diligence watched in wonder as the spot of light
continued its unhurried course above the camp and disappeared beyond the wall of treetops. The whining faded into
stillness.

She looked around the dark ring of vehicles. The guards
seemed oblivious to the strange event; their tall shapes
stood unmoving at their posts in the wagon gaps.

Minutes passed as she waited at the doorway, the wintry
air chilling her through her thin nightcoat. It was hard to
judge the passage of time in the silent darkness. She began
to wonder how long she had been leaning there, and if she
had really seen the golden light pass overhead in its steady
arc. Sometimes, especially if she was recovering from an
illness, or desperately in need of sleep, she had found herself skimming in and out of dreams so quickly that events
of the real world meshed with those of the dreamworld, until she lost track of which was which. Whatever the nature
of this event, it was over now, and her ears were beginning
to hurt from the cold. She was ducking back into the car
when she heard a low booming noise from somewhere beyond the trees. The thunderclap she had anticipated earlier?
As she turned back for another look at the heavens, a shuddering wail sounded from beyond the wagons, making her
jump in startlement. A chorus of harmonious voices quickly
joined in from all around the camp as the choir wolves re-
commenced their interrupted song. Diligence sighed. Back
to normal.

She continued to wait by the doorway, reluctant to return
to her bed amid the renewed sounds of the chorus. Her
gaze fell on the nearer guard, still standing admirably
straight and motionless between two wagons on the north-

west side of the camp. From the broad shoulders and the bowl-shaped haircut characteristic of the Sowers, it appeared to be the tall young man called Huben, with whom she had exchanged smiles on several occasions since the start of the journey. She reached behind her for her bedslippers and a cloak. At least she might enjoy a word or two of friendly conversation before resuming her quest for sleep. She unlatched the lower half of the door, tossed out the ladder, and climbed down to the frost-cloaked ground. She kept close to the wagons as she made her way around the circle, careful not to tread on any of the yeofolk. Her slippers crunched through damp hollows stiff with rime as she came up behind the young man. He remained rigidly at attention, his face turned to the boggy wilderland beyond the camp.

"Huben?" She touched his shoulder. His arm felt hard as stone beneath his black coat. "Are you . . . ?" She let the whispered words trail off, something knotting in her stomach as she stepped slightly to the side, to where she could see his face clearly in the moonlight.

The young man was staring absolutely motionless at something outside the ring of wagons. His eyes were wide and his lips were drawn back in a grimace of frozen alarm.

"Huben?" Diligence swallowed and reached out her hand. His cheek was as cold as polished stone beneath her fingertips; she drew them back quickly with a sigh of dismay. The motion made the young soldier sway slightly in his boots, and she backed away in terror, afraid that he would topple onto her.

She turned and dashed across the camp, the ridiculous slippers making her stagger and slide. She was out of breath when she came up behind the other guard. "Help," she gasped, "it's Huben. He's—I think he's frozen to death . . ." The second soldier had not reacted to the sound of her approach. Like Huben, he stood facing outward, his posture stiff and statuelike.

Diligence refused to look at a second frozen face. With a little cry, she fled back to the center of the camp, turning in a confused circle amid the rounded backs of the yeofolk before racing to the wagon shared by her tutor and the marchmaster. She pounded furiously on the wooden door till she heard groggy voices within. The upper door swung open and Pomponderant leaned out, in his hand a small lantern pulsing with cold fire. The old man scowled down at her.

Then the marchmaster's long, freckled face bobbed into view behind the scholar's shoulder. "What is it—hobs?" He plucked a small plug from his right ear. "Are they attacking the camp?"

"I don't know, I don't know." Diligence waited impatiently as the two climbed down from the wagon. Then she grabbed the sleeve of Pomponderant's nightcoat and dragged him toward the first guard. "I found him frozen— they both are. They've both frozen to death."

"Not likely." The old man shook her hand away and thrust his lantern into Huben's contorted face. Pinkish light illuminated the blank eyes and the gaping mouth. "Not cold enough out here to freeze a marshmouse. Hmm." He cupped the young soldier's chin in his palm for a moment, frowning thoughtfully. "Dead, though. Quite dead."

"What's all this ruckus?" Nury the Hubwoman joined them between the wagons, a gray blanket clutched around her thin body.

"It's hobwork!" The marchmaster's voice rose hysterically. "They've killed the guards!"

"Be quiet, you foolish man." Pomponderant was still examining the frozen soldier, poking the stiff flesh here and there with a crooked forefinger. "No hob ever knew such a trick, to fill a man's veins with ice while he stood and watched."

"Is it ... Amonwelle?" Nury's pale eyes darted nervously among the shadows. "Is this *her* doing?"

Diligence was incredulous. "Why should my mother want to put ice inside our guards?" she asked. "It's her request that started us on this journey!"

"Hush!" Pomponderant was gazing narrow-eyed at the darkness beyond the camp. "I thought to see furtive movement behind those trees—a flick of eyes, a flash of metal—but now it's gone, with all your chattering." He turned his fierce regard on Diligence. "You raised the alarm. Were you the first to see them thus? Why are you not in bed?"

"I couldn't sleep. Then the wolves stopped singing. And there was a light—a golden light in the sky." Haltingly, she told them of the events leading up to her ghastly discovery. More of the travelers were spilling from their wagons as she related her tale, the remaining soldiers emerging to sprint back and forth between their two frozen comrades with shouts of astonishment.

"Evocative and untoward," Pomponderant commented when she had finished. He waggled a finger at the heavens. "In which direction did this floating torch proceed?"

Diligence tilted her head back and frowned at the starry sky. "I'm—I'm not entirely sure. I was at my wagon ..." She turned to the right and pointed vaguely northward.

"You said the guards never moved from the time you first looked out," the Hubwoman said shrewdly. "So they were already changed to ice by the time your heavenly torch passed over the camp. There would seem to be little connection between the two events. Perhaps you saw a flicker hurrying home to its nest."

"No, it was no flicker. It was high in the sky, very bright and very large—I'm sure of that." Diligence scanned the sky to the northeast, wishing she could pinpoint the exact path the light had followed. She felt a crawling sensation at the base of her scalp as she remembered its slow arc above the camp. "I think it *means* something," she said, looking anxiously at Pomponderant. "I—I have a feeling."

Her tutor examined her closely. "A presentiment?" he asked. "A vision?"

Diligence felt a hot flush spread up the sides of her face. "Just a feeling," she said quietly.

Nury clucked her tongue. "Replace the guards," she said. "Put guards behind the new guards with orders to kill anything that approaches the camp. That should put an end to this 'feeling.' "

Pomponderant plucked at the braided strands of his white beardlet with his thumb and forefinger. "I think not," he said. "For I believe I am beginning to share in it myself." He gave a decisive nod and turned to one of the soldiers. "Rouse the alterman," he commanded. "And bid him hasten—we are losing valuable time!"

The alterman was a squabby little man with carefully arranged ringlets of dyed crimson peeping from beneath his bedcap. He listened to Pomponderant's requirements and waved his plump hand at the nearest soldier. "Bring me the tall yellow male with the spot on its cheek," he ordered. "And pay no attention to any grumblings about its leg. It has a slothful and contrary nature."

The alter pen had been erected at the far side of the wagon ring. The soldier returned in three minutes with a scowling man in tow. The alter's blond hair stuck out from his skull in spiky tufts; his long naked body was wiry, more sinew than muscle. He had a purplish birthmark the size of an eight-spot on his right cheekbone and a leather collar around his neck. The alter had been walking with a pronounced limp as he crossed the encampment. When he saw the alterman, he dug his heels in the frosty ground and began muttering under his breath.

"Come, come, don't be recalcitrant. You're not the only one who's been shaken out of a sound sleep." The little man searched in the pocket of his jacket and produced a small gray biscuit, which he extended to the collared man on his open palm. The alter snatched the food with a suspicious glance at the onlookers, and began to devour it with sturdy-looking teeth.

"A moment for the stimulant to flood its body," the alterman said. He unwound a long leather lead from about his considerable waist and clipped one end of it to the small ring of metal at the back of the alter's collar. Then he turned to Pomponderant. "Are we quite ready to begin?" he asked, eyeing the old man's nightcoat and tasseled slippers.

"Five hundred heartbeats," Pomponderant said. The crowd dispersed to their individual wagons to adjust their apparel. When they reconvened several minutes later in the center of the encampment, the alterman was just beginning his work.

Diligence had a distaste for the employment of alters that bordered on revulsion. She grimaced as the little man gripped his charge's wiry arm and leaned in to murmur with his lips close to the other's ear. The alter's face had gone slack, his eyes dull with the effects of the biscuit. He squirmed in the alterman's iron grasp and began to whimper piteously as the murmured commands grew more insistent.

Diligence turned away when the whimper deepened to an agonized moan. She raised her hands to her ears as the muffled crunching sounds began, knowing that the very bones of the poor creature's face and head were slipping over one another and changing proportion in order to accommodate the desired modification of its skull. The moaning continued unabated till the crunching noises quieted to a moist creaking. By the time Diligence forced herself to turn back to the blond man, the sockets of his eyes had

opened to three times their normal size, crowding the flesh
back into wrinkles on his forehead and his cheeks. The eyes
themselves were swollen to the size of treehen eggs; they
bulged from the flattened planes of his face beneath a sheen
of filmy gray.

The alterman pulled his mouth away from the creature's
ear. "Show us the path of fire in the heavens!" he commanded, twisting the alter's head up toward the sky. "Show
us!"

"There!" the alter screamed in agony, raising a trembling
finger toward the northern treetops. "Too bright! It burns! It
burns!" He flung his hands up to shield his bulging orbs.
The alterman lashed at the creature's arm with the end of
the leather leash. The blond man gave a tormented shriek,
peering at the sky through splayed fingers.

"Lead us!" the alterman cried in ringing tones. "Lead us
to the end of the fiery trail!"

Howling, the naked man surged forward into the forest.

FIVE

HATCHLING

Hitch had lingered for several days in the woods beyond the mountain pass, gathering such provisions as he could in preparation for his trek out onto the plains. From what the old woman had told him, he was not likely to find much in the way of food until he met up with one of the caravans. At last he felt ready.

The old woman's instructions had led him to the edge of a wide lake, beyond whose opposite shores the forest was said to turn slowly to bog and marshland and then finally to the open ground of the great plain known as the Siccative.

Most of Hitch's short life had been spent far to the west and north among the craggy peaks surrounding the Silent Falls, and he had never before seen so large a body of bounded water. He decided that it would be interesting to spend his last night in these parts on the lakeshore itself, where the soft lapping of water might bring him unexpected dreams. It seemed a safe enough place; he had encountered no creatures larger than green-gilled minnows in the immediate vicinity.

Accordingly, he drove the jewel-headed walking stick into the sandy ground and officially established his camp for the night. Then he used his striking stones to start a pair of small driftwood fires, where he heated some mint tea and cooked himself a fine dinner of roasted vegetables wrapped in waterflower leaves. He washed out his bowl in the shallows, singing what he could remember of the old woman's traveling song as the minnows made silver flashes in the fading light. Later he carved a shallow depression in the sand to fit his body. He removed his boots and set them by the walking stick. Then he curled up in his long green cloak between the mounds of glowing ashes, on his left side with his backsack under his head.

He dreamt of a great boat shaped like the undershell of a mudcreep, adrift in a stormy sea with winds that howled and churned the water into crashing slopes. People ran and shouted on the tilting decks, but he himself stood unafraid, facing the storm with a feeling of glorious anticipation. Before the dream had found a proper ending he was suddenly awake, shivering in his cloak under a star-dusted sky.

Hitch lay there puzzling, his mind still cobwebby with threads and clots of dream, and wondered how he had reached the shore without a shipwreck. There was no wind, but the air all around him was filled with a whistling whine, as if someone were blowing through a great reed. A cold light was coming from somewhere, though dawn seemed hours away. He knuckled his eyes, but the radiance persisted, throbbing now with the regularity of a heartbeat.

He turned over on his back, then rolled onto his right side and gaped at the marchmaster's walking stick. The crystal embedded in the roots of its head was glowing a bright, unearthly blue that flared and dimmed in a rhythm that was almost hypnotic. He rose up on his elbows and stared at it.

A sound like muffled thunder broke the spell, followed by a flash of brightness that seemed to come from directly above him. He flung his head back and blinked at the large golden star dropping swiftly out of the middle of the sky. Hitch had seen stars dislodged from their places in the heavens before. He watched, waiting for it to wink out like a sunfly caught in the hand of Night.

But the star continued to fall, as the shrill whine grew louder. Hitch wrapped the cloak around his shoulders and got slowly to his feet, his joints still stiff with sleep. He stood transfixed, rooted to the sand in amazement as the star grew larger and brighter, till he was sure he could see orange flames trailing it as it plummeted earthward. At the last minute he understood how large the thing was and that it was actually going to plunge into the lake. "Oh . . ." he said, and raised an arm to protect his face.

He got a clear glimpse of it under his wrist just before it hit the surface of the water. It was not a star at all, but a giant golden egg, its complicated shell afire with a dancing sheen of rainbow colors. It plunged into the lake with a tremendous noise, sending up huge geysers of water and a cloud of hissing steam.

There was a great roiling and bubbling as the object began to sink almost immediately inside its cloak of steam. A dark blotch appeared momentarily on the upper surface of its glowing skin, and something shot up and away in a rapid arc. Hitch heard a splash as the smaller object struck the water. Then other sounds became audible through the hissing: thrashing noises, spluttered cries. Whatever had hatched from the great egg, it was not having an easy birth in the middle of the lake.

Hitch bit his lower lip as the choked, gurgling sounds continued. He tugged the cloak up higher about his neck. The creature's brief flight outside the egg had landed it far from the beach, and the edge of the lake was glazed with ice. His own swimming ability had not been tested for several years, and there was a good chance that he would drown from sheer ineptitude halfway out, assuming the temperature of the water failed to kill him instantly.

The egg was almost completely beneath the surface by

now. Hitch cocked his head to listen as the thrashing and the choked cries grew steadily weaker. In the morning all the wonder would be out of sight on the lake bottom, he reflected, with nothing worth seeing up top but a lifeless body floating in the reeds. He found himself thinking of the old woman in the little house in the valley. *Time to take a chance and find out something new.* He dropped his cloak and sprinted down to the icy shore.

He waded into the frigid water, diving in awkwardly when the sandy ground fell away. Fear fueled his rapid strokes as he swam out to where the dark figure still struggled weakly.

It had a head plastered with sleek black hair, and at least two strong limbs that lashed out at him as he tried to grab it under the armpits. Just when he thought both of them were doomed, the hatchling suddenly gave up the fight and went completely limp in his arms. Hitch grasped a handful of thin hide at the back of its neck and turned back toward shore, beating the water with his other arm and frog-kicking with all his might. The world compressed into a small dark universe of furious motion and freezing water, until at last he dragged the heavy shape up onto the pebbled shore and collapsed next to it. His lungs were pumping like a bellows, wringing small, helpless cries from his throat with each exhalation.

He fought the urge to curl up into a freezing ball, somehow managing to stagger to his feet and up the beach. He knelt between the two firepits and fumbled in the backsack for his striking stones. But his hands were too numb to make the necessary motions, and in the end he clutched the green cloak tight around his shuddering body and made his way back to where the hatchling lay unmoving on the sand.

Out in the center of the lake, the surface of the water still bubbled, while a fading golden light shone weakly up from the troubled depths. Hitch stood watching for a moment before he knelt beside the still figure.

The thing that had flown from the golden egg was a man, with short black hair and a white face, the rest of his body concealed by a strange, slick-looking blue hide that seemed to have no seams or breaks, even where it covered his clenched fingers. It was obviously not his own skin; Hitch was able to work two of his fingers under the odd material where it circled the man's neck. He wondered how a person could eat or drink after being sewn into such a garment—for surely it would be impossible to relieve oneself without first taking a knife to the lower portion of the suit.

There was a large purple bruise coming out on the pale skin above the man's left eye, and he did not seem to be breathing. Hitch grasped his shoulders and shook him. There was no response. He set his ear against the shiny blue surface of the chest and listened for a heartbeat, but it was impossible to catch any sound through the chattering of his own teeth. "Come on," he muttered. "I'm probably going to die myself after that swim—*one* of us should pull through." He used the heels of his hands to pound on the hatchling's chest, as much to warm himself as from a belief that he would be able to revive the man. He had seen a treehen egg toppled from its nest onto the ground once, and watched the brief, fitful movements of the chick that crawled too soon from the sundered shell. Perhaps the creature was not yet ready to survive outside his sunken egg. "Ahhh—wake *up!*" Hitch gave the unmoving chest a final swat and straightened up in disgust. He rubbed his tingling palms together. If he was not able to get a fire going soon, he really would follow the hatchling to an early death.

He heard a wet clicking sound as he was turning back toward the firepits. Cords stood out on the pale neck as the man's head lifted slightly from the sand. The slack mouth fell open and a quantity of lake water spewed out over the blue-clad throat and chest.

Purple-tinged lips moved sluggishly as the boy bent back over him. "He will be with you in a short while," a voice said in clear but oddly accented speech. "At the moment his attention is necessarily focused elsewhere. Continuing to strike his chest will only bring about further skin trauma. Your patience in this matter is appreciated."

The hatchling's eyes had remained shut throughout the utterance, his face muscles slack. Now his mouth closed and his head lolled to one side, his chest beginning to rise and fall in a shallow rhythm.

Hitch stood staring at the man for several long moments, his own jaw hanging open. Then he shook his head and scrambled up the beach to his backsack. After much fumbling and many wasted sparks, he succeeded in building a small fire in one of the pits.

He peeled off his sodden clothes and arranged them to dry on the prongs of a driftwood branch, hunching close to the fire under the green wool cloak. Periodic glances over his shoulder told him that the man in blue remained motionless, stretched out on his back several yards down the shore. At length Hitch's teeth stopped their chattering and his body's uncontrolled quaking diminished to brief bursts of shivering. It was then that he heard the crunch of heavy boots in the sand behind him and realized that he was no longer alone.

SIX

A BOY ON THE BEACH

Diligence had slipped into the pack of pursuers when the alter ran wailing through the trees, leading them along a fiery trail only his modified eyes could follow.

The Hubwoman Nury, and Breitling, the marchmaster, had taken turns ordering her to return to the safety of the wagons, but Diligence had pretended not to hear them, increasing the length of her stride somewhat each time they called out. It was, she reasoned, her golden star they were following, and it seemed only suitable that she be among the first to see what lay at the end of its trail. Besides—with two guards already frozen into startled corpses at their posts, the circle of wagons presented a questionable haven at best.

Six of the remaining contingent of ten black-clad soldiers had been left back at the camp, together with the wagoneer, the cook, and the sleepy-eyed scrivener, who had finally crawled from his bunk just as the star-hunters departed. The woman and the man responsible for the yeofolk had also stayed behind, with orders to prod three of their lumbering charges out of their sleep holes as an added safeguard.

It took all of the alterman's strength to restrain their frantic guide, who scampered like a woodhop over fallen logs and through mires of cold mud, his injured leg apparently forgotten. Diligence bounded along with the soldiers at the alter's back, while the other members of the party kept pace

41

as best they could, Pomponderant wheezing in a most
alarming manner till Diligence began to fear the old man's
lungs would explode in the middle of the chase.

Breitling seemed to share her concern. At the marchmaster's command, one of the quicker soldiers, a lean
woman named Shevoss, added her hands to the leather lead
and slowed the frantic alter to a straining walk. From the
wistful looks exchanged by the other soldiers, Diligence
had the feeling that they had enjoyed the wild pursuit, perhaps as a means of easing rattled nerves after the eerie demise of their comrades.

The searchers prowled the woods for half an hour, the
alter's breath coming in plangent gasps as the collar pressed
tight against his throat. At last they reached a place where
the tree growth became noticeably sparser. Moonlight glimmered from a large stretch of water ahead of them. The alter darted forward, then shrank back from the open area
with a tormented cry, his chin dropping down to his sweat-
stained chest and his palms cupped over the enormous
globes of his eyes.

"Bright!" Diligence heard him protest. "Burning-
burning-burning into the water . . ." He flung his wiry arms
around a rough-barked tree trunk and sank to his knees.

The alterman knotted the end of the leather strap and began to raise it over his head in a threatening gesture. Diligence stepped up to his side.

"Let him be, for pity's sake," she said. "He's shown us
what you asked him to. The path leads down to the lake."

"Bah! It schemes to withdraw from the hunt," the
alterman panted, "when prolonged exercise is what it most
urgently requires." Coloring under Diligence's dark gaze,
he took a firm grasp of the alter's collar, brushed damp
spikes of yellow hair back from one ear, and began his
muttering singsong. At the commencement of the sickening

sounds of transformation, Diligence went to stand by the soldiers.

Pomponderant finally joined them at the edge of the forest. He was breathing heavily, his own eyes bulging beneath their thatch of white brows. "Divide into two parties," he gasped. "One go Wheelwise ... the other opposite. Search the lakeshore for the downfallen star. Mind the evidence of scorched sand ... and be sensitive ... to the odor of charring driftwood." The old scholar sat himself on a weathered log at the top of the beach and endeavored to calm his breathing.

Diligence took a step back into the forest's verge and studied the lake, recalling which direction the alter had been facing when he covered his eyes in agony at the conclusion of the chase. While Nury and Breitling fussed around her wheezing tutor, she trotted off to the left with the anti-Wheelwise search party, a twosome composed of Shevoss and a shorter, stouter individual named Varve.

The pair of soldiers combed the beach methodically, stooping to peer into tide pools and gingerly overturning large shells with the toes of their black boots. Having seen the descendant star with her own eyes, Diligence reasoned that something large enough to shine like a golden beacon in the sky would not be hidden under cockles or behind a snarl of driftwood. She forged ahead of them, her eyes scanning the far sweep of shoreline.

A storm was gathering in the distance; clouds massed and boiled beneath the placid moon and muted flashes betrayed the presence of distant lightning. Diligence tracked the storm's progress as she walked, noting how swiftly it traversed the night sky.

She had left the soldiers a hundred yards behind by the time she discerned the tiny wisp of smoke threading upward from the glowing firepit. Two dark blots stood out like stains on the backdrop of pale sand: one quite near the fire, the other closer to the water's edge. Diligence glanced back over her shoulder to where Shevoss and her comrade still meandered with downcast eyes. Swallowing with difficulty, she approached the dark shapes.

A white-faced man covered chin to sole in damp blue lay on his back not far from the water. At first Diligence thought him dead, until his chest rose and fell in a single shallow breath. Nearly dead, anyway, she amended, when the second faltering breath came some fifty heartbeats later. A short ways up the beach, a hunched figure sat with bare arms outstretched above a small fire, a cloak of green wool tented around it to catch the heat. Diligence crept slowly up behind the creature and stood staring down at it with a mixture of curiosity and dread, her heart tolling like a silent bell at the bottom of her throat. The spell was broken by the crunching of coarse sand as Shevoss and Varve came jogging up in the darkness.

The figure under the green cloak jumped to its feet and whirled to face them. Diligence started in amazement. It was a brown-haired boy a year or two younger than herself, shivering with cold and naked as an alter. She looked beyond; what had appeared to be a group of small carcasses cooking by the fire was in fact an array of damp garments on a frame of driftwood branches.

Shevoss stepped forward, thumbing back the safety catch on her short-handled slicer as she inserted herself between Diligence and the boy. The circular blade spun like a tiny wheel at the end of its ivory shaft. "Check the body by the water," she instructed Varve. Her black-gloved hand struck out like a serpent to clamp the boy's wrist. "Where did you fall from?" she barked. "What mischief are you plotting here?" She emphasized the second question with a sudden wrench of the youth's arm. He gave a yelp of pain.

"*Tch.* This is just a boy in need of dry clothing," Diligence protested. "Look at him shivering, he's cold as the Night."

"That's just what I'm thinking, Daughter," the soldier replied. She looked down the beach. "Varve?"

"Dead as a gutted silverfin," the other soldier called back. "He's got a funny sort of wrapping on, though."

"Ho! And that's the third one dead tonight," Shevoss said. "I'm wagering his bones are cracked full of ice, just like poor Huben and Tarler back there at the camp. You don't know what the Standing Folk can do, Daughter. This little creature's probably made of ice himself, with a bit of thistlethorn as hair and hob dung for color." She gave the thin arm another savage twist. "Speak, hob-son!"

The boy had been holding the cloak awkwardly around his shoulders with his left hand while he squirmed at the end of the soldier's arm. Now the garment fluttered to the ground as that hand made a quick slashing motion toward his imprisoned right wrist.

"Great Black Night!" Shevoss released the wrist with a roar, snatching her arm away as if stung. The leather had been neatly opened across the back of her glove; a streak of bright blood welled over her knuckles in the firelight. She stepped back warily, twirling her slicer. "Little muck's got a fingerblade!" Her eyes flicked down to the water's edge. "Varve! Leave the corpse and tote your slicer up here."

The youth followed her gaze. "The hatchling's not dead," he said indignantly. "Just busy, he told me. Think he forgets to breathe sometimes."

The boy's speech came out with a strong Western burr. It took Diligence a moment to sort through his accent. "He's right," she said. "I saw the man breathing when I got here, but very slowly." She turned to Shevoss as Varve huffed up the beach, his own weapon spinning in his hand. "He hasn't frozen anybody. Think it through: why would his teeth be all chattery if he was made of ice himself? It isn't sensible." She leaned forward and swept up the fallen end of the cloak, pushing it into the boy's shaking fingers. "Here, cover yourself."

The boy wrapped the green wool around his thin frame. Then he pulled a narrow leather belt from one of the prongs of driftwood near the fire and wound it twice about his waist. The effect was slightly ridiculous as he drew himself up, barefoot and shivering in clothing twice his size. "Thank you, Lady," he said formally, bowing in Diligence's direction.

She returned the bow, scowling at the two soldiers who still stood with weapons ready. "Put something on that hand of yours," she told Shevoss. "And stop glaring at him like he's the King of Evil's son. He only hurt you because you were hurting him."

"There's the ringing truth," the boy put in with a nod.

"Oho, and I suppose he carries that blade to peel wartfruit for his breakfast," the soldier muttered, tearing off a white strip from the bottom of her longshirt and winding it around her wounded hand.

Diligence pointed to the man in blue. "Why is your friend lying so far from the fire? Isn't he cold, as well?"

"That's as close as I could carry him," the boy said. "And he's not my friend by any stretch."

A small commotion of voices signaled the arrival of the first search party. Nury strode ahead of the other two soldiers, a sour expression on her pinched features. Diligence moved to stand protectively in front of the boy as the newcomers surrounded them.

"What're these, then?" the Hubwoman asked, looking from the group gathered at the little campsite to the man in blue. "A pair of nightfishers? And have they seen your lapsed star?" She turned her head and squinted toward the motionless body. "Your father's an uncommonly sound sleeper, boy—or has he slipped on a fish back and drowned himself in the moonlight?"

"My father?" The boy hitched the cloak tighter about his throat with a snort of profound amusement. "It's not anybody's father lying there!"

"Answer the Hubwoman plainly," growled one of the newly arrived soldiers. "She's not asking questions to hear you laugh at them."

"Well, she'll need to come up with a better quality, then," the boy retorted. "How could he be my father when he's only just been born?"

Diligence eyed the still figure dubiously. "Just born?" she repeated. "Just now?"

The boy nodded matter-of-factly. "Hatched, anyway. He popped out of a golden egg in the middle of that lake." He cracked his knuckles and studied his twined fingers. "He'd be at its bottom right now if I wasn't so brimful of kindly sweetness."

The two pairs of soldiers exchanged glances, skeptical on the one side, openly scornful on the other. "Here's what his sweet kindness profited me," Shevoss said to Nury, exhibiting her bandaged hand. "And as for that other one—he's either dead or knocking on the door."

Diligence pulled the boy to one side as Varve and Shevoss began to relate their own version of recent events.

"Tell me what happened if you want my help," she said quietly. "Our wagon camp was attacked earlier and they're in no mood for foolish stories."

"Look here, then." He pushed back his cavernous sleeves and pointed to the small depression carved in the sand between the firepits. "It's not so long ago that I'm asleep here in my cloak, dry as a leaf and dreaming high adventure, when a noise like a boiling kettle draws me back to the Night's cold arms." Diligence watched his eyes flick momentarily to one side. For the first time she noticed the gnarled staff stuck in the sand a foot or two from one of the pits. There was a chunk of rough crystal fixed to its head; the licking firelight gave it a dull blue cast. The boy cleared his throat and she brought her eyes back to his face. "Anyways, Lady—up I look out of my dreams, and what's coming down but a golden egg the size of a barn, with no sign of the bird that laid it, though I could still hear her whistle clear and long. Next comes a crash and a splash and the whole world lights up for a heartbeat or two."

Diligence shook her head in wonder. "It truly was an egg?" she breathed.

The boy made a sweeping gesture with his upturned palm toward the middle of the lake. "Spoon the water out and you'll see it for yourself," he told her. "Big and gold and empty—for its chick lies just there on the cold sand, swaddled in blue and breathing as it finds the time."

"And you pulled him from the water." She eyed his damp clothes and cocked her head to the side. "You saved his life. Why, if he's not your kin?"

He took in a deep breath to say something, changed his mind, and let it out. "Because I wanted to see what might hatch from such a wondrous thing," he told her truthfully. He blew out his cheeks. "I took my time, don't mistake me, as it thrashed and coughed by its sinking shell, for the water was cold and I hadn't swum a stroke in years. But in the end my curiosity was stronger than my sense—as it too often is. Ah well, I says to myself, let's follow the green moth and see where she leads us this time."

"Follow the—" Diligence began. Then another figure came bustling up in the darkness. Breitling's long face glowered at them with impatience and disapproval.

"No star, am I right?" He scanned the dark shore. "Right. The time has come to end this waft-hunt and return to our duties."

"Where is Pomponderant?" Diligence asked. "Have you left him alone?"

"The alterman is with him," Breitling said with a sniff. "We are in dire need of decisive action—though I have no doubt the old man would see us camp out in this damp place till sunrise. Unsettling noises taunt us from within the forest: brassy hootings and snatches of wistful song. As marchmaster, I have decided to call an end to the search." He extended a freckled finger at the boy who stood behind Diligence. "What's this?"

"A fisherboy," Nury said. "His father lies drowned by the water's edge."

Breitling nodded. "I see. A dreadful tragedy." He clapped Shevoss on the shoulder and turned from the firelight. "Come now, all of you: back to the wagons."

"Wait!" Diligence grabbed the boy's sleeve and pulled him forward. "Quick," she said. "What's your name and where are you bound?"

"I'm Hitch," he told her. "I was heading for the Siccative and thence to the Aulmad to offer my strong back to the first caravan I meet."

"We're a caravan of sorts. Do you want to come with us?"

"Hold on now," Breitling interjected. "We've wagons to haul our packs and no need of another open mouth on our journey."

"Pomponderant will want to decide that," Diligence insisted. "This boy has an information to relate in regard to my golden star."

"Golden egg," said Hitch. Diligence poked him with her elbow.

Nury leaned in to Breitling's ear. The two conferred for a few moments behind cupped palms. At last the marchmaster gave a short nod. "All right. The tagalong comes as far as the old man's log. But we leave this wretched water hole now." He turned and began to move off down the shore, the others following in his wake.

"Spare us an instant to gather his belongings," Diligence called after them. She turned to find Hitch stuffing his still-damp garments into the large pack that lay at the foot of the driftwood. She glanced about for the wooden staff while he was tugging on his boots, but saw no sign of it. There was a new stiffness to the boy's stride when he hoisted his pack and stepped around the firepit a moment later. Diligence surmised that he had secured the object somehow under his voluminous cloak.

"We'd better hurry," she said. "Or we'll be left wandering. Are you ready?" Hitch was standing motionless on the sand, an expression of pained dissatisfaction on his thin features. "What's the matter?"

"I have to bring him along, you see," the boy said with a shrug of his burdened shoulders. He tipped his chin to the dark blue body near the water. "I can't have done so much straining and shivering just to leave him there in the sand like a clump of watergrass."

"Oh. No, I guess not." Diligence turned and cupped her hands around her mouth. "Breitling!" she called. "Send the soldiers over. We need help to carry the other man."

"You need no such thing!" the marchmaster roared back across the beach. "The boy may come—to the log, at least—but the body stays. I'll not be swayed on this." He turned and muttered something in a low voice to Varve and Shevoss, then looked at Diligence and Hitch. "Now join us at once, or I'll have you dragged the rest of the way!"

Behind her, Hitch clicked his tongue against his front teeth. "I never have got on very well with marchmasters," he said.

The two soldiers had begun to trudge back toward them through the sand. Diligence chewed her thumbnail thoughtfully, looking back over her shoulder at Hitch's unhappy face. A wild wind sprang up suddenly to ruffle their garments. Diligence let her eye stray to the boil of clouds above the dark line of trees bordering the shore. The storm was almost upon them.

As Varve came near, she dropped suddenly to her knees, lifting her arms skyward as if in supplication. *"Yesss!"* she cried as the wind came up again, flattening the blond curls at her cheeks. "Yesss, I hear you!"

The pair of soldiers looked around them, then at one another. "Hear who, Daughter?" asked Shevoss. "To whom are you speaking?"

"Bring the man as well as the boy?" Diligence cried, her eyes rolling back in their sockets as she swayed from the waist like a sapling in the growing breeze. "Yesss!"

"Something ails the Daughter," she heard Varve yell to the others. Boots crunched as the rest of the party approached. A light rain had begun to patter on the sand.

"What is this nonsense?" Nury asked, her voice flat with exasperation.

Diligence let out a high-pitched shriek, closed her eyelids to slits, and peered over the others' heads at the mounting storm. The firelight painted their faces with eerie shadows as a bank of coal-colored clouds drifted in front of the moon. "Yesss, Mother!" she cried. "I understand. The boy must come and the man as well!"

"Mother?" The Hubwoman's shoulders twitched in alarm. "Did she say—"

"O Mother, they do not wish to heed you," Diligence wailed. Above the trees, she glimpsed a flash of white light. "Please restrain your fury!"

"I don't believe—" Breitling started to say. Then a crack of thunder split the night, its echoes rumbling up and down the beach. Nury gave a squawk of terror.

"Bring the dead one!" she ordered. "Hurry, before

Amonwelle drops a whirlwind amongst us!" The soldiers scrambled down the beach toward the blue-clad man.

The moon shone forth once more as clouds raced overhead, hurrying the little storm to the other side of the lake. Some distance from the firepits, the marchmaster and the Hubwoman argued in hushed but heated tones. Hitch helped Diligence to her feet, a thoughtful expression on his face.

"A most enthusiastic performance," he told her quietly. "Who is your mother, if I may ask?"

"Amonwelle of the Land of the Unseen Wall," Diligence replied. She inclined her head slightly as the quartet of soldiers stumbled past with their awkward burden. "We're on our way to pay her a visit."

The pair fell into line behind the others as the party started off again along the shore, Breitling and Nury scouring the sky with worried expressions.

"Evidently a woman deserving of much respect," Hitch mused aloud.

Diligence brushed sand from the front of her nightcoat with a prim smile. "Evidently," she said.

SEVEN

CHANGE OF HEART

Hitch was working hard to make his stiff-legged gait as unremarkable as possible, no mean feat with the jewel-headed walking stick strapped loosely to his waist under the green cloak. He had made a quick decision not to tell the strangers of the peculiar glow that had infused the gem just before the giant egg encountered the surface of the lake; from there it had been a short leap to concealing the very existence of the walking stick. The best way to keep one's treasures, he'd oft been told, was to keep them to oneself. He stalked in distracted silence at the side of the tall yellow-haired girl as the party turned from the beach and headed up to the forest's edge.

Small cages of cold fire had been set here and there on the sand around a felled tree trunk mottled with scarlet moss; they illuminated the immediate area in cool shades of pink and periwinkle blue. An elderly man wearing purple robes and a sparse white chin-braid dozed at one end of the log, his shoulders hunched forward and his elbows propped up on bony knees. At the other end a small, round-bellied individual peered into a palm-sized looking glass and made adjustments to his coif of ringlets with a tiny comb. But it was the third member of the little group that caused Hitch to blink. He nudged the girl.

"What's the matter there?" he asked, staring at the man who sat snoring noisily on the ground a few yards from the log, all four of his wiry limbs wrapped tight around the base of an upright trunk.

"Ah. Poor creature." The girl's mouth twisted in pity. "He led us quite a chase through the woods. Now the alterman's changed him back, I suppose he's doled him out a few moments to build up his strength."

Hitch decided he was missing some subtlety. "But why is he naked?"

"Because he's an alter, of course." The girl gave him a strange look. "Would you put trousers on a minnow?"

Hitch shrugged. "I don't suppose I would," he said, "now that you mention it." He watched the soldiers deposit their burden on a patch of long grass at the forest's edge. Another thought entered his head as he turned back to his young host. "Do you have any other name besides 'Daughter,' Lady? There's too many calling you that already for you to belong to all of them, and I'd rather not add to the confusion—to say nothing of finding myself on the wrong side of this Amonwelle person."

The girl shook her head with a smile. "Daughter isn't my name." Her cap of loose curls had taken on the color of fine ale in the lavender glow from the prisoned fires. "It's more of a title," she told him in her flat Eastern drawl. "My name is Diligence."

"Diligence." Hitch puffed out his cheeks. "That's not a name, it's an aspiration."

"No, it's a child-name," the girl said, leading him by the sleeve toward the weathered log. "When I was born, my mother named me Madawyn, but when they brought me to the Wheel soon after, the Harvesters decided to call me Diligence. In a few months, once I've accomplished my seventeenth birthday and begun to make out the shape of my own circle, I'll be able to choose a name that truly suits me from the Endless Scroll. Then I'll stand in the field with the others at the yearly appellative, under a sky swarmed with kites, and graft my own uncertain turning to some ancient and honorable gyration." Her voice had grown softer as they approached the sleeping elder. Now she leaned over and gently shook the old man's shoulder. "Pomponderant."

"What sort of wheel did they bring you to, and why?" inquired Hitch, who had found much of her explanation strange and abstruse. But before Diligence could answer, the old man sat bolt upright on the log. Narrowing his dark eyes at Hitch, he reached out to snare the boy's chin between a callused thumb and forefinger.

"Hmf," said Pomponderant. "Narrow jaw, angled cheeks, lanky build." He released the startled boy. "Say something."

"What—"

"That's enough. Bred in the high mountains north of the Steppes, for a certainty. Jogjaw Pass, Panumber Peak, perhaps as far west as the Silent Falls."

"How—"

"What are you doing down hereabouts, hm? Sent packing by penurious relatives? Off on your own to roam the level world? Did you see our dropped star?" He twitched his bushy brows at Diligence. "Did he see the star?"

"He says it was an egg—a golden egg, as big as a barn," she told the old man.

"I said it and it's true," Hitch averred as the sharp gaze returned to inspect him. "Though I don't know how large you like to build your barns in these parts. It fell into the lake and hatched before my eyes."

"Hatched?" Pomponderant echoed, looking back and forth between Hitch and the girl. "Hatched?"

"A man—or something in the shape of one," Diligence said, her brows raised high and her tone almost reverential, as if she presented the old man with a great gift. "The soldiers have him over there."

"Oh, then we must see him." Pomponderant pushed his

thin arms against the log, struggling to his feet with the girl's assistance. "Bring me to this egg-man."

The hatchling lay as before, on his back with eyes shut and hands at his sides. The bruise on his forehead had darkened since Hitch had pulled him from the water. It sat above his left eye like a storm cloud. Pomponderant hunkered low to examine the man's face in the cool light, then ran his hands over the slick blue fabric in evident fascination. "What is this, what is this?" he muttered to himself. He peered back over his shoulder at Hitch. "An egg, you say?"

The boy nodded. "I've been thinking this dark stuff might be from the yolk," he said. "A hollowtail's egg has a dark yolk. I was thinking he might be supposed to feed on it till he's old enough to catch his own supper."

"What, like a spitfrog squirmling with its cloak of jelly?" The old man slipped a bony finger beneath the suit's tight collar. The fabric stretched elastically, then resumed its original shape. Pomponderant brought the finger to his nose, touched it delicately to the tip of his tongue. "Not likely," he murmured. "Still, a sound first hypothesis." He leaned back and observed the still figure in silence for half a minute. "Not bothering to breathe very much, is he?"

"Hitch thinks he's busy," Diligence said.

"Busy at what? Who's Hitch? What gave you that idea?"

"He did himself." Hitch chose to ignore the first two questions. "He told me, right when I thought he was drowned-dead. Don't bother pounding on his chest, he says, thank you very much. He'll be with you momentitiously." Frowning, he scratched the end of his nose. "The speaking was right hard to make out at first. He had some of the word sounds wrong—even worse than you folk."

"But those were his exact words—'*he'll* be with you'?"

Hitch gave a nod. "Funny, isn't it? Like he was talking

about somebody who wasn't there. I had a second-uncle who did that sometimes."

Further discussion was curtailed by the intrusion of the freckled man and the pinch-faced woman from the beach. The two seemed to have achieved an uneasy truce, and now both glowered down above the old man's bent back.

"Come along now," the marchmaster said briskly. He tapped his toe impatiently on the sand. "We have a long walk back to the wagons and we'd best begin it. The soldiers think a nighthoot's been weaving its dinner circle around this place, and we don't want to be squatting here like treehens when he decides it's time to feast."

"Shame on us indeed if the Harvester learns how we've endangered his little treasure," added the woman in gray. She reached out a clutching hand toward Diligence, who avoided it with a deft sidestep. "The Daughter should be back at the wagons with the door bolted and her covers over her head."

"Hah. You could surround her wagon with a stack of frozen soldiers and she would still be safer here by my side," Pomponderant said, lifting one of the hatchling's arms to inspect its blue-covered fingers. Hitch leaned forward, noticing for the first time in the pulsing light of the pale fire the odd contours of the hatchling's body. Areas like raised welts stood out along his limbs and torso, as if he wore poultices against his skin beneath the slick covering. And the covering itself had taken on an odd aspect: delicate traceries of hair-thin lines caught the light, vanishing a moment later as the blue surface of the arm was returned to its resting place. "What do you suppose?" Pomponderant muttered to himself at Hitch's side. "Did they dip him in a tar bath before dropping him into the lake?"

"Leave the body, leave the boy," the marchmaster intoned, earning himself a fierce look from Hitch.

"The boy?" The old man lifted his head and inspected

Hitch dispassionately. "Mm. He has put forth some intriguing theories concerning our somnolent visitor, but perhaps his store of insight has been exhausted. As for the body—it comprises a veritable rash of itching questions which we can neither abandon nor ignore."

The marchmaster and the woman in the gray skullcap responded to this assertion at the same time. A three-sided argument began over the merits of toting the unconscious man through the dark forest.

Diligence had been edged out of the little circle of light by the arrival of the gray-clad woman and the marchmaster. "Tell Pomponderant what you said when I asked you why you pulled the hatchling out of the water," she whispered abruptly at Hitch's elbow.

The boy frowned. He was trying—so far without much success—to sort out exactly who was in charge here. In most traveling parties, the marchmaster held ultimate authority, yet the woman they called Nury had so far been treated as a personage of equal importance. The yellow-haired girl had gotten her way earlier on the beach, but here by the log the old man clearly outranked her. If that was true, it did not bode well for Hitch, as Pomponderant seemed to have little interest in him beyond his role as discoverer of the man in blue. Indeed, if only one newcomer were to be chosen to join the caravan, Hitch felt sure the old man would cast his vote for the hatchling.

Diligence made a hissing noise and jabbed him in the shoulder with her knuckled fist. "Tell him!"

"Tell him what?" Hitch responded irritably. "I said that I was curious, that's all."

"Pomponderant, listen to this." Diligence reached out to tug at the old man's purple hood. "Hitch, tell him about the curious part," she prompted. "You remember: Just before you dived in you said to yourself, 'Follow . . .' "

"The green moth," Hitch finished. "That's just a saying. What I meant—"

Pomponderant swiveled around so quickly that he almost fell on the ground. "Where did you learn that phrase?" he asked. "Not on Jogjaw Pass."

"In a valley." Hitch was startled by the sudden intensity of the old man's regard. He gestured vaguely behind him. "In a house. I heard it from an old woman. She was sick, then she died." Hitch had the old man's attention for certain. He paused, casting about desperately for any additional information that might help win him a berth in the caravan. "She gave me this cloak."

"Hmf." Pomponderant fingered the green wool absently. "Died, you say? How long were you with her? Did you hasten her demise?"

"Surely not!" Hitch drew back indignantly, yanking the fabric out of the old man's grasp. "I stayed two nights. I made her some soup and held her hand. She had a shaking fever, and something the matter with her throat."

"Mm-hm-hm ... Marchmaster, Hubwoman!" Pomponderant addressed the two without turning his gaze from Hitch's face. "The blue man and the mountain boy are both to come with us. Ut!" He raised his crooked finger as the marchmaster's mouth flew open. "The longer your disputatious nature has us here arguing, the closer we come to the nighthoot's belly." As if on cue, a mournful, hornlike call sounded from the dark forest to the east, followed by a strange, rapid clacking noise. The marchmaster paled under his scattering of freckles and went to summon the soldiers to resume their burden.

"Thank you, sir," Hitch said, as he and Diligence helped Pomponderant to his feet.

The old man grunted. "Mind you stay interesting," he advised.

The trek through the woods did not take as long as Hitch

had expected. Pomponderant divided the cold fire among the marchmaster and the soldiers, who held the little cages aloft by sliding their fingers through the narrow loops of leather affixed to their tops. Still, it was not far from dawn by the time they reached the wagon camp, a wide circle of towering silhouettes. Hitch, accustomed to the two-wheeled drays employed for haulage by the mountain folk, was unprepared for the size and grandeur of the vehicles: each one like a large bungalow mounted on tall wheels, with a peaked roof lined with brown tiles, and four round windows distributed evenly around the sides. A quartet of black-clad guards hailed them sharply as they approached the camp, then rushed forward to greet their fellows with obvious relief. Hitch looked around, yawning. There was no sign of pull-ponies or any other beasts to draw the heavy wagons. He spied a collapsible pen of withes and fiber mesh at the far end of the circle and supposed they must be quartered there, though the restless figures he made out in the dimness seemed far too slight of build and few in number to do the job.

The center of the camp was mounded with great humps of earth. As Diligence led him around the ring, he thought he saw tremors of movement among the hummocks, and twice he heard a sound like metal scraping on stone.

The tall girl left him for a few moments to confer with a group of shadowy individuals clustered around one of the wagons. Her manner was subdued when she returned. She conducted him to a vehicle halfway round the circle. A black-haired boy in a rumpled sleepshirt sat at the doorway, kicking his legs drowsily above the ground.

"You're to share with the cook and the scrivener for now," Diligence told him. "They've laid a mattress on the floor for you. Try to get some rest. The soldiers are going to bury Tarler and Huben in the sleep holes at sunrise. No doubt we'll be moving again soon after."

A ladder made of slats and rope dangled next to the doorway. The inside of the wagon was warm; it smelled of cooked meat and spices. Thin shafts of rose-brown dawn had begun to slant through the narrow louvers that covered the eastern window. The sleepshirted boy latched the door behind them, then sidled past Hitch into the bunk on the right-hand side. A massive shape lay snoring gustily against the opposite wall. As the younger boy watched in silent curiosity, Hitch removed the damp garments from his pack and hung them carefully on a series of knobs protruding from the left-hand wall. Then he settled onto the floor, his green cloak tucked up under his chin and his backsack beneath his head. Thoughts and questions buzzed in his brain like honeyflies around a disrupted hive, until finally he grew numb to their stings and fell into a fitful sleep.

EIGHT

CHANGE OF HUE

It seemed to Diligence that she had barely touched her head to the pillow silk when she felt a lurch of motion beneath her. She opened her eyes as the wagon began to jog gently from side to side. Daylight streamed in at the windows, investing the ivory-colored wood of the interior with a golden luster. She turned onto her back and examined the familiar image wrought in low relief on the ceiling of the car: a great circle divided into eight segments, embellished in rich color with fanciful depictions of the Advancements and the Inclinations, and fitted discreetly with the elaborate clockwork necessary to provide an accurate representation of the current status of her homeland. The Harvesters were in the third shading of the Eastern Cantle, a location famed for its bountiful rivers; no doubt her father was sitting down at this very moment to a breakfast of roe cake and pickled eels. Hunger knotted in her belly. She sat on the edge of her bed and extended both arms high over her head with a grunt, then padded to the rear of the car and pulled down the ornate panel that concealed the larder.

They had been lucky in their cook, who had shown a flair for invention from the start of the expedition, striving to combine exotic local ingredients with the more standard fare they had brought with them from the Wheel. This morning Diligence had her choice of boiled bogtower stalks served in a briny syrup, crisp wafers of fried sweetmeal, and three small bowls of rootpaste, each flavored with a subtly different fruit essence. Diligence selected the russet paste and a handful of wafers. Pouring herself a mug of dark tea from a steaming silver pot, she retired with her meal to the tiny salon at the front of the wagon. There she sipped the peppery brew and watched the dreary landscape of the wetlands pass by through the forward window.

The day was fair, the sky bright with a lambent sheen of golden brown. The wagons trundled along at a steady pace beneath the sun's urging.

Scooping the last of the paste onto a wafer, Diligence moved to the far end of the car and peered back at the other wagons and, beyond them, at the dusky shapes of the yeofolk, lumbering stolidly in a V-shaped line behind the last vehicle. A flash of warmer color drew her attention to the half-dozen nude figures who chased and dodged one another along the eastern flank of the caravan, their wordless cries coming faintly through the window glass. Diligence tried to pick out the alter who had been used to lead them to the lake last night, but more than one of the males had fair hair, and the group moved so swiftly and in such complexly shifting patterns that it was like trying to track an individual bird in a flock of migrating blackwings. From a distance they had the semblance of a troupe of frenzied men and women, cavorting madly through the umber mudflats; it was only when they passed close by the wagons that the grotesquely swollen thighs and elongated, tough-soled feet became apparent.

Diligence returned to the forward salon for another mug of tea and a solitary game of jump-the-stick on the tiny tabletop built into the wall below the window. After a while, she drew her journal from a shelf beneath the table. Locating a trough of pigments and a fresh stylus, she settled down to record the events of the previous day and night.

The aspect of the land changed almost imperceptibly as

they made their way beneath the sun, becoming progressively drier and more solid, with parch-weed and scattered clumps of ovengrass replacing the marshy flora. The wind rose and fell unpredictably, birthing tiny dust devils that spun alongside the wagons for a few seconds and then dissolved. By early afternoon they had reached a region where the cracked earth stretched out all around them in a vast, sepia-colored plain.

A loose-linked chain of clouds had been massing gradually on the far horizon for the past hour; now the clouds began to pass in slow parade beneath the sun, painting the dusty earth with a succession of shifting, golden-gray shadows.

The marchmaster sounded the signal bell from the lead car. Moments later, the caravan rolled into a wide circle and slowed to a creaking halt.

Diligence clapped her journal shut and knelt to hunt for her sandals under the bed. She hopped down from the wagon without pausing to unroll the ladder, clasped her hands behind her back, and tugged at her shoulders with a groan, twisting her neck from side to side until it produced a satisfying cracking noise. Doors were flung open around the ring of cars, as others clambered to the ground to stretch their own cramped muscles in the cool air.

Diligence surveyed the barren countryside. The yeofolk were congregating not far from the wagons, butting shells with a hollow clanking and crawling atop one another until their dark mound resembled a miniature mountain range. Diligence turned back to the circle and headed for the cook's wagon. As she approached the rear door, a sharp whistle brought her attention to the far side of the car. Hitch stuck his head around the wall of blue-lacquered wood and waved her over. He had strung a slender cord from a pair of ornamental spurs at either end of the car and was in the process of draping the last of his garments over the line.

"They're mostly dry, but in dire need of an airing out."
He wrinkled his nose suggestively, then plucked at the voluminous crimson gown that covered him from shoulder to
shin. "The cook lent me one of his workshirts."

"Now you truly resemble the King of Evil's son," said
Diligence. "The shadowsmith always wears red in the
Fabularies. Were you able to get some sleep?"

"A few blinks. I woke up when Cook stepped on my
collarbone on his way out to deliver breakfast. After I con-
vinced him nothing had been broken, he invited me to join
him on his rounds. Clever, the way you can unlock the larders from the outside . . ." He broke off, his eyes going
wide as the flock of alters came galloping into the wagon
ring, their braying cries turning to yelps of joy when the
alterman appeared in their midst like a benevolent god, a
sackful of green biscuits held aloft. The boy turned back to
Diligence with a shake of his head. "A caravan of marvels.
And the wagons! One of these could make a comfortable
home for a brood of ten back at the Falls. I never realized
till we stopped that they're all roped together." He gestured
to the stout black cable that ran from the rear of his car to
the front of the one behind it. "But who does the pulling?
I noticed the great creatures that followed us, but we were
too far back in line to see what was occurring up front. Is
there another team?" He surveyed the ring with a low whistle and a disbelieving shake of his head. "They must be
mighty beasts indeed to haul all this weight of wood and
passengers."

Diligence was watching him with a look of renewed ap-
praisal. "Pomponderant was right," she said. "You really
did climb down from some far-off mountaintop. And here
I'd thought the Rooted would find our ways dull and
earthbound." She grinned at his expression. Then she
pointed to the sky above their heads. "It's the sun that does
the pulling—or the pushing, rather. The sun pushes every-

thing, so Pomponderant says, urging the world to ceaseless motion." She ran her hands along her bare forearms as gooseflesh erupted in the wake of a sudden gust of wind. "But the sun's cage hangs far away and her urgings are gentle. Only the very sensitive feel the prod and few of them respond to it."

"Is that why we mostly take our rest at night—or in dark corners?" Hitch wondered aloud. "Because when the sun is hanging in the sky above us we're excited to restlessness and movement?"

"Perhaps." She gave a judicious nod. "I do know that we of the Wheel are less subject to the effects of the prodding, for we happily choose to keep ourselves in motion. You Standing Folk are not so tractable, and I've heard your vitals suffer for it." Diligence had unconsciously assumed a didactic stance, setting her right fist against her hip as she gestured to the roof of the cook's wagon with her other hand. "As you can see, each car is crowned with a tesselation of red-brown tiles. The Makers introduce a substance during the fabrication of the tiles which heightens their sensitivity to the presence of the sun and renders them far more amenable to her suggestions than ones composed of ordinary clay."

"The sun encourages the tiles to motion and the tiles are affixed to the wagons . . ." Hitch digested the information, shading his eyes with one hand as warm amber sunlight began to stream down through a widening gap in the sequence of high clouds. He surveyed the ring of colorful vehicles in the evaporating shadows. "Why then do the wagons sit here unmoving, though the sun shines brightly on them once more? Will she not take offense at their stubbornness?"

"Aha." Diligence waggled a finger in the air. "A sound question from the youth in the crimson overblouse. Hidden beneath the tiles, you see, are tiny roots which grow down between the inner and outer walls of the car. The roots lead below the floor to a brace of sturdy metal hands mounted in such a way as to grip the axles. You can see them for yourself, should you care to lie down upon your back beneath the car." Enjoying her role as instructor, Diligence had begun to pace in a measured circle as she spoke. She paused to indicate a small furze of purple-black leaves with the toe of her sandal. "Now you know that water is commonly induced to travel upward through a root in order to slake the thirst of a patch of ovengrass. Well, in the case of the wagons, it's the impulse of the tiles toward motion that must traverse the roots downward to the clutch of metal hands. The hands turn the axle and the axle propels the wheels." She curled her fingers around an invisible bar and twisted forward. "When the marchmaster wishes to halt the caravan, he exerts pressure on a lever in the lead wagon, thus causing a temporary separation between the tiles and their roots. The tiles lie mute, the impulse is lost, and the metal hands fall into idleness. As an obvious consequence, the cars come to a stop." She opened her hands and spread them wide. "There. A simple explanation for a simple feat."

Hitch executed one of his elaborate bows with a skeptical chuckle. "Your simple student thanks you." He raised his eyes doubtfully to the nearest red-brown roof. "Yet the lead wagon sits seven cars away ... How then does the marchmaster's lever induce the tiles of the cook's wagon to part from *their* roots? And if the lead car alone fell into idleness, would not its followers crowd into it from behind?"

Diligence stepped back and raised her hands. "Too many questions!" She pointed past the blue wall toward the inner circle. "Yonder green and golden wagon is shared by Pomponderant and the marchmaster; the wagoneer resides in the ultramarine car next in line after yours. Kindly address your further inquires to one of them. I've had my fill for the day."

"Meaning you don't exactly know," said Hitch with a smug grin.

"Hmf." Something caught Diligence's eye. She leaned back to peer around the corner of the car. "There appears to be a small commotion outside the second guard wagon. Isn't that where they stored the blue man?"

They crossed the dry ground to the scarlet and silver car.

Pomponderant was sitting in the sun on a collapsible chair at the foot of the wagon's ladder. Other members of the caravan crowded around him with a babble of conversation. Diligence pushed her way to where the old man basked with eyes half closed, ignoring the hubbub. She plucked at his purple sleeve. "Is it the blue man?" she asked. "Is he all right?"

Pomponderant opened one eye. "There has been a development," he said sagely.

"Here now, get down out of there!"

Diligence turned at the marchmaster's bark in time to see two soldiers heave Hitch's struggling form from the doorway of the scarlet wagon. The boy struck the ground awkwardly, scrambled to his feet with as much dignity as the crimson overblouse would allow, and threaded his way through the crowd to Diligence's side. "It's changed color!" the boy declared in a tone both wondering and accusatory.

"Indeed," Pomponderant confirmed. "Most intriguing."

"What are you talking about? Let me see." Diligence strode toward the ladder. Breitling moved in a halfhearted attempt to intercept her, changed his mind, and fell back. "Mind she doesn't get too close," he instructed the soldiers as she swung herself up and ducked into the doorway.

It took a few moments for her eyes to adjust to the dim interior of the car. The hatchling lay in one of the lower bunks, wrapped to the chin in a bright green coverlet. Diligence approached with a frown, unable to detect any change whatsoever in the pallid hue of the sleeping man's face. She leaned forward and gave a startled exclamation. No coverlet lay across the unmoving form. The dark blue material of the hatchling's slick-looking clothing had been replaced by a rich teal green. She examined it closely, noting the pattern of nearly invisible lines that covered the garment, sparsely in some areas, heavily in others. Was it the same clothing he had been wearing when she saw him on the beach last night?

Diligence returned to the brightness outside with a thoughtful expression on her face. Pomponderant inspected her keenly as she hopped down from the wagon. "So! A theory, founded on observable data? A supposition, moored to whimsy?"

Diligence considered. "Is there pertinent information to add to what we have just observed?"

Pomponderant measured a small quantity in the air with his hands. "Little of substance. The soldiers claim that his condition was unchanged and his garment's color as before when the car grew light. They busied themselves with tea-drinking and games of dig-the-ditch in the forward salon till midafternoon, when one of them chanced to pass by the bunk on her way to the relief room. *Oho!*"

The old man spread his fingers dramatically. "During those several hours, last night's somber hue had drained entirely away, leaving the attractive green you have just observed. After a brief discussion, the soldiers communicated news of the alteration to the marchmaster, who took advantage of the sun's obscuration to call a halt."

"Ink, perhaps?" Hitch chewed at his lower lip, his eyes on a point between two of the wagons. "Blackfruit ink spilled on the hands will eventually wear off. Perhaps he tossed and fretted in his bunk while the soldiers laid their wagers, and so rubbed away the outer color."

Diligence watched her tutor. "Have the bedclothes been changed?" she asked.

"They have not."

"Then the hypothesis is insupportable, for it requires a sizable stain on the bedsheets beneath him, when in fact they remain unblemished white."

"Good," said Pomponderant. He poked Hitch in the side with his bony forefinger. "Other thoughts?"

"Many fabrics become darker when exposed to dampness," the boy offered. "Perhaps his garment is unusually acquisitive and retained the lake moisture until recently."

Pomponderant looked at Diligence, who shrugged. "It seems possible," she ventured.

The discussion produced no additional theories. At length the other passengers drifted away from the wagon to their own pursuits. Chores were performed: relief buckets emptied into a small furrow some distance from the circle; axle mounts oiled and wheels inspected; provisions for a light snack of desiccated fruit and hopwater distributed to the larders by the cook with Hitch assisting. After half an hour, Breitling's bell announced that they were ready to resume their journey.

Pomponderant and Hitch joined Diligence in her wagon for the next leg of the trip. After the three had rehashed the sudden metamorphosis of the hatchling's apparel, Diligence and her tutor discussed the mysterious attack on the camp which had claimed the lives of two guards the previous night. Several theories were propounded in connection with each event, but no conclusions reached.

Hitch made inquiries concerning the wheelwork that decorated the ceiling of each wagon. He listened in rapt attention, eyes turned upward, as his two hosts took turns describing the purpose of the device and the unusual land that was mirrored in its functioning. When asked about his own origins, he made vague responses, leading Diligence to conclude that he held little warmth for the mountains of his birth. Listening to him, she had come to the decision that Hitch could no more be considered Rooted than she herself, and that he was in fact a Wander Man—one of those unfathomable beings who chose to spend their lives walking away from their points of inception with little desire to return.

Vivid swirls of orange, plum, and lavender in the western sky heralded the arrival of sunset some four hours later.

The nine wagons drew their circle for the night on a plot of dry earth that was not noticeably different from the place they had stopped that afternoon. The alter pen was erected and Cook began dinner preparations. When Diligence and Hitch went to check on the hatchling, they found his physical condition unchanged, with the exception of the bruise on his forehead, which had faded almost to invisibility. His garments—as well as they could be judged by lamplight—had grown even greener.

The air chilled rapidly once the sun disappeared. Dinner, served on collapsible tables arranged about a central fire ring, consisted of a stew of leeks and a salad in which ovengrass was prominently featured, followed by braised chunks of pinkish meat wrapped in waterflower leaves. Chewing sticks and mugs of evergreen beer were passed around the circle.

Hitch had resumed his own dried and freshened garments shortly before the meal. He declined Diligence's offer of a fur-lined blanket and huddled in his green wool cloak close to the shuddering fire ring. Pomponderant dozed in his chair for an hour after dinner, roused himself with a great snort, and sought out his wagon. Diligence watched Hitch in silence, pondering the contrasting aspects of his nature; the young man's attributes seemed to fluctuate within the space of seconds, now marking him as a common pack-man with limited experience of the world, now as a keen-witted pupil whose efforts pleased even Pomponderant.

Time passed. Stars began to wink through the tattered cloak of Night above them. At last the fire ring was broken down and the remaining passengers folded up their chairs and made ready to retire. The two handlers responsible for the yeofolk led their shambling charges into the center of the circle to dig their sleep holes. Diligence took note of Hitch's fixed attention as the creatures fell to their burrow-making with the usual creaking and clanging of body parts. She recalled his bemused response to the sight of the racing alters earlier in the day. Considering the two reactions, she felt it safe to assume that the boy had never before encountered representatives of either race—a remarkable thought in itself. The Silent Falls must occupy a distant arc of the world indeed, she reflected, as she gathered up her blanket and mounted the ladder to her car.

Diligence slept surprisingly well; choir-wolves were disinclined to range this far from the wetlands, and night on the vast plain was still. In the morning she was awakened by shouts from outside the wagon. Sometime during the night, unobserved by marchmaster or guards, Pomponderant had vanished from the camp.

NINE

SOMETHING IN THE WIND

Hitch awoke considerably later than was his custom. The safety of four stout walls and a belly lined with good food could work a change on anyone's habits, he reflected ruefully as he pulled on his clothing in the cook's empty car. Strange dreams had occupied his night; they vanished like wisps of colored smoke when he tried to recall them.

The wagon sat motionless, daylight slanting in through the open louvers. Hitch knelt on a bunk to peer out one of the side windows: dry earth stretched endlessly away beneath a sky the color of brass. He stowed his pack in the space set aside for him beneath the right-hand bunk, confirming in the process that the jewel-headed walking stick remained where he had hidden it at the rear of the cubby.

He found the scrivener boy sitting cross-legged on the wooden landing just outside the door of the car, copying alphabets onto his talking board from a frayed brown scroll. Hitch lowered himself alongside the younger boy and dangled his boots over the edge, surveying the ring of quiet wagons. The camp appeared to be deserted, except for a pair of black-clad soldiers idling in conversation by the alter pen. He peered over the boy's shoulder, comparing the marks on the ancient scroll to those just applied to the sheet of vellum stretched across the talking board.

"You do careful work," Hitch observed after a moment.

The scrivener shrugged. "Each letter has but a single correct shape," he said without taking his eyes from the board. "One learns to reproduce them with precision, or one is swiftly guided to another Inclination. I myself prefer writing to clearing brush or transforming dead fish into fertilizer."

Hitch snorted in amusement. "I take it you don't work your craft for the love of it, then."

The boy lifted his gaze to the horizon with a sigh of deepest melancholy. "I loved the Wheel, and the turning, and knowing where my center was," he said with unexpected fervor. "Now all that's gone. Since we passed through the Northeastern Gate, I've been a Wander Man like the rest of you, cursed to amble off in a tangent that may never bring me home." He squeezed his eyes shut as if he felt a stab of pain, then blinked them open again. "At first I tried mightily to make this awful journey a part of my turning—but it's impossible to chart." He rolled back the thin parchment on his talking board to show a previous section, where a dozen wavering ellipses had been overlaid on a sketchy map of the Wheel and its nearest neighbors. "One consolation: If by some prodigy I do return, surely I will have advanced far beyond my given circuit, and find myself that much closer to serenity than when I was plucked from my gyre." He twisted the knobs that returned the board to its previous state.

Hitch sat blinking, taken aback by the outpouring of words and feeling from the hitherto taciturn youth. "Well," he said after a moment. "I hope so, for your sake. My name is Hitch."

"I'm Alacrity." The boy lifted a shallow bowl of shelled nutmeats from the other side of the landing and passed it to Hitch. "The white ones are bitter," he said.

Hitch tipped a palmful of brown kernels into his mouth and squinted at the amber sun, already halfway to the zenith. He stretched his legs out in front of him. "Perhaps I'll take a stroll around the wagons and see what's doing with the other folk. I'm usually up and out much earlier than this."

"I'm not." The scrivener fisted a yawn and unrolled another length of the age-darkened scroll, pinning it flat to the landing with a pair of polished stone weights. "I couldn't sleep through all the noise," he added.

"Noise?" Hitch scanned the placid camp. "What noise?"

"Well, the first uproar came when they discovered the old teacher had gone missing." The boy dipped his stylus into the pigment trough and returned it to the vellum, where he slowly executed a series of complicated whorls in rich turquoise. "Then the green man woke up, and everyone had to exclaim over that for a while." He raised his head from the talking board and squinted speculatively at the eastern sky. "It might be a good time for a nap, now that things have quieted down again."

Hitch's boots struck the ground with a thump. "And where am I when he finally comes to his senses?" he muttered as he started across the wagon ring. "Sitting here waggling my feet and popping nutmeats, like a dwindlewit on his rock!" He cupped his hands to his mouth. "Diligence!"

The scrivener watched him hurry away with a raised brow. "But we're off the Wheel," he said in a listless murmur. "What could any of it matter?"

Hitch headed straight for the scarlet and silver wagon where he had last seen the hatchling. He repeated his call for Diligence as he neared the car, attracting the notice of the two guards by the alter pen. A big-shouldered woman named Ottshent dropped the handful of seeds she was feeding an orange-haired female and waved her arms at him. "Hoy!" she bawled. "No one's to go in there!"

"*I* am," Hitch called back from halfway up the ladder. "Ask the Daughter—ask her mother!" He ducked inside.

His excitement cooled rapidly as he negotiated the shadowy interior of the car. Nothing seemed to have changed. The hatchling lay as before: on his back with his hands at his sides, his sleeping face turned toward the decorated ceiling. As Hitch came closer, his attention was drawn to the strange body wrap. Apparently, its coloring had undergone a further alteration overnight, dimming from yesterday's bright viridian to a soft leaf green. Hitch wondered absently if exposure to daylight could be responsible for slowly leaching away the fabric's vivid hue. The hair-thin lines that subdivided the supple material like veins in a new leaf stood out more clearly in the paler garment. Hitch was reminded of the scrivener's board: could this be writing? He traced one of the markings with his forefinger and saw a sudden flicker of motion out of the corner of his eye. Startled, he looked up.

A bar of shadow fell across the top half of the white face, making it difficult at first for Hitch to credit what he'd seen. Then the hatchling's eyelids gave a second rapid flutter—and this time they stayed open. Oddly colored pupils twitched to follow the boy as he moved to the head of the bunk.

"Well, then!" Hitch said with a forced heartiness. "Awake at last! At the least, you make me feel better about my own tardiness in rising." He cleared his throat when the man made no reply. "Is there anything you need? Water—a change of clothes?"

The shadowed eyes studied his face with no sign of comprehension, seemingly drawn only by the movement of his lips.

"Don't you remember me?" Hitch asked. "Or is it human speech you've forgotten?"

"Mountain boy!" The soldier's head and shoulders appeared in the doorway behind him. "You'd better crawl down out of there! The far-turners are on their way back in and no one's looking exceptionally cheerful."

"One moment," he told her sternly. "My friend and I debate the disposition of weighty matters." He peered down at the silent face with a grimace of frustration. The hatchling might well be awake, Hitch reflected, but he seemed in no mood for conversation. As he watched, the eyelids drifted shut again, eclipsing the odd green-gray stare. Hitch gave a disappointed sigh. Perhaps Diligence had managed to get something out of him. As he was turning away, a pair of strong hands shot out from the bunk and encircled his left forearm in an iron grip. He gave a grunt of surprise as he was yanked suddenly forward.

With eyes still shut, the hatchling raised his head and shoulders from the thin pillow and propelled them outward, burying his face in Hitch's loose jacket. Drawing in a shuddering breath, he began to speak in a low monotone, his words muffled by the garments.

"What?" Hitch twisted in the bizarre embrace, trying to pry the hatchling's forehead back from his chest with his free hand. "What did you say? Turn me loose!"

"Preliminary olfactory evidence identifies the individual who performed the aquatic extrication," remarked a flat voice from the vicinity of his breastbone. The statement was followed by a soft snuffling sound as the pale face burrowed deeper into his jacket and blouse.

"Hey!" Hitch struggled against the straining head, searching unsuccessfully for a handhold in the cap of short black hair. "I aired them out yesterday! Stop smelling me!"

The uncomfortable pressure against his chest abruptly ceased. With a slump of green shoulders, the hatchling cocked his head to one side and blindly addressed the shadowed wall: "Auditory sampling lends considerable credence to the theory." The hands released their painful grip, sending Hitch stumbling backward several paces to land heavily on the opposite bunk.

The hatchling's head fell back against the pillow silk. The eyes remained shut in the white face, which lay as blank and unmoving as a mask of carved saltwood beneath the ceiling's ornate wheelwork.

The boy took in a shaky breath and pushed to his feet. "Night's hairbrush—you might've just asked me," Hitch said, feeling gingerly along his midsection for evidence of bruised ribs. "I would have told you I was the one who pulled you out of that lake."

"Identity confirmed. Pending information to the contrary, an undetermined quantity of goodwill is assumed," the green man murmured. Then his voice strengthened, the words snapping out with a curious rapidity, like someone tapping impatiently on a tabletop: "Physical recovery has been effected, as clearly manifested in the account of the instrument suit—yet there is an irrefutable indication of memory loss, similar to that reported by Lastique and Brouderben during the early trials. In that case, the condition was found to be contingent on the immanence of the auxiliary consciousness. Immediate withdrawal therefore presents itself as the optimal solution."

"Hitch?" Diligence's voice came from outside the wagon.

He turned a quick glance over his shoulder. "In here—hurry!"

"Automatic retrieval will occur at the conclusion of one local revolution," the hatchling continued in his rapid staccato. "Should it become desirable to hasten the event, you may inform him of this sequence. As always, your cooperation is noted and applauded." The hatchling's right hand rose from his side and moved to briefly touch the pale green garment at throat, navel, and left shoulder, in each case pressing the first two fingers on the hand within a small circular area formed by the pattern of lines. His pale head stiffened, then lolled to one side on the pillow silk, a faint moan escaping the slack lips.

"Here you are." Diligence stood in the doorway.

"Did you hear that?" Hitch wheeled around. "What could it mean?"

"I'm not sure." She walked to his side. "He was groaning like that earlier. I thought it meant he was in pain, but we couldn't find anything wrong with him. Then he calmed down and went back to sleep."

"No, no. Before that." Hitch shook his head impatiently. "He was talking again—like on the beach! A few things I could make out, and then a lot of queer grummidge about revolutions and old factories." He paused, squinting at her face in the shadows. "Ho, you didn't hear a word he said, did you? You think I've been sniffing puffballs."

"Hitch, he was making a little groaning noise when I came in." Diligence chopped the air with the side of her hand, a gesture of finality. "That's all I heard. If you want to tell me he was reciting the Elucidaries backwards, I'll believe you." She glanced over her shoulder as voices were raised somewhere outside the car. "We're getting ready for an argument and I need your help. Did you hear that Pomponderant vanished sometime during the night? The Hubwoman and the marchmaster came banging on my door just after dawn. We've been out walking the plain. I made them look for him, but there are no tracks, nothing to say where he's gone. The soldiers swear they never saw him leave." She paused for a breath. "Nury and Breitling are understandably upset. First the two guards, now this."

Hitch felt the skin tighten at the nape of his neck. "Are the events connected, then?" he asked.

"Who can say? I told them it was Pomponderant's way as a member of the Society: to go when he wanted to, and not waste time with elaborate farewells. Now they want to move on—right away, this morning—without waiting for him to return."

"Sensible." Hitch nodded. "Sitting out here in the midst of nothing only puts you further behind in your journey to your mother—not to mention making you easy prey for whatever froze your guards." He glanced down at the still form on the bunk. "For my part, I'm going to stay in this wagon and try to rouse him again. If nothing else, he must be wanting food and water."

"No, you have to come to the meeting with me. We can't abandon Pomponderant like this. He may be somewhere nearby, in dire need of our assistance."

"Dire need?" Hitch blinked in bewilderment. "I thought you said this dropping out of sight was perfectly normal behavior for him, that there was no cause for concern . . ."

"But I didn't *mean* it." She twitched her shoulders in an exasperated shrug. "I was just trying to maintain some appearance of knowing what was going on. Pomponderant has always said that knowledge—or the semblance of knowledge—is power."

"Look, Daughter." Hitch nudged the hatchling's legs to one side and seated himself at the end of the bunk. "You have to clear something up for me. Who exactly is in charge of this caravan? One minute it seems to be you, the next it's the marchmaster; an hour later it's Nury, then Pomponderant. I'm surprised one of the alters isn't making the decision to move on."

"Evidently things are done a bit differently in the Standing Lands," the girl said stiffly. "Back on the Wheel many voices are heard when there's a decision to be made. Often a consensus must be achieved among kings and Hubmen, Advancements and Inclinations. Affairs may turn more slowly as a result, but it's the continual round of discussion and compromise that has driven the Wheel for centuries." She sighed and ran a hand through her blond curls. "This time I have the feeling I'm alone in my arc. Will you come as my supporter? Remember: With Pomponderant gone, few voices will be raised in protest if Breitling decides we've one mountain boy too many and leaves you out here to cultivate ovengrass."

"There's the ringing truth." Hitch looked glum. "What do you want me to do?"

"Just sit by my side and look wise," she told him. "Agree with me when it seems appropriate and look askance at the marchmaster's propositions."

Hitch considered the task. "All in all, not a difficult assignment—particularly that last bit."

The meeting took place in the lead wagon. Hitch was afforded his first glimpse of the interior of the green and golden vehicle as he and Diligence climbed the ladder and joined those already assembled. The car was spacious, the marchmaster's belongings stored in a row of niches set in the left-hand wall; of Pomponderant, who had shared these quarters as recently as last night, there was no sign. In addition to the intricate wheelwork on the ceiling above the sleeping area, Hitch was surprised to note a second elaborate fabrication, this one a crisscross of colored lines and crabbed notations both carved and painted on the sloping wall above the large circle of the forward window.

Awaiting them at the broad round table by the window were pinch-faced Nury, Breitling, and Welleck the wagoneer. The first two made no effort to conceal their disapproval as Diligence led Hitch to the table, while Welleck looked on impassively with pursed lips and a smooth brow. Diligence placed her hands on the back of the single unoccupied wicker chair. She cleared her throat. "I see we're lacking a place at the table for my adviser," she said.

"Adviser!" Nury gave a snort of disbelief. "Your humor is ill timed, Daughter." The Hubwoman narrowed her eyes at Hitch. "In truth, a place has been made for everyone who is entitled to be at this table."

Diligence gazed imperiously at the other woman. "Meaning that if Pomponderant were present at this moment, you would expect an old man to stand? Or am I the one who would be left leaning in the corner?"

"Pomponderant has flitted off on his own course, as you yourself have stated," Breitling said in a soothing tone. "Therefore—"

"Therefore I have chosen this young man to advise me in his stead. You know that my tutor was most interested in his opinions."

"His opinions on what?" Nury jeered. "Mountain fishing? Golden eggs? That blue man—or green man—or whatever hue he's ripened to this morning? Hah! All matters that have been outside our proper purview from the start." She waved her hand in a gesture of dismissal. "Tell your playfellow he's welcome to hang outside on the ladder if he wishes to hear our counsel."

"I see." Diligence appeared to seriously consider this advice for several heartbeats. At last she nodded her head and pulled the wicker chair out from the table. "Very well." She stood to one side, motioning Hitch to come forward. "In that case, I shall be the one to stand."

"Daughter, please!" The wagoneer got hastily to his feet and pushed his own chair toward Diligence. With a reproachful glance at his companions, he stepped to a cubby in the nearby wall and brought forth one of the collapsible chairs Hitch had noted the previous day. He unfolded it and seated himself at the table, then waved Diligence and Hitch to the two unoccupied places. "May we begin now?" he beseeched them all.

The meeting itself was not the shouting match Hitch had been expecting, but rather a long and somewhat tedious restating of events and opinions. The marchmaster was for

getting under way without further delay; at Nury's prodding, he spoke of timetables and an audience with someone
called the Dreamwright—a vitally important audience for
which they must make every effort to arrive on time. For
her part, the Daughter requested that they allow Pomponderant a mere two days in which to confirm that he had
truly left the caravan for good. She reminded them of the
easy distractibility of Society members, and put forth the
theory that he had merely wandered off to inspect some local oddity that had caught his attention on the previous day.

Hitch remembered to nod sagaciously whenever Diligence spoke, and soon came to enjoy the opportunity to
sneer and goggle his eyes at statements made by either the
Hubwoman or the marchmaster. The mustachioed wagoneer
seemed a decent and sensible fellow; he voiced concern for
the missing old man in an accent that betrayed his own
Western origins, and sided more often with Diligence than
with the two on his own side of the table.

In the end it was decided to spend the rest of the day and
following night waiting. Breitling unrolled a thin sheet of
vellum on the tabletop. If Pomponderant did not return to
the caravan by the next morning, the wagons would push
on toward their immediate destination, a sort of way station
in the midst of the waste that the marchmaster referred to
as a ramble house. Breitling traced their route with a polished fingernail. "Straight northward for a day, then northeast for two more should see us safely moored at
Paddifraw's Repose, here at the junction of the Maroon and
Mustard Lines," he said. "At that time we shall replenish
our supplies and the first leg of our journey may be considered complete—though not, I regretfully acknowledge,
without incident." His severe gaze swept the cabin and the
rear window, taking in Diligence, Hitch, and the red and
silver wagon behind them, where the hatchling lay in his
bunk. Ignoring the implied accusation, Hitch left his chair

to peer over the mountain range of shoulders bent above the map. He searched the sheet of vellum for maroon and mustard lines, but found none. Puzzled by the marchmaster's remarks, he finally glanced up at the strange configuration of brightly colored scratches and notations above the forward window. Another sort of map?

"We'll be skirting the edge of the Aulmad if we go that route," Welleck observed in a bleak voice.

Hitch turned to Diligence with a frown. "The Aulmad?" he whispered. "I thought we'd been traversing the Aulmad these past two days."

"No, we're barely into the Lower Siccative." She gave him a sympathetic smile. "World's a bit bigger than you thought, eh?"

Harvest's Daughter Diligence accepted the compromise with dignity. At the conclusion of the meeting, she left the lead wagon with Hitch in tow and went straight to her own car. There she retrieved from beneath her bunk a small object bound in blue leather.

"The latest volume of my journal," she explained. "Pomponderant gave it to me just before we left the Wheel. He made it himself, so I'm hoping some of his scent still remains on it." Book in hand, she led the way to the fourth wagon, where they found the alterman popping dandytarts and holding forth on a variety of subjects. The pair of yeofolk handlers who shared his wagon sat across from him at the table, munching their noon meal in stolid silence.

Muttering peevishly, the little man accepted the small bribe of silver hairbeads Diligence had brought him, and allowed himself to be conducted to the alter pen. Minutes later, Hitch watched aghast as a trio of the naked creatures were led forth on leather leashes, their newly modified heads swinging this way and that in the light, cool breeze that had sprung up from the south. It was the first time Hitch had watched the alterman at work, and the results had all but turned his stomach inside out. Cavernous nostrils now dominated the distorted faces, frantic eyes peering out of small bony caverns to either side of the great juts of splayed cartilage, while the mouths had been reduced to nubbins of pursed flesh.

The sun had attained the zenith by the time they left the camp. It had taken the alters a few minutes of intense inhalation to separate out the various scent residues lingering on the journal. After satisfying themselves—with some urging from the alterman and his lash—that Diligence was not to be their quarry, they surged out from the wagons in a ragged line to the southwest, heads flung back, huge nostrils trembling in the breeze.

Diligence had recruited Shevoss and a bristle-bearded guard named Dopple to help handle the creatures, the alterman preferring to return to his dandytarts and the comfort of his wagon. For two hours they searched the barren earth around the camp, often doubling back and crossing over their previous trail, until Hitch came to believe the old man had been either severely inebriated or wandering blindfolded when he departed the camp. At length their zigzag course brought them to the edge of a large circular area where the sandy earth was stained a dark reddish brown. The alters refused to venture beyond the outer perimeter of the circle, flapping their distended nose cups and twittering to one another as they stamped the ground with their unshod feet.

Hitch dug idly at the blood-colored earth with the toe of his boot. The soil had an odd consistency, as if it were permeated by some sticky fluid. He walked to the place where Diligence and the soldiers were attempting to calm the skittish creatures. "What's the problem?"

"The soldiers think it's an old wormhole." Diligence eyed the patch of stained ground somberly. "Probably dead for years, but the smell is strong enough to panic the alters in their present state."

"Wormhole?" Hitch peered across to the opposite rim of the discolored soil. The circle was at least twenty yards in diameter. "How many worms would it take to make this?" he wondered aloud.

"Only one, I'm afraid," said Diligence. She gave a defeated shrug. "We may as well go back to the wagons. The alters are ruled by their noses at the moment, and without the alterman here to coax them into a new form we have little chance of getting them to investigate further."

The soil looked progressively more friable nearer the center of the circle, as if it had been recently overturned. "You don't think something happened to Pomponderant out there, do you?" Hitch asked. "If you want me to do some digging . . ." He stepped onto the dark area.

"No!" Diligence pulled him back. "Best not to venture very far. It's a wormhole. There's no telling where the ground might refuse to bear your weight."

When the small search party was about halfway back to the camp, a strong breeze sprang up from the west. The trio of alters halted in their tracks, nostrils expanding like sails in the wind, then turned as one to scan the western horizon with their shrunken eyes.

"Pomponderant?" Hitch asked, drawing close to Diligence.

She shook her head. "Look at them. They're scared to death." The alters stood quaking in the breeze, pawing one another and gabbling back and forth in high-pitched interrogatives. Hitch felt a shiver travel up his own spine. He turned to Shevoss and Dopple, who were conducting their own conversation in tones of quiet foreboding. "What do you think it could be?"

The soldiers peered across the barren expanse to the west. "Most anything, this close to the Aulmad," answered

Shevoss. "Though nothing good. Rockrasps swarm the dead cities to the north of here, while Dry Pirates and bone-takers haunt the wastes." She lifted her chin as the wind blew chill. "Now that winter's coming, we might even encounter a blaze of candlemen heading back to the Blasted Lands."

Marshaling the alters with stern tugs of the leashes, they continued on their way.

They reached the camp without further incident. The alters fled into the pen, where they stood huddled against the far mesh, whining softly for their master and his biscuits. A disconsolate Diligence returned to her wagon to brew some tea, while Hitch continued on to retrieve something from the cook's car. "You may join me if you like," she told him at the foot of her ladder. "Maybe together we can figure out why he left."

She was writing in her journal at the table near the front of the car when Hitch came puffing in, his bulging pack slung over his shoulder. "I have something to show you." He heaved the backsack onto the tabletop and began to rummage through its contents. "Here it is." He lifted out an oblong object and handed it to her. "See? I have books, too."

Diligence took the bulky package and turned it over, exclaiming in surprise as she discovered the tiny latch and folded back the cover to reveal three identically bound volumes in a slipcase of black and green tortoise skin. She slid one of them out into her hand. The book fell open to a place marked with a green silk ribbon. On the right-hand page was a meticulously executed sketch of the diminutive flicker known as a waft, while the text on the facing page described the elusive creature, listing what little was known of its disposition and preferred habitat. "But these are wonderful!" Diligence looked up from the page. "Where in the world did you get them?"

"I . . . inherited the set from someone who had no more use for it," Hitch said, inwardly delighted that he had succeeded in diverting the girl's attention from her vanished tutor.

He joined Diligence at the table, leaning with his chin propped on his elbows as she paged through the book, marveling over the quality of the illustrations and reading aloud from the more memorable descriptions.

The day passed quietly and a quiet night followed it, both without untoward circumstance or an appearance by the absent Pomponderant. The hatchling's garment had continued to pale overnight, assuming by daybreak a soft yellow hue with just a tinge of green that was not unlike that of a ripened river squash. When the wagons started to move again the next morning, Hitch elected to ride with the guards in the red and silver car, where he might keep an eye on his fading charge.

"He's got his eyes open again," he reported to Diligence at the midday break. "Keeps drawing his tongue over his lips like he's parched—but he won't take water. I'm going to ask Cook for a little white-berry wine." He grinned in anticipation. "Maybe that'll catch his interest."

"Better make certain it's a good vintage," Diligence advised archly. "Perhaps it's his elevated tastes that have so far prevented him from sampling our fare." She accompanied him to the cook's wagon, where they talked the large man out of a quantity of sweet red cheese and some fruit crackle for themselves, in addition to the hatchling's libation. At the end of the half-hour stop, the girl climbed into the guards' wagon along with Hitch. The yellow man blinked up at them gravely as they drew their chairs up to the edge of his bunk. He refused to part his lips when Hitch held a mug of the pale wine up to his chin. Diligence tried two minutes later, to no greater effect.

"Ah well, let's peruse a few more of nature's grotesques," Hitch said, "then try again." He reached to lift the bulky slipcase from a cubby in the wall beyond the bunk. A fragment of fruit crackle had lodged in the corner of his breast pocket; as he extended his arm, it dropped onto the hatchling's breastbone. A yellow-swathed hand scuttled spiderlike across the chest and retrieved the morsel instantly, conveyed it to the expressionless face, and popped it into the hatchling's mouth. Hitch and Diligence sat amazed for a few seconds. Then the boy let out a whoop of delight.

"He ate it!" he called, earning a curious glance from the quartet of soldiers playing kick-the-rock at the forward table. "He finally ate something!" He turned back to the hatchling in time to see the placid face screw itself up in a grimace of fastidious distaste. The next moment the yellow man spat the chewy morsel out onto the bedclothes and turned his head toward the wall like an obstinate child.

Hitch shook his head in weary defeat and handed Diligence the first volume of the guidebooks.

"Look here," she said, opening to the page where they had left off the previous day. "A diamond-patterned bogsquat. And doesn't he have a wicked set of ankle spurs . . ."

That night, asleep on the floor of the cook's wagon, Hitch found himself in the grip of an oddly familiar dream: he stood on the upper deck of a rolling ship beneath a sky black with clouds and rain, while waves pounded the hull and swept over the sides. All around him, people cried out in terror, cowering back from the sea and the storm. Hitch alone felt no fear. Holding fast to a swaying line, he pointed ahead to the sliver of rocky land lit by flashes of purple-white lightning, a jagged shoal looming in the darkness.

Abruptly he opened his eyes. Light came spilling from somewhere, a cold, pulsing radiance. He rolled his head to

the side and peered into the storage space under the cook's
bunk, where he had stowed the jewel-headed walking stick
and covered it with his backsack as best he could. Bright
blue flared and dimmed against the far wall. Hitch stared at
the throbbing glow, his belly prickling with anticipation.
The last time he had seen that light . . .

He eased out from under his cloak and crept to the rear
of the car. With a glance over his shoulder for the sleeping
cook and scrivener, he opened the door and slipped outside.
The camp seemed quiet enough. He looked to the south
first, toward the guards' wagon where the hatchling resided.
Nothing. Then he lifted his eyes skyward. There was no
moon and the stars blazed silently overhead. He searched
for signs of movement, but no golden egg traversed the
heavens.

Approaching dawn filled the east with a bright nimbus
above the curve of wagons. Hitch looked away, then looked
back again a second later with a frown. That way lay the
north, not the east. As he watched, the luminous halo began
to change, tightening at its base and flaring up and outward
to become a wide, twisting funnel of light that flickered and
undulated through a series of brilliant colors: gold, green-
gold, rose, crimson.

Hitch was not the only one to witness the eerie spectacle.
He heard cries of wonder from the guards on the north side
of the camp, and answering voices raised in consternation
from within the wagons. People stumbled out of the cars as
the alarm spread, their faces turned northward. A great
wailing clamor began in the alter pen, to be quelled a minute later as the alterman scurried over, his bedcap aslant
and his plump cheeks pink with fury.

Hitch sat cross-legged on the wooden apron outside the
wagon door and stared at the sky until his eyes began to
ache. The funnel of light writhed and bellied like a sail in
the wind, colors shifting in great waves from east to west.

In the middle of the funnel, scattered points of light pulsed and grew like flower buds opening, adding star-flashes of pink and white and brilliant emerald.

A lantern flared to life unnoticed in the window at his back. Then the cook came bursting out of the door behind him, swerved sharply to avoid tripping over Hitch, and sat down heavily at his side instead as huge wheels creaked in protest. His fleshy jaw dropped open. "What is it?" the large man croaked, staring at the play of lights. "Is the top of the world on fire?" The wagon yawed to the right as he lowered himself down from the little porch and hustled off to join the others.

A moment later the door swung open again and the scrivener boy peered out of the car, his black hair standing up in disordered clumps.

"Alacrity!" Hitch said over his shoulder. "Just look at that! Isn't it a wonder?"

The boy blinked owlishly at the shimmering display. "I want no part of it," he announced with a shake of his head. He ducked back into the car, slamming the door shut after him.

Most everyone else had deserted the camp circle to congregate beyond the northernmost car. Hitch saw Diligence standing with her hands at the collar of her nightcoat, blond curls glowing in the shifting light. He clambered down from the wagon and started diagonally across the dark expanse to join her. He stubbed his toe immediately on something hard and stepped back toward the perimeter of the circle with an oath, remembering the yeofolk in their sleep holes at the center of the camp.

He was almost at her side when he thought of the walking stick. Looking back to the cook's wagon, he saw that the lantern had been extinguished. The scrivener was probably safely under his covers by now, his eyes squeezed shut against an unpredictable world. But if the boy did keep his eyes open, he would be almost certain to notice the pulsing light from beneath the other bunk.

Diligence was just turning in his direction as he pivoted on his heel. Hitch grinned and pointed down to his bare feet. "I forgot my boots," he told her, the truth coming first to his mind. "Don't want any toes to drop off in the cold, while I stand here transfixed by the glory of whatever it is."

The radiance from the north sent his shadow bobbing and stretching crazily in front of him as he picked his way back around the circle. He was halfway to the cook's wagon when he heard a faint clanking noise, as one of the huge creatures shifted position beneath the soil at the center of the ring. Glancing over at the sound, he thought he saw something that did not quite belong amid the jumbled murk of overturned earth and rocks.

Hitch stopped in his tracks, drew his head back, blinked, and squinted; all was still. Perhaps it had been a trick of the sky lights. He glanced away for a moment and saw it again out of the corner of his eye: something much smaller than either yeofolk or human, flitting stealthily among the mounds of dirt. Hitch tiptoed toward the sleep holes and paused again, eyes narrowed in the flickering dimness. Nothing moved.

He was in the middle of another step when something made him stop in his tracks. He balanced awkwardly for a second with his bare foot upraised, then danced backward just as something sinuous lashed up from beneath him, whipping under his leg to catch in the long green cloak. He stumbled back with a cry and landed on his backside in the mounded soil.

Hitch reached out his arm reflexively as the thing darted past him. Catching hold of a leathery limb, he yanked the small body toward him out of the shadows. The shifting radiance brought him a mangled glimpse of impossibly long arms, pale eyes the size of saucers, and a mouth that glittered like a sack full of broken glass. The creature doubled over in his grip and emitted a high-pitched, chattering shriek that sent Hitch's hands flailing toward his ears. At the same time, something delivered a painful sting to the heel of his left hand. He tried to shake it off, but the thing was latched firmly to his wrist and palm. Tightening its grip, it bit deeply into the underside of his wrist and began to rock back and forth.

The pain was like nothing he had ever felt before.

Hitch howled and pummeled his captive arm against the ground at his side. At last the squeezing grip was broken. He saw the thing clearly for a second in the shifting glow, before it loped across the wagon ring and fled yammering into the night.

The noise had drawn the others. People crowded around him in a ring of dark faces, many voices shouting questions and demanding explanations. Hitch sat blinking and holding his wrist. Things were happening too fast. His tailbone was sore, his mind still spinning. At last Diligence shoved her way through the crowd. She brought her face close to his. "What happened, Hitch? Are you hurt?"

He explained it to her as clearly as he could. His thoughts were getting harder to turn into words as they blossomed and faded in his head. It felt as if his wrist were wrapped in a bracelet of cold fire; he kept trying to find the clasp and take it off. Somewhere nearby, somebody had begun to moan in a low, mournful keening that sent chills crawling up his spine.

Then Welleck's broad, mustachioed face loomed next to the girl's. The wagoneer took Hitch by the shoulders and gave him a shake that jarred his bones. "This small biting thing you found—did it have long, rubbery limbs and a great mouth brimmed with fangs?"

Hitch nodded dumbly, remembering the yawning maw and the gleam of too many teeth.

"Astilfe. That's it for certain," he heard Welleck mutter to someone. "Take him inside. I'll go for my poison kit."

Poison? Hitch looked out over the dark circle of heads to where the funnel of colored light still pulsed and burned in the northern sky. "No, thank you," he heard himself say as the light began to fade. "I think I've already had some . . ."

TEN

TO THE IMPERY

At home on the Wheel, care of the sick or injured was the exclusive province of those Inclined to Bodymending. Diligence had never had the opportunity to nurse anything larger than the pet lizard that had swallowed one of her brooches after mistaking it for a sunfly, and she eagerly volunteered for the task of looking after Hitch. She found the experience instructive, though not quite what she had expected. Following the poisoning, the mountain boy spent most of his time asleep or unconscious in the bunk opposite the hatchling's in the red and silver wagon. Rather than spooning broth into her patient's mouth and stroking his forehead while he murmured phrases of sweet gratitude, Diligence found herself changing mountains of soiled bed linen and listening to the erratic rhythms of his snores.

Once the wagoneer's antidotes had prevailed against the poison, once Hitch's fever had broken and he had stopped making the violent swimming motions that left his bed-clothes in knots, it was not all that different from looking after Hoppy, she reflected—although the lizard had died two days into his treatment, whereas Welleck confidently pronounced the boy well on the road to a full recovery after the first night.

Her patient finally came to his senses during a halt for repairs, around midmorning on the third day after the attack. Bored with writing in her journal, Diligence had been amusing herself by mentally connecting the freckles that dusted Hitch's wide cheekbones into fanciful animal shapes, when his eyelids flew open and she found herself staring into a pair of dark eyes not six inches from her own. Startled, she sat back suddenly, her arm striking the bowl of cold broth on the folding table by her stool.

"Ow!" She rubbed at her elbow, watching ruefully as half the contents of the bowl spread into a large yellow patch on Hitch's coverlet. "I just changed that linen, not two hours ago."

"Sorry," Hitch said huskily. He cleared his throat. "I didn't mean to open my eyes so carelessly."

"It's all right," Diligence told him with a gracious nod. "Comes with the job." She dabbed at the yellow stain with the edge of the pillow silk. "The important thing is, you're awake."

"Mmmm." Hitch stretched languorously. "I guess I am. I got bit by something, didn't I? Something small and mean. How long was I out?"

"The astilfe poisoned you three nights ago. Welleck gave you a sanative, but he said it would take a while to work all of the venom out of your system."

"Three nights! No wonder I'm so hungry." Hitch pushed up onto his elbows and looked around the interior of the car. His gaze fell on the hatchling lying silently in the other bunk. "I'm in the guards' wagon. Have you been tending me all this time?"

Diligence nodded. "Not much to do except keep you clean and on top of the bed. The first day you kept trying to climb up the walls—a lot like a little lizard I once had. After that, you just slept."

Hitch winced and turned his face toward the wall. "With all this trouble," he muttered, "I'm surprised they didn't just shove me into one of the sleep holes and leave me there. Certain parties wanted to, I'll bet." He had a thought and turned back. "What was that thing doing in the middle of the camp, anyway? Was it trying to poison the beasts?"

Diligence rocked her head from side to side, considering. "Only in a manner of speaking. An astilfe's toxin isn't immediately harmful to the yeofolk—but it does stimulate them to bring forth young. Yeofolk have no fixed gender, you know, so any one of them would have been susceptible to the venom. Luckily, the creature only managed to get to one before you discovered it. Welleck says your intervention probably prevented it from infecting the whole troupe."

Hitch narrowed his eyes. "So one of those things is going to have babies now, just because that little creature stung it?" He lifted his arm and inspected the ring of yellowish bruises still visible on his left wrist. "It only works that way with yeofolk, right?"

"Right. And that's why we've had to change course. We're detouring to the nearest impery to trade in the prospective mother before the young come forth. She's already pretty much immobilized, and Welleck's had to rig up a litter. Luckily, we've got the rest of the troupe to haul it."

"Does this mean another delay in your journey?" Hitch managed a weak chuckle. "Heh heh. The marchmaster must be in a ringing rage."

"If Breitling's feeling wrathful, he has only himself upon which to vent his ire," said a deep voice from the doorway. Welleck climbed into the car and made his way to the side of the bunk. "Oh, I've seen him grumble a bit to the Hubwoman, but other than that he's kept his mouth shut about the incident. He knows any marchmaster with a firm hand and his head on straight would've stopped the guards from deserting their posts to watch the blazing sky. That's how the damned thing was able to sneak in and muck with the yeofolk, you know. Now Breitling's got you to thank we didn't lose the lot of them . . ." The wagoneer grinned and gave Hitch a friendly swat to the side of his head.

"Welcome back, mountain boy! You're looking less like a maffle and more like a man this morning."

Hitch nodded, rubbing his right ear. "And I guess I have the two of you to thank for that. Diligence says you'll have to lose more travel time because of the yeofolk. Will you still reach the Unseen Wall in time for your audience with the great and remarkable?"

Welleck blew out his cheeks beneath the ends of his grandly curling mustache. "We should, we should. There are always a few days strapped on at the start of any trip, you know, for just such a reason. Of course, it's a foolish marchmaster that ever lets on to it before he has to. As for the detour . . ." He gave an unhappy shrug. "It means an even closer scrape with the Aulmad, and that's a piece of danger. But this caravan has proven we can find ourselves in the middle of trouble anywhere, haven't we? Especially when it seems to be sniffing so earnestly at our trail . . .

"Not much choice at all, when you come right down to it. Without twice-seven yeofolk as part of our fee, we might as well end the journey now. At first we'd thought to head due north for Tustable Impery. But Tustable's been in decline for some time now, and the yeofolk handlers tell us it's been overrun this past half year by a coalition of rockrasps and Little Winding Men." Welleck had raised his hand to the rim of the wheelwork on the ceiling above the bunks, sketching the alternatives with his forefinger while he spoke. "In terms of proximity, that meant Behelda was our next choice—but to go that route would actually have us doubling back to the southwest, over ground we've just covered, and the resultant delay would be prohibitive."

Hitch raised an eyebrow. "Little Winding Men?" He murmured to Diligence.

"A type of miniature blue astilfe, according to your guidebook," she told him, "noted for their habit of burrowing up beneath their prey to implant poison barbs in the foot or ankle by means of a muscular constricting limb. They didn't have a picture."

"Thanks," Hitch said with a shudder. "I don't think we're needing one."

"Weighing our options, we finally settled on Old Hopshog, up here to the north and west," Welleck went on in a musing tone, his eyes still traversing the ceiling. "At our present pace we should see its plumes before sunset tomorrow." He let his hand drop to his side with a shrug. "I'd allow another day and a half at the impery to conduct our business before we're rolling again. Assuming we've good sunny weather—and nothing worse than a bad smell blowing over from the Aulmad—we'll be back on our track in no time. Well!" He slapped his thighs with his palms and turned back to Hitch and Diligence. "Enough time yapping in the sickroom. There's a wheel with a weak axle that needs replacing before we're under way." The wagoneer winked at Diligence. "Mind you boot dawdlebones here out of this silken luxury as soon as he can crawl, Daughter."

He favored Hitch with another good-natured swat and departed the car.

Hitch looked after the man with a thoughtful frown. "Have I still got a dream or two snagged in my locks, or was he proposing a link between the funnel of light and what happened to the yeofolk?"

Diligence nodded soberly. "It's what they're all saying. Everybody thinks the sky lights were a diversion, to get us all out of camp so the astilfe could sneak in. As for who could arrange such a distraction, or why they'd want to . . ." She clucked her tongue and shook her blond curls. "Lucky for us you forgot your boots."

"Mm." Hitch was chewing his lower lip. "Diligence, I have to tell you something. It wasn't only my boots I was heading back to the wagon for."

"It wasn't?"

He looked chagrined. "Remember the night when you found me on the beach—what I told you about waking up to a whistly, whining sound, and then catching sight of the egg as it fell? Well, it wasn't only the noise that got me up. I had a walking stick with me—a bequest from a previous employer, as you might say—with a great gemstone the size of a salver's nose fast to its head. I'd stuck it into the sand not far from my little camp, and when I opened my eyes that night I saw it glowing all bright and blue, waxing and waning like an icy heartbeat. Then the egg came down and the hatchling popped out, and I forgot all about my shining stick. When I thought to look at it again, the head was just a piece of cloudy crystal. I brought the thing along when we left the shore—though I may have neglected to mention its existence to anyone. With everything that's happened since then, I gave no thought to any connection between the gemstone lighting up and wonders dropping down from the sky—but then, three nights ago ..." He paused to suck in a breath, his gaze turned inward. "Three nights ago I come awake in my little sleeping patch on the floor of the cook's car and there it is again, throbbing its frozen light against the wall. I get up to peer outside and this time I see a skein of twisty colors in the northern sky."

Diligence nodded slowly, remembering the shifting glory of the light funnel. "Do you think we should tell someone?"

Hitch shook his head. "Not now, I don't. Perhaps later—Wagoneer Welleck, at least. He's a clean-spoken Western man and I trust him. But I'm sure if I told them just now—if Nury or Breitling found out—well, the jewel makes a pretty bauble, and you know they'd try to take it away from me. Most likely they'd say it was summoning bad fortune or some such, when truly I figure it has the opposite effect: to warn me when there's something momentous about to take place." He lifted his head and shoulders from the bunk, then lowered them again with a sigh of exhaustion. "Thing is, I left it under the cook's bunk, and someone's bound to come across it there sooner or later—especially if there's any more strangeness in the sky and the stone feels obliged to flare up with its beacon light."

"Do you want me to go get it?" Diligence slid off the stool. "I could hide it in my wagon. No one will find it there."

"If you wouldn't mind." He pushed up feebly from the covers as she made for the door. "But wait—it's bright daylight outside. How will you manage it without being seen?"

She gave him an indulgent look. "The same way I watched you manage it back on the beach, I imagine. I don't reckon this group has gotten any more observant since then, do you?" She gathered up her long cloak and draped it over her arm. "At the worst, they'll think I've caught the same peculiar limp that afflicted you that night."

The wagons were getting ready to roll and the cook was out making his rounds restocking the larders. The scrivener boy sat hunched over a collection of alphabets on the little porch outside the door to the wagon. He barely glanced up as Diligence climbed the ladder. She found the jewel-headed walking stick where Hitch had told her it would be. Tucking it into the back of her waistband, she unfurled the cloak and settled it over her shoulders. Before she left, she stooped to retrieve Hitch's backsack, grunting under its unexpected weight. Lowering herself down past the scrivener, she made her hobbling way to her own car, where she stowed the walking stick in the cubby beneath her bunk.

When she reentered the guard wagon, Hitch and the hatchling were propped up on their elbows in their respective bunks, staring silently at each other across the few feet that separated them. It was an eerie sight: some trick of the light and shadow had turned their expressionless faces into mirrors of one another. Diligence set the pack down with a thump, breaking the spell. Hitch looked up at her with a tired smile as the hatchling's head bobbed back onto his pillow silk. "Not much difference here, I see—except the yellow's just about gone." He gestured at the hatchling's garment, the color of old bone this morning beneath its dim tracery of lines and symbols.

"I'm surprised to find him looking so alert. He's been fast asleep these past three days," Diligence said. "At least, this is the first time I've caught him with eyes open since we brought you in here."

Hitch was amazed. "What—still no food, then? How does he live? No water?" He licked his own dry lips.

"Nothing. And speaking of which . . ." Diligence poured half a mug of water from the carafe on the table and brought it to the mountain boy's lips. The hatchling lifted his head slightly, watching with silent interest as the boy swallowed. He pushed his jaw forward when Diligence turned to set the cup back on the table, and parted his own lips as if requesting the same service.

Diligence and Hitch exchanged a glance. She refilled the cup and brought it to the bone man's bedside with cautious wonder. He allowed her to pour a small quantity down his throat, odd-colored eyes staring into her face the whole time. When she turned to exclaim to Hitch, she found him snoring peacefully.

The mountain boy recovered rapidly from his ordeal. For the rest of the day he slept and woke in alternating blocks of two or three hours. The hatchling was either tied to the boy's schedule in some imperceptible manner, or he had evolved into an extremely light sleeper, for every time Diligence found Hitch awake, a glance at the other bunk would confirm that its occupant had opened his eyes as well. More changes were evident. Each time she offered Hitch a drink of water, the hatchling also accepted one— though unlike his model he never showed the effects of having consumed what was becoming a considerable volume of liquid. Nonetheless, Diligence thought it advisable to store an extra relief jug as near as possible to the bone man's bunk.

A few disastrous trials proved that Hitch's stomach was not yet ready for solid victuals; the two decided that Diligence should continue to offer them to the hatchling in the hopes of ending his alarming fast. That evening they watched with clinical interest as their subject tasted a variety of small portions of fruit, flesh, and grilled legumes—invariably spitting out each offering with a sour expression within a few seconds of ingesting it.

The next morning, Hitch followed his wake-up drink of water with his first spoonful of bland grummidge. He waited with a watchful expression until he was certain the food had found a secure resting place in his stomach. His triumphant smile turned wry as he tipped his head toward the other bunk. Diligence turned on her stool to find the hatchling up on his elbows, mouth open like a baby treechick awaiting its allotment of grubs. She spooned the lumpy substance onto his tongue and sat back. The hatchling's blank expression turned instantly skeptical, but he swallowed the nearly tasteless gruel, his pale eyes on Hitch, and made no effort to regurgitate it. "Finally!" Diligence and Hitch traded the weary grins of relieved parents.

Old Hopshog Impery came into view several hours later, in the form of a trail of hazy smoke slanting off into the mild afternoon breeze. "The breeding grounds are always situated at the base of a volcanic cone," Welleck had told them during his visit to the convalescents that morning. "The little ones require prodigious amounts of heat when they come into the world."

Diligence left Hitch and the hatchling sleeping in identical poses after their midday meal. She leaned on her elbows in the front of her car and gazed out the window as the wagons trundled across the dusty plain toward the imposing structure. A trio of multicolored pennants flapped beneath the plume of smoke: violet, yellow, and ultramarine; ocher, purple-brown, and rose; black, vermilion, and pale green. According to Welleck, the colors were flown to indicate the current status of the impery, the combinations specifically denoting the tally of recent births, the number of surviving imps, and projections of their estimated utility and worth. A flexible mast fixed with line and pulley had been raised atop the lead car during the last halt, allowing Breitling to fly his own rippling semaphore in reply.

The impery itself was a thick-walled fortress of black stone, hewn from the base of the smoking basalt cone that towered in its midst. The circular outer walls were sunk to a depth of several feet in a wide apron of glassy black— testimony to the fact that the volcano had brought forth more than smoke at least once since their erection.

The wagons halted a hundred yards from the wall, while a succession of bright flags rose and fell above the marchmaster's car. Diligence realized that she was holding her breath as the seconds ticked away with no response. She released it in a low whistle when a pair of thirty-foot gates swung slowly outward to admit the caravan.

The wagons drew into their customary circle just inside the walls in a broad courtyard that stretched off to left and right, the gates closing ponderously behind them. The yeofolk had gathered to one side of the caravan in a loose circle of their own, mouthparts clashing with excitement. The expectant mother lay immobile on her makeshift litter, its swaying, sagging beams supported on the backs of four of her fellows. Diligence peered out the corner of her forward window at the towering black walls and wondered what would happen next.

The impery had been laid out in a series of concentric rings; after half an hour's wait, a second, somewhat smaller pair of gates eased open directly in front of the mammoth creatures. A moment later, the two handlers strode from their wagon in full regalia, their red-brown helmets connected by slender black threads to the swaying, whiplike poles that buzzed in their gloved hands. The pair urged the shambling creatures forward with expertly aimed taps and prods, the whip-poles reminding Diligence of a sugarfly's proboscis: one second tightly coiled at the handler's side, the next extended rigidly to a length of five yards. She shaded her eyes as the litter was borne past her wagon, easily making out the lumpy encrustations that rimmed its occupant's dorsal surface. The swellings, which ranged in size from pellets to bristling spherules twice the circumference of her head, were darkly translucent; she thought to see a quiver of activity in a few of the larger nodes.

One of the handlers was a pale-skinned woman whose head was crowned with a nimbus of fine hair like pinkish down. Diligence remembered her words from dinner break of the day before: "The chick has two imperatives when it quits the node. Inward. Upward." The woman had used her flattened palm to indicate the movements, first parallel to the ground, then abruptly perpendicular. "Once they have gorged on their first repast, the survivors seek the sunlight to harden their carapaces."

"Survivors?" Diligence asked.

"The first to break free of the nodes begin at once to eat their way through the mother's flesh; before rising to the light, the most successful finish off their meal with whichever of their less developed siblings they encounter in the husk."

The handlers coaxed their flock through the second opening amid a cacophony of creaking and clanking. The gates drifted shut. Stimulated by the notion of food, Diligence went to her larder, where she extracted a handful of green-black berries and two loaves of fragrant bread. She devoured the berries, licked the dark juice from her fingers, and stuffed the loaves into the pockets of her cloak.

She found Hitch at the forward table in the guards' wagon, demonstrating some sort of trick involving a pair of identical ammunition horns and a quantity of small blue pebbles. The three guards who had been sitting opposite him rose to their feet as Diligence came into the wagon and edged past her to depart the car with noises of disgust. Hitch chuckled and drew a mound of fine yellow glint toward him across the table. He smiled up at Diligence as he began to divide his spoils between a pair of small leather pouches. "Five- and ten-spots in this one, grains and lesser shards in the other . . ." he explained happily. "Welleck tells me we'll find items both bizarre and wondrous at the ramble house—and that each one has its price." He paused to weigh one of the pouches in his palm. "I want to make sure I can meet it."

Diligence gave the table a skeptical glance. "You'll meet the turning end of a slicer if you persist in cheating the guards." From the corner of her eye she saw the hatchling sitting upright in his bunk, his hands moving through a series of odd gestures. It took her a second to recognize the movements; the man in white was imitating Hitch as he sorted his winnings.

"Cheating?" Hitch pushed back from the table and stood blinking in wide-eyed innocence. "Why, Daughter, you wound me."

"That's nothing to the wounds the soldiers will inflict if you're not careful." She tugged at his sleeve. "I'm going to do some exploring. According to what I've read of imperies, this courtyard should extend around the whole place in a perfect ring. Put your boots on and come along if you want to join me. I have bread."

Hitch knelt to stow his winnings in his backsack, thought better of it, and tucked the ends of the pouches under his narrow belt. "Might as well," he said. "I've plucked the golden pelt from that trio right down to their naked skin. Besides, my little white shadow is starting to get on my nerves." He gave a perfunctory wave to the hatchling as the two filed past the bunk. The white man returned the gesture, his face impassive.

"Why do you suppose he does that?" Hitch asked as they walked out into the black stone courtyard.

"Maybe he thinks you're his mother," Diligence suggested. "After all, you're the first person he saw when he came out of his egg. You're lucky he didn't burrow right in and make a meal of you." She slid her palm forward and angled it sharply toward the sky. "You know—inward and upward?"

They found Welleck conferring with Nury and Breitling over a tableful of charts not far from the inner gates.

"My legs are cramped," Diligence told the wagoneer. "We're going to walk around the wall a bit."

Nury did not bother to lift her eyes from the charts. "See that you don't wander out of earshot," she ordered. "Don't go skulking where you're not welcome, and touch nothing that seems to be alive. And mark the time: make sure you're back in your wagon before sunset."

The Daughter twitched her lips in annoyance and turned on her heel without deigning to reply. She handed Hitch one of the loaves from her pocket as the pair set out to explore the impery.

The cook leaned out as they passed the blue wagon. "Ho, what do you think of the bread?" he called. "I culled those herbs from the undersides of certain flat rocks while the young hero lay poisoned."

"We haven't tried it yet, but it smells very nice," Diligence called back. "What do you have for supper?"

The cook raised a trio of blunt fingers. "Oyster-cake, served on a bed of curried drymop; a pudding of amber grannets cast in the shape of rare seashells; sausages from Emshwell."

"My mouth is watering already," Diligence said through cupped hands.

"And my stomach is doing jump-rolls," Hitch muttered, his face contorted in a bilious grimace.

Diligence set a brisk pace, her arms swinging at her sides as they followed the wide path between the featureless black walls. "Uplifting to find an edifice constructed on such soundly circular principles out here in the dry wastes," she remarked around a mouthful of the herb-flavored bread. "Not to mention how comforting it is to be able to stroll along like this, and know that before too long we'll be right back where we started." She raised her brows at her companion's dubious expression. "Hm? You don't agree?"

"You're beginning to sound like Alacrity now," Hitch said. "He'd give his two forefingers to be back on the Wheel, spinning circles with the rest of 'em."

"Ah, the poor sleepy scrivener. He needs to learn to adapt. Look at me—I was raised among the Turning Folk, yet here I am on the edge of nowhere, striding outward into the unknown without a backward glance." Diligence clucked her tongue. "It's all a matter of mastering one's apprehensions and putting predisposition in its proper place."

"I think you'll have to do the rest of your striding without me," Hitch said. He stopped and rested his hand against the smooth black stone, his chest rising and falling in deep breaths. Sweat stood out in beads on his brow. "Oof. I'm not so ready for a trek as I thought."

"Oh." Diligence's concern was tinged with disappointment. "I guess we'd better turn back, then."

"No, no." He shook his head. "You complete your circuit. I think you need to." He put his shoulders against the wall and leaned back with his eyes half-closed. "I'll rest here just a moment, then skip back to the wagons."

"Are you sure?"

"I'll be fine." He waved her on. "Enjoy the comforting gyre."

Diligence left him with reluctance, checking back over her shoulder several times to make sure he was still standing. She was relieved to see him straighten up and take another bite of his bread. The two exchanged a final wave just before she lost sight of him around the bend.

The circumference of the impery was greater than Diligence had first supposed: the sky began to grow noticeably darker as she made her way between the high wall on her left and the even higher one to her right, while the clouds that drifted overhead showed a luster of orange and lavender on their nether sides.

Still, it was a joy to tread an honest circle again; for all her protestations to the contrary, Diligence was a true child of the Wheel, and as she walked she felt as if her soul had dropped back into its rightful track after a long and senseless digression. She was just finishing the last of the bread when she saw a glimmer of yellow light spilling out onto the smooth black stone from somewhere up ahead. She quickened her pace.

The light was coming from the left, above an area where the floor had cracked and buckled to a distance of several yards out from the inner wall. Half a dozen fractures added wrinkles to the smooth black, now threaded with gold like a flicker's net full of sunflies. The light itself leaked from a half-inch crack that ran straight up from the base of the wall to a point just above her head. Diligence traced the breach with her fingertips, marveling at its regularity. The stone slab to the right of the seam of light protruded slightly from the wall, and she took a step back as she realized that she was looking not at a natural break but at some sort of deliberately crafted opening. She leaned forward to inspect it with interest, wondering at its connection with the patch of dam-

aged floor. Welleck had told them that the Siccative was rife
with volcanoes, a good portion of which experienced active
intervals from time to time. Could a recent eruption have
caused the earth to shift and thus jogged open a long-sealed
passageway? She pressed her eye to the crack, her pulse
quickening as ideas swarmed her brain. A chamber of unknown dimension lay before her, fashioned of black stone
and bathed in a yellow light whose source was not immediately evident.

The edge of the rock slab stuck out no more than an
inch. Diligence pressed the heel of her palm against it,
more out of frustration than intent, and gave a reflexive
shove. Like the walls in which it hung, the door slab measured a good foot in thickness. To her amazement, the slab
moved easily under her touch, swinging outward as noiselessly as had the towering front gates.

Diligence found herself gazing at another black wall six
feet in front of her. She chewed the knuckle of her right
thumb in momentary indecision, then leaned her head cautiously through the opening. A gust of heated air struck her
face. The yellow light shone from a rectangular cage of unusually vigorous cold fire, bracketed to the ceiling of a corridor of black stone that stretched off into dimness to the
right and the left. The tunnel was nearly circular in cross
section, its walls flowing into floor and ceiling without a
seam, as if the passageway had been hollowed out of the
rock by some natural force. Squinting at deceptive curves
of glossy black under the yellow light, Diligence realized
with a start that the tunnel ran at a considerable angle, in
addition to following the curve of the outer walls. From the
level area directly in front of her, the floor rose to the left
and descended sharply to the right. Interesting . . . She en-
visioned the center of the impery as a vast cylinder, sunk
deep in the lap of the volcano and wrapped around with a
pleasing, down-spiraling corridor. She took a tentative step

inside the doorway, but turned back at a sudden thought to wobble the open door back and forth between her palms. The slab swung freely at her lightest touch, and remained where she left it. Still, she needed to be sure it would not gradually swing shut, should a breeze come up while she was off exploring. The interior of the tunnel was a good deal warmer than the open-air passage she had just left. She removed her cloak and folded it lengthwise several times, then placed it on the floor against the stone jamb and brought the door slab gently to rest against it.

She stepped to the right, determined to continue on in the same direction—if not at the same angle—as she had been following outside. Quarter-inch ridges mounted crosswise every foot and a half on the rock helped prevent her from losing her balance and sliding forward on the tunnel's slick, steep floor.

It was uncomfortably warm; Diligence was dripping with sweat after her first two minutes in the tunnel. She had not descended far when she came upon another level area, and a narrow opening in the wall on the inner side. She turned sidewise and squeezed slowly through. The heat struck her like a physical force as she staggered out the other side. She found herself standing on a small balcony with a waist-high parapet, looking down on a huge circular chamber that was floored with—soil? She blinked in surprise. Three round pits, each filled with rich-looking dark loam, made up the floor of the room. Each soil pit had a rim of alternating gray and green tiles; three feet of slick black stone bordered the circumference of the chamber itself.

The ceiling curved high above her head. Greenish light trembled in a score of widely spaced receptacles. A large, cranelike apparatus fitted with wide leather harnesses and adjustable straps stood on a small island of tile and stone at the centerpoint of the three circles. An outline of disturbed dirt in the soil pit nearest to the balcony indicated that something large had recently been deposited or removed.

Diligence had heard one of the handlers mention a clutching chamber in connection with the impending birth. She stood swaying in the heat and wondered how far down the soil went. From here the pits resembled empty growing plots about the size of the summer spice garden back home. Were they really deep enough to conceal one or more yeofolk?

She became aware of a thick film of dust around her booted feet. It had been a long time since anyone else had tried to squeeze onto this balcony.

A small noise drew her attention back to the chamber. Peering over the edge of the parapet, she saw a line of figures coming into the room from a side doorway to gather almost directly below her, some twenty feet beneath the balcony. She counted about a dozen of them, identically dressed in bulky breeches of a damp-looking gray material. A swath of stiff, dull green fabric was draped across their shoulders with a hole for the neck; it dragged on the ground to front and back, creating a constant dry, rustling sound as they shifted their weight at the edge of the nearest soil pit. Their faces were concealed by flat-topped, cylindrical hoods that covered the head completely, with a glassy, transparent insert over eyes and nose. About half of the strangely garbed company grasped long, sturdy-looking poles topped with complicated fabrications of mesh and wire. Enormous gray-green mittens made them look like children's mannikins dressed for war.

The group's attention seemed to be focused completely on the pit. Confident that she would not be noticed, Diligence craned her neck out over the parapet and saw that the two handlers from the caravan were there as well. They wore the strange gray hoods over their red-brown uniforms, along with the stiff shawls and the outsized mittens. An air of excitement was growing in the chamber. The handlers conferred in hushed tones with the folk of the impery as they watched the soil pit. Diligence strained to hear their comments, but could make out only an occasional soft sibilance. There was something different about the way the gray-green figures moved. Diligence studied them in the flickering light, trying to discern the proportions that lay beneath the oddly styled garments.

A muffled exclamation from one of the handlers drew her attention back to the center of the pit. Something unseen thrashed and squirmed just below the surface of the soil. There was a faint rippling distortion, as of rising heat waves in the air over the disturbed area. Diligence got a sudden whiff of an intensely acrid odor. Stinging tears started immediately at the corners of her eyes. She ducked back into the doorway and pushed her way through, willing herself not to cough until she was once more in the tunnel. She breathed deeply for a minute in the relatively cleaner and cooler air, then pulled her overblouse up tight over her mouth and nose and sidled back onto the balcony.

The group on the floor had fallen silent, watching the activity in the soil pit with a fascination that bordered on reverence.

Diligence squinted down through the greenish flicker. Something small and dark pushed its way awkwardly past a clump of soil. Her eyes had begun to sting again, and a maddening tickle was growing at the top of her throat. She clamped her hands over her mouth. Her throat spasmed. There was no way she could remain in the chamber without making a considerable amount of noise.

With a final glance at the roiling earth in the pit, she returned to the tunnel, where she immediately doubled over in a fit of uncontrollable coughing. Wiping her eyes with her knuckles, she leaned against the opening and tried to listen above the sound of her own gasps. She heard voices raised in the clutching chamber, but could not tell whether their exclamations were in reaction to the emergence of a newborn imp or to the sound of an intruder's coughing fit.

Better to be safe than to be hauled unceremoniously back to Nury in the hands of the gray-green attendants: she hurried off to the right, descending as quickly and quietly as she could on the slippery black surface. The spacing of both the caged lights and the floor ridges seemed to increase the farther she descended. She was sliding from one tiny ledge to the next in yellow-black dimness by the time she came to another opening in the inner wall.

The second portal was located some fifty feet below the clutching chamber. It was much wider and lower than the first, and hung with a stiff black curtain. There was no level space before this opening; Diligence would have passed it by unnoticed had her hand not brushed the rough surface of the fabric as she fought to maintain her balance. Taking a deep breath of tunnel air as a precautionary measure, she heaved the heavy drape to one side and stuck her head through the opening. She found herself on the floor level of a much smaller room. The air beyond the curtain was hotter than that in the tunnel, but free of the clutching chamber's caustic edge. No pools of dirt marred the smooth floor, which was hewn from the ubiquitous black stone, with inlaid tiles in gray and dull green depicting familiar-looking creatures Diligence could not readily identify. Dim, bluish light came from a single cage set in the center of the ceiling. As in the chamber above, she had the impression of great age, though the floor here seemed relatively free of dust. The room was shaped with three sides like a slice of cheese, the wall in which the door was set curving slightly to follow the shape of the outlying cylinder, and the other two coming together at a right angle about twenty feet in front of her. A jumble of odd shapes lay against the right-hand wall. The flash of colored lights caught her attention from a long, low plaque set on the left. She was debating which to investigate first when she heard a noise from the tunnel behind her.

She pulled her head back out from under the thick curtain and froze. Something large and ponderous was rounding the bend below her, ascending from below with a slow, swaying gait. It was too late to run; she would surely be seen. She eased her way in through the drapery, her mind racing furiously. Maybe the thing in the tunnel had business above—though she was sure it was far too bulky to fit through the entrance to the balcony in the clutching room. There was still a chance it would pass by this chamber. The heavy sounds approached, barely audible through the curtain. Diligence scanned the room. The right-hand wall was obscured by tumbled heaps of unidentifiable artifacts, some of them leaning several inches out from the wall. She half ran, half slid across the slippery floor, insinuating herself into a narrow space between the wall and a large, many-sided device just as the stiff black curtain at the door began to bow inward.

She shrank back against the polished stone and attempted to calm her breathing. The hot air scalded her lungs and sweat streamed down her cheeks and forehead.

The thing that entered the room proved no easier to identify at close range than it had from a distance in the black tunnel. It was large and wide-bodied, its bulk completely shrouded in the folds of a loose, purple-black covering of complicated construction. It came into the chamber with a ponderous, side-to-side swaying motion that suggested that its lower limbs were articulated in a radically different fashion from those of a human being. Diligence's skin prickled as its shuffling gait brought it close to where she hid. The sheer lumbering size of the thing made her think of the yeofolk, although it bore the unmistakable aura of intelligence as it made its way to crouch with a creak of joints before the colored plaque on the left-hand wall.

Diligence studied the peculiar wall design from her new vantage point. At first glance it had reminded her of a piece of wheelwork, except for the flat smoothness of its surface and the stippling of fiery colors that changed before her eyes. She leaned forward through the metal latticework that concealed her, fascinated in spite of herself. The bright colors came and went, as if an invisible artist spattered the surface with successive layers of glowing paint that faded to nothingness almost as quickly as they appeared.

The thing in black stood before the board, swaying massively as it contemplated the play of darting colors. Small shapes, pinpoints, streaks of light zigzagged in the wall design. The creature slouched closer to the apparatus and extended an arm. Diligence learned nothing of the limb's construction; the purple-black draperies rendered it as shapeless as the rest of the body. The concealed appendage manipulated a row of small toggles along the base of the plaque, then dropped to a flexible rod that reminded Diligence of the tiller in the marchmaster's wagon. She started as the sound of faraway bells came from the device: a reverberation of small chimes and weighty gongs, their noises mingling dolefully in the small chamber like the evening call echoing over the hills of the Western Cantle. A doorway, wider than it was tall, had appeared in the black wall alongside the flashing colors; clots of dark soil tumbled out onto the floor as it slid open with a hiss.

Diligence stared, sweat dripping steadily from the end of her nose and chin, as a pair of oddly jointed metal arms protruded suddenly from the orifice, something small and wet-looking twisting and creaking in their grasp.

Diligence pried her gaze from the squirming thing. The attention of the purple-shrouded creature seemed equally divided now between the tiny newcomer and the bright board. Diligence felt certain it would be unable to hear any sounds she might produce above the din of the tolling bells. She slunk out from behind the rubble, took a deep breath of hot air, and scurried across the slick floor to the tunnel door.

She eased up the stiff drapery and flung herself into the tunnel. The skin of her face felt clammy and her arms turned to gooseflesh at the touch of cooler air. She crouched for a few seconds to regain her wind.

The muffled chiming sound from inside the chamber abruptly ceased. Diligence straightened up and began to scramble up the slick black slope. She paused when she reached the first bend and peered back.

Her blood froze.

The thing had emerged into the corridor. It was carrying something small that squeaked and twisted in its grasp. After a short pause outside the curtain—during which Diligence's heart threatened to pound through her chest—it turned and began to descend, swaying ponderously, into the dimness of the tunnel. Diligence blew out her cheeks and headed back up the spiral as rapidly as she could, dancing by the opening to the clutching chamber on tiptoe when she came to it.

She retrieved her cloak and passed through the doorway to the outside, then pushed the heavy door back into place. Dripping and shaking, she headed off to the right, still stubbornly determined to complete her circuit. The sky was almost completely dark now, a scattering of stars already glowing near the zenith. The air felt chill after the intense heat on the other side of the door. She wrapped her cloak around her sweat-soaked body and continued on.

The black walls stayed featureless for the remainder of her walk: no more spilled light, no more enticing passageways. After a while, the lack of discernible landmarks became oppressive in itself, as it began to seem as if the journey would truly have no endpoint. Diligence almost cried out in relief when she reached the dark circle of the wagons, their windows glowing in a chain of cheerful lights. Nury called to her in angry tones as she hurried past the lead wagon to the red and silver car.

Hitch was asleep in his bunk, the hatchling curled in a matching pose on the other side of the aisle. Three black-clad soldiers examined a pair of ammunition horns and a quantity of blue pebbles at the little table. Plates laden with sausages and silvery oyster-cake steamed at their elbows. They raised their brows at Diligence as she stood shivering uncertainly near the door of the car.

The fragrant smells decided her. Mouth watering, she retreated to her wagon, where a change of clothes and her own hot supper awaited.

She was drowsing in her bunk several hours later, journal drooping in her hand, when a flurry of voices drew her to the window. The massive inner gates were gliding outward in the darkness. Diligence pulled her cloak from its peg as the two handlers strode out through the opening, once again wearing their helmets of burnished red-brown.

By the time she reached the lead wagon, the meeting was already in progress. She slipped in behind Welleck, who gave her a quick smile and made room for her next to his own place at the table.

"The chicks came forth shortly after the planting," the orange-haired woman was reporting in clipped tones. It seemed to Diligence that she and her partner had taken on a new air of cool aloofness during their absence: ambassadors returned from a mysterious land. "The clutch consisted of eighteen viable nodes of prime quality, yielding twelve fully formed imps," the man in red-brown added. "Of these, five survived the birthing."

"Six," Diligence murmured under her breath.

Welleck stirred at her side and shot her a questioning glance. "Did you say something, Daughter?"

Diligence shook her head. "Just thinking aloud."

In her mind's eye she saw a massive, shrouded shape move ponderously off down the black tunnel, bearing its tiny burden into the sweltering darkness beneath the impery.

ELEVEN

CONFLICTING REPORTS

The yeofolk handlers had selected two hardy adolescents from the wallow, along with additional compensation in the form of victuals and supplies, in exchange for the five imps that would be left behind. The troupe, now numbering fifteen, emerged through the black inner gates the following dawn.

Hitch awakened with a clear head and a voracious appetite as the wagons rolled out of the impery. One of the soldiers pointed out the new additions to him through the rear window of the car while he breakfasted on golden scones laced with currants and a peppery nettle broth. Hitch made an attempt to memorize the subtly different markings on their dorsal surfaces as the massive creatures plodded along behind the caravan; by the time they halted for the midday break, the two newcomers had become indistinguishable from their fellows.

Diligence appeared at the door to his wagon shortly after the marchmaster's bell, her blue-green eyes alive with hidden knowledge. Hitch ushered her outside with a sour backward glance for the hatchling watching alertly from his bunk. "He's been mocking me all morning," he grumbled. "The soldiers are overcome with hilarity each time he scratches his backside or yawns when I do." He accepted a mug of dark tea and leaned against the spoke of an eight-foot wheel. "I slept right through dinner last night, so I had to eat twice as much breakfast," he informed her, patting his flat midsection. "How was your gyre? Did I miss anything?"

"Ha!" Diligence examined the hem of her sleeve, waiting with feigned nonchalance for a pair of guards to climb down the ladder and head off to help their comrades erect the alter pen. Then she pulled Hitch around to the other side of the wagon.

Here on the far side of the impery, the landscape had begun to show a bit of variation from the arid wasteland known as the Siccative. Dales and narrow ridges gave the earth a rumpled look, while unusual growths sprouted from the soil like the fanciful face-poles at a mountain festival. The two went to sit on a patch of moss at the base of a tall, bluish gray plant whose rubbery trunk was topped by a crown of flexible golden spines.

Hitch listened gape-jawed as Diligence recounted her adventure inside the impery. "D'you think the handlers are in on it, then?" he asked when she was done. He leaned to one side and narrowed his eyes at the orange-haired woman who was moving with her partner among the troupe of yeofolk, bathing their dusty joints in oil and scraping galls from their ventral plates. "Do they know about the missing imp?"

Diligence shrugged. "I don't think so. I got the impression nobody in the clutching chamber had any idea that something else was going on down below."

"I wonder if it eats them," Hitch said softly. He gave his head a quick shake that was part shudder. "Sounds like something from one of the Fabularies: a hideous monster under the ground, stealing babies for its supper and nobody knows."

"Maybe we can ask the Dreamwright about it. I know Nury's brought a whole list of questions from the kings and the Hubmen, but who's to say how long it'll take him to answer them?" Diligence rubbed her shoulder blade absently against a ridge of the resilient trunk. "I've been thinking I should be ready with a query or two of my own if he has the time."

Hitch drained his mug and nested it in the springy moss at his side. "He would know a thing like that—whether or not someone's carrying off yeofolk chicks beneath Old Hopshog Impery?"

"The Dreamwright knows everything—at least that's what I've always heard. He lies asleep in his Glass Castle, dreaming the world to come, and nothing escapes his notice."

"Not a bad vocation." Hitch twined his fingers together at the back of his head and stared up at the honey-colored midday sky. "To slumber all day and have folks looking up to you for it." He frowned in speculation. "Now, do you have to pay a fee in order to ask him a question?"

"Only if you want an answer back," Diligence told him dryly. "What do you think the yeofolk are for? Not to mention the seven alters, the thrice-three tine buds, and some old sword they dusted off from the great storehouse in the Hub."

"Hmph." Hitch was indignant. "It's not as though he was being asked to pitch the First Moon back into the sky. The man spends his working hours asleep—why should he require such grand booty to answer a few simple queries?"

"Swindle the soldiers out of another bag of glint and maybe you can afford to ask him yourself," Diligence suggested.

"First cheat, now swindle. You do me an injustice with your slander," Hitch complained. "Pebblehorn is known as a game of chance, because that's what you're taking when you set your wager down. Truly, everyone has an equal shot at winning. That's the beauty of it."

"Everyone?"

"Well, everyone on the other side of the table, at least. As the man hiding the pebbles, the odds are slanted somewhat in my favor, because I know the trick."

Diligence pushed to her feet with a snort of amusement. "And you don't see that as cheating?" She shook her head, mystified, as she started back toward the wagons.

"I see it as *chance*," Hitch insisted, ambling after her. "There is a chance that I may fumble with the horn, a chance that I may sneeze and spill the pebbles from my sleeve, a small chance that my wits will desert me entirely . . ."

Hitch toted his pack back to the cook's car before the wagons started up again. With his recovered health, he saw no need to remain with the soldiers—especially when the hatchling's irritating penchant for mimicry showed no signs of abating.

By the end of the day, their new trail had taken them perilously close to the borders of the Aulmad. A guard with a scattergun rode on each wagon, occupying the small observation platform located to the fore of the peaked roof. Watching from the side window of the cook's car, Hitch could see no outward evidence in the landscape to signify that they were approaching that place which seemed to spark such profound trepidation in the other members of the caravan. A great gorge with steep slopes and a wild river in its bottom split the land to the east of them, forcing a circuitous route that would take them nearer still over the next few hours. Eager to reach safer ground, Breitling did not call the usual halt at sundown, but kept the caravan moving through the darkness, relying, so Diligence explained to Hitch, on the wagons' recollections of the sun's prodding to push them onward. The moon showed his full face late in the evening, but apparently had little to say about the caravan's progress—though his pale illumination did make their nighttime travel easier over the rugged terrain. The wagons chugged on until a few hours past midnight, when the sun's exhortations finally faded from their memories and they slowed to a creaking halt.

After consultation with the alterman, Breitling ordered a pair of mounted soldiers sent out to reconnoiter just before dawn, the task relegated to the least massive members of the guard, so as not to overly burden their makeshift steeds.

Hitch sat sipping tea with Welleck on the porch of the supply wagon that doubled as the wagoneer's quarters, and watched the waking sun infuse the eastern horizon with a flush of gilded rose as they waited for the scouts to return.

According to Diligence, a mighty kingdom had once ruled this region, though no sign of it remained that the mountain boy's eye could detect. In truth, it seemed a pleasant place after the awful dry bleakness of the Siccative, and Hitch said as much to the wagoneer as he refilled their mugs. "Why does everyone cringe at the mention of the Aulmad? It seems no different from the land we've been traveling—aside from being a bit cooler and damper and more inclined to growing things."

Welleck rumbled his assurances to the contrary, swearing that the territory that lay to the north and west of them was cursed, and home to a veritable stew of monsters, as well as to predatory humans of every classification. "For all its hoary age, the Aulmad is like a fresh-killed corpse," the barrel-chested wagoneer declared, "with still a twitch here and there from those parts as haven't yet warmed to the idea of stony death. And like a corpse, it breeds all manner of pestilence and sordor throughout its long decay: Dry Pirates; face-stretchers and flaymen; packs of eviscerators, who'd burgle the organs from your living body just to add a few lumps to their morning grummidge; solitary bonetakers, with their whetstones and their scalpels; rockrasps aswarm in the ruins; Stalking Claws; trammelers and two-touches; the blind remnants of the Dark Commanderies, mustering in the night gardens; golden-haired Noose Women, trembling for the moon to rise ..."

He lapsed into moody silence as dawn spread scarlet and amber above the hills. Hitch was formulating a request for amplification concerning the moral nature and physical attributes of a Noose Woman when all at once the guards came pounding into camp with a mad swirl of dust and noise. Dopple and Brevny leapt from their near-exhausted mounts and stumbled into the circle of collapsible chairs and tables where the rest of the camp sat at breakfast.

Oblivious to the excitement generated by the soldiers' precipitate arrival, the alterman swallowed a final pastry and went clucking off to his wheezing charges. He stroked their coarse hair, muttering intimately into twitching ears as the foam dried on their chins and their wild eyes roved the brightening sky. Hitch sidestepped the distorted forms with a grimace and hurried after Welleck toward the fire ring.

The soldiers gasped out their story in alternating chunks. Riding into a wide, shallow basin not more than a league ahead, they had suddenly found themselves at the edge of a fierce battle between two huge and unknown armies. The conflict had clearly been raging for hours, and by the time the two guards arrived it had become little more than mutual slaughter. "Warriors were dying all around us," the two reported, their faces stricken above their damp black collars. "The floor of the hollow was heaped with the fallen. They took little notice of us in their agonies, and we were able to leave the field without pursuit."

The news plunged the caravan into a turmoil of consternation. Who were these savage combatants? Did their presence mandate another lengthy detour? Would armed survivors be returning home along the caravan's prospective route? Welleck advised the dispatch of two more soldiers on fresh mounts, to climb the hills around the basin and spy out the current situation. If a preponderance of the warriors of both armies were truly dead or dying, perhaps there was no need to change course. The alterman grudgingly worked his will on a second pair of alters, and Varve and Shevoss departed for the east.

An hour later the two came trotting back, their expressions guarded as the marchmaster and the others gathered round to assault them with questions. Finally Shevoss raised her black-gloved hand for silence.

"There was no battle." She carefully avoided the incredulous gaze of her two predecessors as she climbed from the yellow-haired alter. She gave her mount an absentminded pat on his sweat-stained flank and strode over to where the wagoneer and the marchmaster waited. "We made our way up into the hills and surveyed the basin, peering down from half a dozen vantage points on a scene of unremarkable tranquility. We rode down through the pass and well into the hollow itself without sighting a soul." She shook her head, her lips compressed into a thin line. "All was silent, the dusty ground smooth and unmarked save for the tracks of the first two alters."

"No battle? By Night's hangnail, there was!" Dopple marched up to stand stiff-backed and quivering before his erstwhile comrade. "Brev and I picked our way across the rivers of their blood. The air was full of moaning and the dead were piled to our chins!"

Shevoss turned her lean face toward Breitling. "I say what we saw, Marchmaster, nothing more."

"And I say you lie!" roared Dopple. He spat on the ground by Shevoss's black boot and put his hand on his slicer. Welleck's thick fingers closed over Dopple's as the wagoneer stepped in between the two soldiers. "Enough! No one need twist the truth here in order to recount marvels. Do you forget? This is the Aulmad, cauldron of sorcelment. Perhaps you saw a detachment of the Dark Commandery at their grim sport. More likely, the basin hides a trammeler's nest, and nets of false seeing were flung over your eyes as you rode through the pass."

Dopple lifted his black-bristled chin. "If that's so, then whose sight do you name as false—ours or theirs? We witnessed a battle, with fierce warriors and much wild death. What prey could a trammeler hope to snare with so frightening a vision?" He shot a vehement look at the silent Shevoss. "Only a madman would venture into such a place as we saw."

"Unless your vision came not from a trammeler," Varve suggested, "but from some other whose lair lay nearby, and who wished to dissuade you from crossing the basin." He looked toward the east, his lips pursed in speculation. "There are tales of great treasure hoards concealed in the Aulmad ages ago and still guarded by dark means."

"Why then were you allowed to trespass?" Dopple sneered. "D'you think yourself blessed with a babe's honest face, where Brev and I have the look of thieves?" Welleck stepped in again before words turned to blows, declaring the dispute at an end and banishing the two pairs of guards to opposing corners of the camp.

The maps were hauled out of their cases. Their evidence was clear: the wide rumple of hills that collared the hollow was impassable by wagon. Two more days at the least would be lost if the basin had to be circumvented by a more circuitous route. In the end it was decided to continue on as originally planned, weapons at the ready.

Low clouds had been gathering to dim the brightening morning. A light rain began to fall as the caravan uncoiled and set off, a black-clad guard hunched stolidly on the roof platform of each car. The wagons lurched and swayed through the grassy dales, moving sluggishly as if still fatigued from last night's marathon.

Diligence had informed Hitch after breakfast that the hatchling was refusing to eat, now that the mountain boy had resumed his quarters in the cook's car. Hitch reluctantly agreed to return to the guards' wagon long enough to serve as a model for the man in white. He sat staring out the side window, munching on toasted honeyloaf and a small salad while the hatchling dined similarly across the aisle. "He's doomed for sure if you find no other way to convince him to take his food," Hitch said around a forkful of flower-heads. "For I'll tell you now, I have no intention of reshaping either my life or my belly for the convenience of this tiresome mimic."

Diligence was examining the hatchling's garment criti-cally, her head tilted to one side. "He's becoming a bit dingy-looking, don't you think? Looks like we're headed for gray next."

A tangled outgrowth of forest had appeared to the north of them. Hitch rested his chin on his folded arms and stared into its dark depths, searching for mysteries through the slanting rain as they lurched across the hills.

Tension vibrated like an inaudible song through the wag-ons when the pass came into view. Hitch pressed the side of his face against the window, straining to see in front of them as they moved cautiously forward. One by one, the cars rolled down into the narrow gap.

The basin was empty as far as could be seen: a wide, flat expanse filled with rain-dampened earth and a few scraggly fir trees. The yeofolk shambled into the hollow behind the last wagon, and a wave of relief swept away the tension. Hitch found that he had been holding his breath and re-leased it. "*Whoof!* It must have been a trammeler's trick, after all," he remarked to Diligence over his shoulder. "The rain's nowhere near heavy enough to have washed away the evidence of such a battle as Brevny and Dopple reported."

The girl turned in her seat at the opposite window, with a shake of blond curls. "But why entrance the first pair of guards and let the second walk in clear-eyed? It doesn't make any sense."

Hitch was framing his reply when a great noise split the air.

TWELVE

IN SPURIOUS BATTLE

It took several long moments for the earsplitting clamor to sort itself out into shouts and curses, the sound of mighty horns bellowing, the shrieks of panicked animals, and the hoarse cries of wounded warriors.

Her head ringing, Diligence gaped in disbelief at the roil of bright shapes that twisted and lunged just beyond her windowpane. A second ago there had been nothing but rain between her and the sloping walls of the basin. Now armored warriors were everywhere, their battling shapes blotting out the gray sky, filling the empty hollow like a mad tide from edge to edge.

"Where—" She lifted her arm to shield her face as a pair of elaborately costumed combatants—the nearer clad in overlapping plates of jet and scarlet, his opponent a shimmer of gold mail dressed with green—came together in a fierce clash of arms directly outside her window. Hitch flinched back from his own observation post on the other side of the car, as two mounted warriors reared high on massive steeds. A quartet of hooves shod with spike-edged metal slashed the air inches from his nose.

Diligence stumbled to the rear of the car and cracked the door, staring without comprehension at the noisy chaos of crowded violence. "They're all around us! Where did they come from?" She was thrown against the near wall as the car lurched sharply to the left. Far ahead in the lead wagon,

Breitling was employing the master tiller to draw the caravan into its defensive circle.

The rear door had swung open to flap widely in their circling wake. Diligence pulled herself back to the doorway and yanked it shut to a crack again.

Welleck the wagoneer was bawling orders from the last car, his bass voice barely audible above the din: "Make ready to release the gases! Defend your vehicles! Employ your scatterguns at will!" The guards hunkered down on the rooftops, scrambling to level ponderous weapons at the nearest combatants. Diligence eased her head out the door and peered up at them. In the confusion of sound and motion, she could not make out whether they had fired yet, and if so, whether they had struck anyone on the ground.

Hitch came barreling down the aisle to crouch at her side as the battle swirled around them like an ever-deepening flood. "Look at that!" he exclaimed. "They're riding giant pull-ponies!"

"Warbucks," Diligence corrected him, as a huge beast charged riderless past one of the narrow gaps left between the circled wagons. "I've only ever seen them in pictures before, in the Histories," she added, turning to follow the progress of the magnificent creature as it leaped back into the fray. "I thought they were all extinct ages ago."

This close, there could be no mistaking the fabled mount for anything else. Its curved, six-pronged horns had been wrapped with gold and silver wire and spangled with flashing emblems. A caparison of stiff, figured cloth draped the muscular body and proudly arching head. Like the tail, the long chestnut mane was plaited with colorful ribbons, several of these now stained with a seep of dark blood.

A detonation of bright white light followed by a loud report caused them to jerk their heads back into the car. Half-blinded, Diligence squinted through the rear louvers, while Hitch raced back to alternate between his own posts at the inner and outer windows.

Something was going on inside the circle of wagons. At a frantic signal from the wagoneer, the soldiers began to leap down from their high perches. A low hum that seemed more vibration than sound traveled through the wagons, followed by a harsh grinding noise.

Hitch dropped his jaw in amazement as the peaked roofs parted neatly from the wagons along their inner edges, flailed high into the air like layers of bark curling from a tree, then swung out and down to land with a solid thump against the outer wall of each vehicle.

He gazed up at the ceiling of their own car as the humming stopped, then looked to the outer window. To his consternation, the battle still raged unobstructed beyond the glass, while something large creaked and spasmed fitfully atop the red and silver wagon.

Hitch hurried back down the aisle. Squeezing past Diligence, he unlatched the top half of the rear door and flung it open. He twisted around to hook his fingers over the jutting lintel and pulled himself up over the edge.

The guard called Ottshent crouched at the far end of the roof, her heavy shoulders straining as she grappled with the half-unfolded panel. Hitch grabbed the nearby edge and began to push and pull, slowly jogging the sheet of metal-backed ceramic back and forth in unison with the soldier. He jumped when a pair of gray-white hands appeared from nowhere to grip the rooftop alongside his own. Swiveling in surprise, he found the hatchling hunkered down on the roof next to him, blank face set with effort as he heaved his own weight against the stubborn hinge.

"Stop it! Get inside! You'll both be killed!" Diligence's blond head thrust into view above the edge of the roof, bobbing in agitation behind the man in light gray. She tugged resolutely at the hatchling's slippery ankle.

"Wait, give us a second," Hitch protested. "He's helping to un—"

The rest of the utterance was swallowed by an awful cracking sound as the hinge came abruptly unstuck. The freed roof jerked wildly and began to rise shuddering into the air. Ottshent dove for the inner circle with a startled cry. Hitch lost his footing on the narrow wooden platform as the heavy panel wrenched itself from his grasp. There was a moment of terrible, muscle-wrenching imbalance. Reaching out blindly, he grabbed hold of the nearest pale arm. The hatchling stood his ground for a second, then obediently released his own grip on the flailing rooftop and clamped his fingers firmly onto Hitch's opposite forearm. "Oh, no . . ." Hitch said with a moan.

Her left hand still securely wrapped around a gray-white ankle, Diligence had boosted herself up into a precarious squatting position on the lower half of the rear door. She was pulled along as Hitch and the hatchling tumbled off the far side of the roof.

The recalcitrant roof plate swung into position with a loud thump just as the three of them landed in a heap outside the circled wagons.

Diligence had ended up on top. She scrambled to her feet and began yanking on Hitch's vest. "Get up! We're outside the ring!"

Hitch raised his head dazedly. Horns rang out over the basin, echoing brassily above the thud of hooves on packed earth and the bray of animals. He fought the urge to clap his palms over his ears and shut out the clatter of swords on shields, the snap and whine of power-whips, the groans of the wounded and the shrieks of the dying. The hatchling was sprawled inertly across his chest. The space in front of the red and silver wagon was momentarily clear of fighting. The colorful wagon itself was almost unrecognizable. The red-brown tiles that had formerly covered the roof were gone, concealed now beneath the underside of grayish metal that formed a shield of heavy armor around the outside of the circled wagons.

"Look there!" Hitch shrugged away Diligence's insistent hands, pointing to the three-inch space between the armor plate on the guards' wagon and that of the car closest to it. Dim figures swarmed through the curtains of rain. Somehow the armored circle had been breached, and battling soldiers from both armies now crowded the inner ring, some on foot, others atop the massive warbucks.

"How could they—" Diligence backed away from the wagons in shock, whirling around when she remembered the bulk of the battle still going on behind her. A nearby bleating call caught her attention above the din.

Whether through intention or sheer laziness, the alterman had refrained from restoring their original forms to the two alters that had served as mounts for Shevoss and Varve. Instead, he had instructed the naked creatures to run alongside the caravan for exercise while the rest of their band traveled inside the wagons. The rain-sodden pair were huddled tight against the shielded car occupied by their fellows, yammering to each other in terror and confusion. The battle swirled near once again.

"Quick!" Diligence grabbed Hitch's belt with both hands and hauled him out from under the hatchling. She dragged him to his feet and pulled him stumbling after her toward the frightened pair. "Calmly now," she murmured, trying to keep her gestures soothing as they shied away from her touch. "We don't want to startle them."

The alters had been fitted with leather harnesses and cushioned back pads. A metal ring for the rider's boot dangled from each side of the pad. Hitch dug his heels into the ground as they approached the shivering creatures, his face twisting in disgust at the grotesquely lengthened front limbs and unnaturally arched spines. "What?" he said, "get on their *backs*?"

"Unless you know of some way to ride atop their heads," Diligence snapped. The alters bent their jutting elbows and sank to their knees as she tugged authoritatively on their ear clips. She boosted Hitch onto the nearest one with a grunt of effort, then swung herself up onto the padded back of its partner.

Hitch shook his head in defeated disapproval as the alter rose swaying beneath him. His previous riding experience had been confined to brief, forbidden jaunts as a little boy on the small, tough pull-ponies of his native peaks. Instinctively, he sought to take control of his mount by digging his sturdy boots into the narrow flanks. The alter gave vent to an angry, throbbing wail: "Off! Off! Off!" Locking her hind legs, she began to shake rhythmically from side to side in an obvious attempt to dislodge the offending passenger.

Diligence had headed off immediately toward the pass that led out of the basin. Looking back over her shoulder, she saw Hitch oscillating helplessly on the back of his indignant mount. She wheeled her own alter around and bounded back.

"It's trying to k-kill me," Hitch gasped when they were close enough to communicate. "H-how do you steer these th-things?"

"Like this!" Diligence extended her right arm and pointed in the direction in which she wished to be carried, at the same time giving her mount a light push below its shoulder blade with the heel of her other palm. "This way!" At once the alter swiveled about and began loping toward the pass.

Hitch pulled his boots away from his mount's sides, gratified when the warbling demands stopped immediately. Then he stuck out his own arm and gave a tentative tap to the rain-wet back beneath him. He was amazed when the alter lowered her head and took off in rapid pursuit. They threaded their way through the wall of combatants between them and the pass, almost blinded by the vast clouds of dust kicked up by the warriors' exertions. Once Hitch became accustomed to the loping, half-upright gait, he was surprised to find that the alter performed quite satisfactorily as a steed.

The dark figures of the yeofolk loomed out of the dust in front of them. Left to their own devices in the midst of the bewildering chaos of the basin, the massive creatures had begun to excavate a shallow, circular trench to the rear of the wagon ring. Diligence and Hitch gave the clanking behemoths a wide berth and plunged into the grass.

"This way!" With Diligence in the lead, they urged their mounts up the steep hillside toward higher ground, the alters complaining as they slipped and scrambled on the rain-slick grass. The hill was dotted with upthrusts of rock like rotted teeth that periodically obscured the action taking place in the hollow. Finally they paused next to a slab of upstanding granite and looked down on the seething basin.

"Did you see anyone following us?" Hitch gasped, still fidgeting uneasily on the back of his panting alter.

"I couldn't get a very good look with all the dust. But nobody even seemed to notice we were there," Diligence replied. "Will you sit *still*? You'll rub the skin off her spine."

"It just doesn't seem right, that she should have to carry me," the boy grumbled. Rain dripped from his nose and chin. "She's not much bigger than I am—even if that little dye-pated reek has stretched and angled her into his own idea of a pull-pony."

He turned his gaze back to the unrelenting madness below them. Bodies littered the ground. The remnants of the opposing forces had marshaled together for a final furious clash as he and Diligence were retreating through the pass.

Dust was rising in clouds that almost concealed the wagons.

Hitch felt a pang of guilt as he thought of the hatchling. The space in front of the guards' wagon where they had deserted the man in gray seemed empty, but it was hard to be sure. He flattened his palm above his eyes to shield them from the driving rain as he searched in vain for some sign of their comrades.

"Hey." Hitch lowered his hand and narrowed his eyes in sudden wonder at the droplets pooling on his knuckles. "Hey," he said again. "That's not right."

He heard a sigh at his side. "I told you, Hitch, she's an alter. She truly doesn't mind having you on her back." Diligence was also peering beneath her hand, trying to ferret out familiar shapes in the noisy chaos.

"No, no, not that. The dust, the rain." He waggled his hand in the air between them, splattering her face with raindrops. "Don't you see? It's practically pouring out. How can there be so much dust down there?"

She regarded him blankly for a moment; then her brows knit as she turned to reexamine the scene below them. Thick clouds of red-brown dust motes churned and drifted in the basin, seemingly unaffected by the ever-increasing downpour. "You're right," she said. "What could it mean?"

"It means Welleck and Varve were right—it *is* just a vision. That's how all those warriors could end up inside the wagon ring. They're not really there at all!"

"No, it can't be true." Diligence watched as a gold-clad fighter stumbled out of a swirl of dust, her fingers clawing at the gleaming lance that protruded from her abdomen. The woman gave a shriek of despair and pitched forward onto the ground. "Listen to it, Hitch: the battle noise, the horns, the screaming." Diligence's uncertain scowl betrayed her inner conflict. "A trammeler's trance works to confuse the eye alone. No conjured vision could summon up such a commotion."

"Then find me a better—hey!" Hitch stabbed the air with his forefinger, pointing past Diligence toward a spot farther up the hillside. Whether by accident or design, his hand fell on his alter's shoulder blade, and boy and mount sprang into sudden motion.

"What is it now?" Diligence scanned the crest of the hill as the pair shot by. There was nothing in view but a great, lichen-wreathed boulder, standing starkly against the gray sky. She prodded her alter into action and went scrambling up the hill after her companion. "Hitch! What did you see?"

He was leaning out from his padded seat at a precarious angle by the time she caught up with him. He searched the ground at the base of the boulder intently, a dumbfounded expression on his face. Diligence followed his gaze. The rain-softened soil was unmarked. "I could have sworn . . ." he began.

"Well, now. You've strayed considerably from your chosen path."

The voice came from a spot directly behind them on the wet slope. Hitch gave a start that threw him sideways on the alter's back, his arms flailing. He teetered for a moment, then tumbled onto the ground, one foot still snagged in the metal boot ring. The boy scrabbled in the soft dirt, the frightened alter wailing and kicking at him until he managed to extricate his left boot from the stirrup. Hitch pushed to his feet with an oath, one side of his vest and trousers plastered with gray mud.

"*You!*" he exclaimed. He charged forward, only to lose his footing on the slippery grass and tumble backward again.

Diligence had leaped down from her own mount. She nudged past the mud-smeared boy with a cluck of her tongue. "Where have you been all this time?" she inquired sternly of the purple-robed figure standing before them. "And what's that sitting on your head?"

Pomponderant touched a bony fingertip to the strange object perched at a rakish angle on his skull. The bronze toque was set with cabochon rubies and tiny tablets of burnished metal. "This is an extremely ancient relic of uncertain origin and properties," the old man announced. "I have been wearing it in hopes that it might suddenly manifest its capabilities. You will note, however, that it is a bit too small to properly conform to my cranium. I wonder if this might indicate that the ancients were a diminutive people in comparison to ourselves—or merely that it was designed to be worn by a child?" He looked off into the distance, his lips pursed in speculation as Hitch stalked up to him.

"What do you mean, sneaking up on us like that?" the boy demanded. "And why are you skulking around up here like a windlewisp, while your friends and comrades are besieged down below?" He gestured to the basin, still choked with dust and battle through the rain.

"Ut! I have not been skulking and no one is besieged." Pomponderant dismissed both notions with an airy wave of his hand. "Now, I believe I have yet to answer my former pupil's initial question. Be so good as to wait your turn." The old man took a small step back and to the side, focusing his attention once more on Diligence. "As to where I have been: I was summoned several days ago to a location several leagues from where we now stand—not far within the borders of what was once widely known as Auldemar the Shining, Lord of Nations, and which is currently little more than a verminous rubbish heap, a midden prowled by Stinging Whips and the odd bone-taker."

"What about Noose Women?" Hitch looked up from scraping streaks of odorous gray muck off the seat of his trousers. "You know—with the golden hair and all? Have you come across any of those?"

Pomponderant turned the boy a curious side glance. "Not this trip."

"But why did you leave the caravan in the middle of the night?" Diligence asked. "We were all worried about you."

The old man snorted. "I suspect you guilty of an imprecision in your employment of the word 'all.' At any rate, I was fast asleep in my bunk on the night in question when a small singing waft of a type found only in the forests of the Lower Aulmad crept into the car by way of a loose window frame and made its way to my pillow silk. What with the marchmaster's cacophonous snoring, it took some time for me to become aware of the presence of the tiny creature. The waft, which had assumed the form of a blue-tailed lizard after the fashion of its kind, finally roused me by perching on the tip of my nose." He rubbed the appendage in thoughtful recollection. "Its song, which it repeated rather insistently until I agreed to leave my bed, was in fact a summons in verse from a colleague of mine, bidding me to join him at a place not far from here to assist in the inspection of some curious artifacts." The old man removed his unusual headgear and scowled at it critically, using his purple sleeve to wipe at a dusty smudge on the gleaming surface.

"Ask him what's going on down in the hollow if no one's under siege," Hitch whispered at her side. "He won't answer me!"

Diligence shushed him. "It was another member of the Society that sent for you, then?" she prompted.

"Mm? Oh, yes—just so." Pomponderant raised his eyes from the toque. "One of my fellows was inspecting the ruins of an ancient pavilion from the Second Empire Period, when a fierce windstorm gave him no choice but to seek shelter beneath its partially collapsed roof. While excavating a shallow chamber in the rubble in which to lie protected from the brutal winds, hé happened upon a hidden door and a treasure room containing several interesting devices. He summoned me at once and we two fell to evaluating his discoveries.

"As I stated previously, we have so far been unable to discern the exact purpose of this artifact." He hefted the bronze helmet into the air. Hitch noticed that the rain did not seem to be adhering to the lustrous metal surface. "However, by our combined efforts, we were able to prod a remarkable historical repository into temporary functioning, as well as a related device used for the transference of visual and auditory images. Hence the spectacle which now fills the basin below. Eh?" The old man glanced over his shoulder with a distracted look, nodded to the empty air with a murmured phrase, and turned to hold the helmet out behind him at arm's length. When he drew back his hand it was empty. Hitch and Diligence exchanged a wondering glance.

"Unfortunately, the heart of the machine is rotten," Pomponderant continued, "irreparably damaged both by the passage of time and by the incursion of numerous minute, hard-bodied insects who have constructed a breeding nest at its core. Even now, Derbelderhed labors mightily to prolong the current sequence." He cast a scholarly eye out over the desperate battle that still raged in the hollow. "We have witnessed this conflict three times over the course of the past day and a half. Most likely we will not see it again in its entirety. Now we strive to set details in our own memories, later to compare our assessments with the official accounts in the Histories, and to correct any inaccuracies present in the old records."

Hitch had been squinting down at the devastation in the basin while the old tutor spoke. "Are you saying that what's taking place down there is some sort of magical storytelling—an illusion wrought with sound and sight? That the wagons have been drawn into battle formation for naught, and the members of the caravan are even now being frightened out of their wits, merely so you and your imaginary friend can take notes on some old set-to?"

" 'Old set-to' hardly does justice to the conflict below," Pomponderant protested. "Come. I suppose we should reassure your marchmaster as to his relative safety, before his heart gives way 'neath fear's unreasoning lash." He turned and began a loose-limbed amble down the damp slope toward the pass, the two alters trotting obediently after him at the snap of his fingers. "Well, come along," he said over his shoulder, on his face the mischievous grin of a young child. "This is far more difficult for me than you can imagine. I at least deserve some company!" After a moment's hesitation, Diligence and Hitch joined the small parade.

"This spirited engagement is in fact the Rout of Red Harra, which took place in yonder basin some eighteen centuries past." Pomponderant's didactic phrasings drifted back to them through the lessening drizzle. "Notice the energetic individual in the blue-crested morion." The old man paused to allow them to catch up, pointing to a spot near the center of the fray before resuming his odd, almost skipping gait. A warrior in green and golden armor stood atop a slight rise, which apparently did not exist in the present-day basin, giving him the distinct semblance of floating several inches off the ground as he held at bay at least a dozen of the red-clad enemy. "That is El himself, the so-called Hero of the North," Pomponderant observed. "The implement he wields to such great advantage is the sword Manscythe, which until very recently resided in the subterranean storage chamber at the Wheel's Hub and, coincidentally enough, currently lies beneath Nury's bunk in the white and brown wagon assigned to her use."

"How did such a thing find its way from this desolate

spot to the center of the Wheel?" Hitch asked. He watched, heart racing, as the subject of their conversation turned to a golden blur in its wielder's hands, striking among the black-and-reds in a dance of lopped limbs and sheared-off heads.

Pomponderant continued his unorthodox descent of the hillside as he responded. "Although El carried the field to victory in this particular contention, as well as many a previous and subsequent contest, he did not fare as well in every battle in which he strove. Manscythe was lost in a much later age when its master fell at last to the candlemen, who incinerated him brain and body during the Battle of the Stolen Air." He tipped his white head back toward Diligence. "As my erstwhile student can no doubt tell you, the battle itself ended badly for the Effulgency, taking a fateful turn when Amonwelle of the Unseen Wall renounced her sworn neutrality, and entered the fray against the candlemen following the immolation of her lover. In the ensuing confusion, the golden sword was removed from the battlefield by persons or creatures still unknown, eventually making its way into the hands of a metals merchant from Gaughanwell, who deeded it to the Wheel in exchange for free access to certain trade routes bordering the Western and Northwestern Cantles."

"Amonwelle—her mother?" Hitch looked back and forth in bewilderment between the old man's bobbing back and the fresh-faced girl at his side. "I thought you said this all took place in an age long dead."

"The Rout of Red Harra was accomplished eighteen hundred years past," Pomponderant confirmed. "The demise of the Hero of the North, however, took place a mere six centuries ago. Still—we are discussing the strivings of the great powers here. You must accustom yourself to dealing with a more flexible temporal framework, now that you have climbed down out of your western peaks. After all: an age is an afternoon to the Wielders, a year an eyeblink . . ."

They continued on in silence, Diligence contemplating the damp grass at their feet while Hitch struggled with the notion that his companion had been born of a mother who was at the very least six centuries old.

Pomponderant skipped forward confidently as they rounded the hillside and started through the pass. Hitch and Diligence found themselves hanging back slightly at the edge of the noisy battle. "Are you sure none of this is real?" Diligence called above the screams and bellows.

"Eh? Oh, it's quite real," Pomponderant told her. "But it is also eighteen centuries gone." He strode out into the midst of the chaos, the alters gamboling behind him. Diligence and Hitch followed, doing their best not to flinch each time a warbuck charged through them, or a warrior fell spurting blood across their path. "Wait a minute," Diligence said as they neared the circled wagons. "We've seen this part before." She watched in awe as two warriors came together just outside the guards' wagon in a clash of richly ornamented steeds. "Soon comes a great flash of light and a loud explosion."

Pomponderant cocked his head to one side and nodded sagely. "Derbelderhed informs me that the device is now presenting only the last stages of the battle in ever-shortening cycles. Unless we can revive its power chamber, this may be the final reenactment."

As if in direct response to his words, the entire battle suddenly vanished, the vivid colors and the cries of anguish replaced instantly by empty gray skies and a vast, ringing silence. There was a long, skeptical pause before Hitch saw figures peering cautiously between the gaps in the wagon ring.

"That got their attention," the mountain boy said. "No doubt they'll have a few carefully phrased questions to put to you. Will you be staying on with the caravan for a while?"

"I think not," the old man replied. "There are one or two more artifacts Derbelderhed and I wish to investigate."

"Just as well," Hitch said with a shrug. "Nury's taken up residence in the marchmaster's wagon these past several days. I doubt they'd be eager to see you back in your old bunk."

"What?" Diligence spun around, aghast. "Nury and Breitling—are you sure?"

"Sure as bad weather. Cook told me. It's been going on ever since your tutor quit the caravan." Hitch grinned at her horrified expression. "World's a bit darker than you thought, eh?"

"I am toying with the idea of meeting you at the Unseen Wall," Pomponderant continued, unruffled. "A rather intricate pattern of deeds and portents has been forming during this journey and I am hopeful that your mother will be able to add a thread or two to the design."

"Uck." Diligence shook her head, her eyes on the gray mud. "Nury and Breitling. I don't even want to think about it."

The armor was being drawn back with a heavy creaking sound from two of the cars as they approached. Caravan members stepped through the gap in the cars to gather in front of the wagon circle, some gaping in disbelief, others scowling darkly with arms folded, looking as if they were certain the entire recent unpleasantness could somehow be laid at the feet of their former traveling companion. Hitch found himself looking forward to watching the sparks fly, as Pomponderant coolly explained his role in staging the spurious battle to the confused and angry group that awaited them. Nury and Breitling in particular seemed discomfited, detaching themselves from the muttering mob and striding forth to meet them.

"This should be an entertainment," he said softly to Diligence, pulling her back slightly to allow Pomponderant to take the full brunt of the attack from the Hubwoman and her paramour.

"Have you noticed how he's walking?" Diligence whispered back. "Or the fact that his head and garments are not in the least damp?"

Hitch looked at her blankly. "Heh? What's that got to do with the color of Night's sleeprobe—"

At that moment Pomponderant came to a halt several yards from the glowering mob. He turned an abstracted gaze to the emptiness at the center of the hollow and his lips moved, though Hitch was not close enough to catch any of the words. Then the old man gave a curt nod and raised his brows placidly at Diligence and Hitch. "It seems I must truncate this glad reunion and assist my colleague. The insects have all but strangled the device's inner workings. Perhaps we will meet again at the Unseen Wall." He took a single step backward and disappeared.

"Well—*he* wasn't here, either!" Hitch exclaimed. He turned an accusatory eye on Diligence. "Did you know this all along?"

"No, I just figured it out a few minutes ago. When we came down the hillside, I noticed that his feet weren't quite touching the ground. I think he was just marching in place somewhere back there in the Aulmad, and moving the image forward with one of those instruments they discovered."

After a stunned several seconds, the marchmaster and the Hubwoman rushed forward with howls of thwarted anger. Diligence and Hitch did their best to pass along Pomponderant's explanation of the bizarre illusion.

Breitling insisted on a thorough inspection of the area before he would believe that the old man had not slipped into hiding somewhere nearby. An exhaustive search failed to come up with Pomponderant, but it did locate the hatchling, who was discovered sleeping peacefully on his back on top of the red and silver wagon. Hitch and Diligence escorted him blank-eyed back into the car and restored him to his bunk.

It took a while to convince everyone that it was indeed safe to travel on—whether or not the long-dead combatants reappeared. In the end, the false battle flickered back into being one last time, a few minutes after the wagons had uncoiled and resumed their trek across the basin. The image seemed to grow weaker as they passed through it, the armor's gold becoming less scintillant and the scarlet of the fresh-spilled blood noticeably more pallid. Even with Pomponderant's reassurances fresh in their minds, the marchmaster and the wagoneer steered the wagons along the far outside edge of the fighting as best they could, all eyes turning to the eerie sight of the fading warriors.

Once out of the hollow the land changed even more dramatically, the weather growing abruptly colder and the vegetation becoming thicker and more varied as they left behind their glimpse of the land once known as Auldemar the Shining, Lord of Nations, and entered into that area called the Madescent.

Two days into that verdant region, the caravan caught sight of a band of dark-clad strangers, skulking silhouettes against the far horizon who paralleled their course for a while, always keeping their distance across the moors. The guards tracked them warily from their posts atop the cars.

More ancient phantoms? Hitch was not so sure. Once he climbed up on the roof of the guards' wagon and watched along with Ottshent, the hatchling sitting between them and dangling his silver-gray legs. Hitch felt a cold flutter of unease along his spine: either it was a trick of the setting sun, or the hunched figures bore a familiar-looking black carriage swaying in their midst.

The vegetation thinned as they headed south again, soon passing out of the Madescent and back into the Siccative's warm upper reaches. The land grew arid and dusty. Late on the third day after their encounter with the ghostly skirmish in the basin, their spirits lifted as the ramble house finally hove into view on the eastern horizon. The wagons quickened their pace, Welleck having previously informed them that it would be against custom for them to attempt to dock at the way station in other than complete daylight. But they were still some leagues away, and it became obvious as the afternoon wore on that it would be twilight before they reached the outermost mooring ramps. Instead, they chose to halt within half a mile of the sprawling edifice and once again draw their circle in the dry earth.

The evening was calm, with a warm breeze wandering up from the south. Hitch sat close beside Diligence on the small porch outside the entrance to the cook's car. Cook was off engaging in a game of leap-the-log with some of the guards, while the scrivener boy had retired to his bunk directly after dinner.

The two sat on the porch in companionable silence, speaking only in occasional whispers as they gazed at the ramble house. The mountain boy found the way station a fascinating and mysterious vision in the deepening darkness, its spangle of softly glowing orange, yellow, and pale blue lights giving it the semblance of a glimmer-haunt of the ancient days, when it was said certain of the larger flickers had resided in fantastic structures cobbled together out of sugarwebs and evening dew.

The wagons had filled their water stores at a placid forest lake during their sojourn through the Madescent. Hitch was profoundly conscious of the scent of Diligence's freshly washed hair as he sat next to her, and of the warmth of her bare skin pressing against his own where their forearms touched. Keeping his eyes fixed on the soft lights, he slowly lifted his left arm and draped it lightly about her shoulders. Neither one spoke for several heartbeats.

"Well," Diligence said finally, as if shrugging off a daydream, "we'd best be seeking our rest if we're to mingle with civilized folk in the early morning. Don't stir yourself—I'll look in on the hatchling on the way to my wagon."

She gently disengaged Hitch's arm and returned it to him as if it were a borrowed shawl. "See you in the morning ..." She climbed down the ladder to the dusty earth.

Hitch watched the pale glow of her blond curls as she made her solitary way across the camp. He took a deep breath of the evening breeze and turned back to the glowing edifice. Resting his chin in his palm, he contemplated the colored lights until dreams claimed him.

THIRTEEN

THE RAMBLE HOUSE

By the brassy light of morning, the glimmer-haunt was revealed as a tumbled pile of oddly shaped boxes that seemed to have been cobbled together by a careless child. A central wooden tower thrust up several blocky stories, each painted a different faded color, above a sprawl of angled dwellings and passages on many levels, while the outer edges of the way station had an unraveled look, bristling with multicolored piers set at varying heights on wooden pilings. The ramble house was in fact a huge, rambling, houselike structure, enlarged with each addition to the constantly swelling family that had occupied it for many generations, until it now comprised a stupefying number of interconnected chambers of differing sizes and dimensions.

A host of landfaring vessels were already docked at the way station. The shorter piers were lined with single wagons, while the longer ones sprouted great circular platforms like flower faces at their ends, around which curled the caravans, from modest assemblages of four or five cars to huge wagon trains composed of a score or more vehicles.

Diligence awoke early; she sat at her breakfast and watched the preparations with interest. Welleck and Breitling had been up and conferring before the sun. Noticing the Daughter warming her hands around a mug of tea on the back porch of her car, the wagoneer invited her to accompany him when he went on his morning rounds, checking the undercarriages and making sure that all of the roof panels were in working order.

"Look at that now. A bad bit of business." The big man gestured sharply toward the north, from which direction another, larger caravan had arrived sometime during the night, drawing its camp circle almost exactly the same distance as theirs from the single vacant mooring dock. "By rights, we've got the green pier for ourselves, but Captain Spit-in-your-face over there seems ready to make us race." By squinting, Diligence could make out a small figure clad in gray and yellow seated grandly on a collapsible chair atop one of the garishly painted northern cars.

The ramble house itself seemed devoid of inhabitants until the precise moment when the lower rim of the sun's lambent disk rose free of the eastern horizon. Then a small green door creaked open and a slim girl dressed in sandal-scuffs and a brown smock appeared at the top of the unoccupied dock. She carried a tall, burgundy-colored pennant down the sloping ramp and fitted it into a socket set in the last plank of the pier. The ramble house was officially open for new business.

The wagons of the Turning Folk had hummed to life as the first ray of amber sunlight struck their peaked rooftops. Welleck and the others had long since returned to their cars to make ready for this moment, with Diligence watching curiously through the louvers of her side window. Breitling gave his signal just as the girl stepped back from the pennant, and the caravan crawled swiftly out of its circle while the echoes of the bell still hung on the cool morning air. The northern wagon train uncoiled moments later, and the two caravans dashed for the dock like racing skitterbugs. Diligence held on to a stanchion and chuckled to herself as the wagons shook and jostled; if Hitch had chanced to oversleep again, he'd be smack in the middle of a very rude awakening just about now.

The race was over in a matter of minutes, when Breitling's wagon touched its nose to the pier while its rivals were still several hundred feet away. With a grand flourish, the marchmaster leapt from the rear door of his car onto the canted platform. The girl in the brown smock stepped politely forward and offered him her hand for a brief ceremonial shake. With their preeminence thus officially confirmed, the folk of the Wheel disembarked from their cars and made their leisurely way up the ramp, ignoring the angry gesticulations of the other caravan's wagonmaster, who sat fuming in her own lead car some distance from the green pier. "Ha! Captain Dust-in-the-eyes, she is now," Welleck was heard to rumble beneath his mustaches. "Teach her to put *my* wheels and wagons to the test!"

Half the guards stayed back to watch the wagons. Diligence joined the small group of travelers that followed the girl through the green door and into the ramble house proper. They were led down a long, sideways-tilting corridor into a big, green-yellow room. The girl smiled sweetly and left them there.

Diligence found herself standing in the first ranks along with Welleck, Breitling, and Nury. She contrived to search for Hitch by turning her head slowly this way and that, as if stretching stiff muscles. At last she spied him near the back. Her mouth dropped open.

The mountain boy had obviously dressed with unusual care this morning. His breeches were newly pressed and his green cloak hung from his shoulders in regimented folds. As Diligence watched in disbelief, he moistened his fingertips with spittle and began polishing the tiny red gems on his double-wound belt. He had skinned his unruly hair back from his face and twisted it into a brown knob around one of the scrivener boy's discarded styluses. Diligence had not realized before how far his ears protruded from the sides of his head. She turned hastily back to the front of the room, coughing into her fist in an attempt to conceal her amusement at her friend's decidedly un-Hitchlike appearance.

A door opened before them to allow a great barrel of a man to squeeze into the room. He had pendulous jowls, and the irises of his eyes were clouded with cataracts. He moved slowly, the slender girl from the pier leading him to a carved wooden podium, against which he propped his bulk with a heavy sigh. Diligence nudged the wagoneer's arm, her brows raised in a questioning glance.

"That's the master hostler, old Paddifraw himself," Welleck informed her. "It's his custom to give the welcoming lecture to each batch of new arrivals, presenting the tariff, explaining the rules of the house, and so forth."

The girl rapped for attention on the podium with a sturdy gavel of gray wood. Scowling out over the crowd, the large man spoke to them at length in a gruff but pleasantly modulated voice. Diligence's attention wandered to Hitch lounging in his finery at the back of the room, while Paddifraw enumerated a long list of fees and surcharges for the various commodities and services provided by the ramble house; listed consequences ranging from the symbolic to the dire for infractions of what he termed "house decorum"; and finally wished them all a pleasant and restorative stay beneath his many roofs.

Each member of the caravan was issued a colorful badge incised with his or her identity and status, length of stay, and affiliation, to be worn at all times within the walls of the ramble house. Money was collected by a young man in brown tunic and breeches; Diligence watched as Breitling doled out the Turning Folk's glint with obvious ill humor. She turned her head at the sound of a hushed altercation. She crossed the yellow-green room to where Nury and Hitch stood trading murderous glances, the brown-smocked girl looking on impassively to one side.

Hitch turned his red-faced gaze on Diligence. "Younger visitors need a sponsor, and your father's servant won't authorize my presence here!"

Nury's hollow cheeks receded an additional half inch. "This shamble-shanks is no true member of our party," she declared. "We have no desire to be blamed for his obstreperous behavior."

"Nury, Nury." Diligence shook her head. She lifted her brows at the girl in brown. "What is the tariff for this lone thin boy?"

"Two shards, thirteen grains for a day's unlimited access to all yellow, blue, and medium green areas of the Repose, Lady," the girl told her.

Nury began an immediate squawk of protest. "Daughter, we are simply not authorized to make such a sizable disbursement, even on your generous behalf. Our finances were calculated to the demi-grain before we departed the Wheel."

"Yet since that time our party has grown smaller by two brave guards and one esteemed tutor," Diligence observed. "No matter. Hitch, do you have personal funds sufficient to gain access to the ramble house once you're recognized as a valued member of our caravan?"

"Truly I do, Daughter." The boy hefted a small leather sack at his waist with a sour grimace. "Though it leaves me little more than dust in my purse." He loosened the mouth of the sack and counted out the required fee.

"The glint is sufficient," the girl declared. She raised sea-flower blue eyes to Nury. "Will you or your marchmaster vouch for this youngling?"

The thin-faced woman assented ingraciously. "But don't come crying roughscuff to me," the Hubwoman directed, "if he's broken half your ordinances before he draws his hundredth breath within your walls. It's your affair if you open your door to him after hearing my admonishments."

"Thank you, Ladies and Sir." The girl in brown doled out their badges with a perfunctory curtsy. "A brief tour of the Repose will commence momentarily," she recited. "Complimentary refreshments are available at its conclusion in the yellow refectory. Please respect our customs and enjoy your stay." Hitch handed over his money with a wink that Diligence found unnecessarily intimate, and the slender girl moved off to distribute the remainder of the badges.

"Mind you tell your grandfather of our forebodings," Nury called after the girl. "If the boy commits a hanging offense, sadly he must hang alone for it." She left their side with a huff of disapproval and went to rejoin the marchmaster in the front of the room.

"Well, what do you think?" The mountain boy swirled his cloak in a half turn before Diligence. "Am I fit to mingle with civilized folk?" She was spared the need to reply by the approach of one of the Turning Folk guards, with a curt summons from Breitling himself.

"It is customary for a personage of your importance to join the caravan leaders in taking tea with our host," the marchmaster told her. "The rest of our group will be enjoying the twelve-grain tour provided for them by the Hub's generous coffers."

"I'll meet up with you later in that yellow dining hall," Hitch whispered to Diligence. To her annoyance, he made an about-face and set off in hasty pursuit of the brown-smocked ramble-house girl.

Breitling, Nury, Welleck, and Diligence were conducted up a creaking spiral rampway to a room near the top of the central tower. There Paddifraw sprawled in a vast cushioned chair and offered sour-sweet tea and bowls of swaddled nutmeats to his guests.

Diligence sipped disinterestedly at her tea as the wayfarers exchanged pieces of news and gossip with their massive host. She pricked up her ears when Paddifraw began to

speak of recent northbound travelers bearing reports of un-
steady ground and worsening weather among the lands of
the South. The large man inquired as to the purpose of their
own journey, in a manner that seemed to Diligence to be
excessively roundabout.

Nury and Breitling exchanged uneasy glances.

"We go to seek the Dreamwright," Welleck announced
bluntly. "To ask his explanation of the very phenomena you
have just described. The Wheel itself has been plagued by
queer disturbances of the air and ground for some months
now."

Nury had been conferring with the marchmaster in rapid
whispers. "We were not aware the strangeness had spread
to neighboring lands," she remarked in her clipped speech.

"Tales of unusual storms and dancing earth have reached
us from many lips," Paddifraw confirmed. He fell silent for
a long moment, his clouded eyes narrowed in a skeptical
frown. "Some say the Shadowsmith is astir again in his lair
to the far south," he said finally, his gruff tone growing almost defiant. "Some others that he ranges northward even
as we speak."

Welleck heaved a great sigh. He looked around the table,
his own eyes filled with doubt and hesitation. "I myself
heard such claims from several sources before we departed
the Wheel."

Breitling's face had grown pale at the mention of the
Shadowsmith. Nury sat at his side in stony silence.

Diligence could scarcely believe her ears. The
Shadowsmith was a creature from the Fabularies, the monster children feared when the last candle was blown out at
night. It seemed unthinkable that grown men and women
could discuss the King of Evil's son as if he were something other than a fable used to reinforce discipline or
threaten the wayward child.

The group sat quietly for half a minute, each member

immersed in his own thoughts, until a woman in dark blue appeared from somewhere with a pot of fresh tea. Paddifraw refilled their bowls of nutmeats, and the conversation turned to lighter matters.

At the end of their audience with the old hostler, they were given a tour of the ramble house that left Diligence feeling completely confused and turned around. Paddifraw's many children and his legions of grandchildren swarmed everywhere within the labyrinthine structure, identifiable by their garments, which were dark blue and pale brown respectively, and their strikingly similar features. The travelers were told repeatedly to ask for directions whenever in doubt, until Diligence began to feel that they were being led around in circles, as part of a strategy that was designed to leave them disoriented and dependent.

At last they were shown to the refectory. The great yellow room thronged with foreigners, vibrated with their unexpected aromas and the queer sounds of their speech. From her lessons with Pomponderant, Diligence was able to recognize many of the peoples seated around them. Taciturn glasshouse builders from Toime sat cheek by jowl with garrulous Sand Rafters; gray-faced Steppemen cast contemptuous glances at unctuous salvers from the far west—the latter relegated to an isolated serving board against the farther wall.

Diligence was shown to her place of honor at the hostler's board. She spotted Hitch half the room away, sitting by himself at one of the common tables. She had little time to send more than a smile in his direction before one of Paddifraw's elder sons engaged her in earnest conversation concerning the Wheel and its age-old system of Inclinations and Advancements. By the time she was able to steal another look, the mountain boy was chatting amiably with a clutch of the brown-clad grandchildren. Subsequent sidelong glances indicated that he had not only managed to catch up with the slender girl from the green pier, but that he was finding her laughing comments particularly congenial.

Paddifraw's son Leddaken had begun to expound on the virtues of the wide variety of victuals available for purchase at the Repose, producing from the pocket of his dark blue vest a large illustrated pamphlet that Diligence was obliged to appraise for several minutes. The next chance she had to scan the common tables, she found that neither Hitch nor the slender granddaughter were in evidence. Fuming, Diligence announced her intention to do some exploring within those areas of the house to which her brightly colored badge guaranteed her admission, and excused herself from her tablemates.

The ramble house was a masterful maze, with a profusion of ramps going up and down and around; corridors that divided suddenly into four different branches, three of which seemed to lead nowhere; tiny rooms crowded with ancient furniture and large ones that were nearly empty.

She was about ready to give up when she trudged down a long, narrow corridor and peered into the L-shaped cul-de-sac at its end. Hitch and the girl were seated on a low bench with Hitch's open pack between them. They murmured back and forth in tones too soft for Diligence to make out. As she watched, the mountain boy lifted a pair of fine lace undergarments from the backsack with a muttered comment. The granddaughter accepted the tatwork with an appreciative grin and folded it into her lap, where another pair already resided. Diligence leaned silently away from the corner of the cul-de-sac, turned in her tracks, and stalked back down the corridor.

Her mind filled with dark thoughts, Diligence spent the afternoon inspecting the many small shops and kiosks that dotted the interior of the ramble house like mushrooms in a cave. She saw no further sign of Hitch until nightfall, when she exited the green door and returned to her wagon. He was sitting at the end of the pier, on the rim of the platform just beside her car, half dozing with his arms clasped around his drawn-up legs. He opened one eye as she attempted to slip past him into the wagon.

"Good evening," he said with a yawn.

"I have a headache," Diligence replied stiffly. "I'm going to lie down." She stepped from the platform and tugged open the rear door of the wagon.

"I'm sorry to hear that," Hitch said. "What did you think of the ramble house?"

"It's very large." Diligence stood in the doorway, one hand on the door.

"Isn't it? I had a wonderful time poking around. I tried to find you for a while, but you were busy with the far-turners." He cleared his throat with a grimace of discomfort. "I've run into a small problem. I used up all my glint, so they've taken my badge away and told me I can't go back in tomorrow morning."

"There's a pity." Diligence tried to keep her lip from curling. "I'm afraid you can't look to me to pay your tariff." She nodded her head toward the black-clad soldiers huddling around a lantern on the other side of the dock. "But it's early yet. There are plenty of guards about. I'm sure you'll find a way to relieve somebody of enough wealth to win your way back inside." She turned and stepped into the car. She had a thoroughly satisfying view of Hitch's wide-open mouth as she slammed the door shut in his face.

FOURTEEN

END OF A GYRE

Hitch sat at the table in the red and silver guards' wagon and poked the sharp end of his eating stick at a bowl of sticky grummidge studded with flakes of sandfish meat, the wreckage of the midday meal he'd been toying with for the past half hour.

"Well." Shevoss stood at his side, hands on her hips. "If it wasn't completely killed to begin with, you've certainly worried it to death." Hitch lifted his stick and dropped it into the mottled mush, then pushed the bowl away from him with a sigh.

"I truly need to get back in there." He looked up at the soldier, his eyes beseeching. "I was in the midst of conducting a business transaction, and it's been left incomplete. Are you sure you haven't any glint to loan me?"

"Not a grain," she said with some satisfaction. "I spent it all yesterday on bark board and picture-paints to bring home to my little son. Now I'm comfortably cleaned out—which is all to the good, as today's my day to watch the wagons." She retrieved her slicer from a wall cubby and strapped it to her hip. "Time for patrol," she told him. "Good luck. Maybe you could burrow in beneath the floorboards."

Hitch gave another gusty sigh. He pushed back from the table and walked to the rear door, where he watched the guard's dark figure retreat through the louvers. Opening

160

the top half of the door, he hopped up onto the lower half, balanced, and boosted himself onto the roof. The hatchling lay stretched out in the sunlight, his peculiar eyes shut and his arms and legs spread wide, looking like a man who'd been run over by a heavy wagon. His mutable garment glistened pale silver-gray. Hitch went to sit at the edge of the rooftop in the shade of the canted tiles. He kicked his heels lightly against the side of the wagon and stared at the far horizon, where brown-umber earth melted into amber-bright sky.

After a while he heard the creak of footsteps on the pier. He stuck his head around the edge of the roofslant. Alacrity was climbing onto the porch of the cook's wagon, his thin shoulders hunched high and a black look on his young face. The door swung shut behind him.

Hitch frowned. He climbed down from the roof, picked up his boots and cloak, and crossed the end of the dock to the cook's car.

Several moments later he was back on the pier, a bright badge flashing on his chest, a whistled tune on his lips as he headed up toward the green door.

He came close to getting lost several times as he roamed the undercorridors of the ancient structure. He ran into the occasional Paddifraw in brown or dark blue, but saw no sign of anyone from the caravan. At length he found his way, half by accident, into the L-shaped room at the end of a long corridor.

The girl in the brown smock was sitting there. She set down the book she was reading and gave him a sunny smile. "I thought you might not be coming," she said.

"I almost thought the same," he admitted. "But there's a melancholy scribbler boy—a scrivener, they call him—who's part of the group from the Wheel. He came back to the wagons a little while ago and told me he had no desire to mingle further with any Wander Men till the end of his life's gyre."

The girl laughed at Hitch's expert imitation of Alacrity's lifeless drawl. "Besides," Hitch continued, "he said some brazen girl in a brown smock pinched him."

Paddifraw's Semmalyne spread her hands. "Don't look to me. I've been sitting here waiting for you all morning, when I should have been upramp folding pennants and scrubbing out the bathing urns. I do have some very brazen cousins, however, and my sister Coroboth will pinch anything that doesn't smell like a sandfish."

"Well, whoever it was, she did me a favor. Alacrity was only too happy to turn his day-badge over to me, while he spends the rest of his time here practicing his loops and serifs in the cook's wagon." Hitch set his backsack down on the bench and pointed to the small package wrapped in paper by her side. "Is that it?"

Semmalyne nodded. "I got the blue one, like you wanted. It's a little bigger than the other, but I talked my uncle into making it the same price."

She untied the string and slipped a small, gleaming disk carefully from the wrapping.

"Excellent!" Hitch crowed. He held out his hands and Semmalyne dropped the object into them. The disk was made of beaten copper, its surface bisected by eight radiating lines and set with alternating wedges of ivory and rich-looking turquoise. It carried an aura of great age. The boy reached into his pack and brought forth a fold of lacy white cloth. "Here's the last one. Are we even now?"

Semmalyne unfolded the undergarment and held it up to the light that streamed in golden through the high window. "Even and done," she said. She tilted her head toward a small doorway set flush with the far wall. "Do you want to go walking with me in the under-undercorridors again?"

Hitch dropped the disk into his pack and straightened up. "Thanks," he said, "but I've got to find somebody."

Semmalyne shrugged. "I'll see you later, then." She tucked the garment into the waist pocket of her brown smock. "My aunt is going to love these. I hope your present is a success, as well."

"Thanks," Hitch said again. "So do I." He touched his forehead in a quick salute and headed down the long hallway.

He searched the lower levels, got genuinely lost for nearly an hour in a vast network of rooms that somehow seemed to turn back in on itself every time he thought he had found the way out, finally did stumble onto the exit, and emerged into the upper corridors. He had left his green cloak back at the cook's wagon, but he was still sweating by the time he made his way to the refectory. To his disappointment it was nearly deserted, the only occupants two corpulent female salvers off by themselves in one corner and an aged-looking individual of indeterminate race and gender bending its hooded head over a bowl in another.

He ladled a cup of clear water into a mug, scraped the last three grains of glint from his pouch by way of payment, and retired to a small table that was roughly equidistant from the room's other occupants. He took out the disk, inspecting it in the warm glow from the many skylights set at odd angles in the broad ceiling. Tiny curlicues of script crossed both the turquoise and the ivory wedges. He would have to consult Alacrity later to see if it was really writing and if it had anything of interest to say.

"Not many of those around," said a wavering voice from his side. Hitch jumped. The aged individual was now sitting next to him, most of its countenance save for a rather large nose concealed by a voluminous hooded cloak. Wrinkled hands clasped a shallow bowl filled with something stringy and yellow that emitted an odor that made Hitch's nose wrinkle.

"I hope not," he replied. "I was told it was a rare and ancient artifact."

Narrow shoulders shrugged. "Rare, yes. Ancient? Twenty-eight hundred years old at the oldest."

Hitch whistled. "That's plenty old for me. Are you sure?"

"Quite sure." The cloak rustled, accompanied by a dry sound that might have been amusement. "What do you think of this pile of tunnels and boxes, then?" The nose, hands, and now the voice were still not enough to give Hitch any clue as to the person's origins, nor even whether it was male or female.

"The ramble house? It's, um, very large," he replied, trying to see past the shadows that thronged inside the shapeless hood. "I like it."

"Yes, the ramble house remains one of the more successful adaptations of those families forced from their native soil during the Second Dispersal. A carefully managed breeding program incorporating selected visitors enables them to avoid most of the problems inherent in such isolated pocket societies—though close inspection reveals that the Paddifraws have nearly developed into a sub-race over the centuries." A bony hand pointed to the trio of brown-and blue-clad servers on the other side of the room. "Note the strong jaws, the relatively small ears and slender torsos. A rather well favored people, all told, though the lack of variation soon grows tiresome to the—"

"If you'll excuse me, I have to go look for someone," Hitch interjected. He drained the last drops from his mug and pushed to his feet. "You're very knowledgeable, and I'm sure it's been a pleasure chatting with you."

"Likewise." The clawlike hand closed with surprising

strength about his left wrist. "Did I mention that all this fiddling with the Wire will soon be coming to a head?"

"The wire?" Hitch struggled automatically in the obdu-
rate grip. "I'm not sure I know what you're talking about."

"Trouble in the south and worse in the north. It'll be
more than bad weather and a lurching landscape if certain
parties get their way," the wavering voice mused. "It's been
tried before, of course, but never with such ferocity—nor
with such allies. Your somnolent friend may hold the key in
the end, depending on when you decide to wake him up.
Oh, here . . ." The hand withdrew for a second, sending
Hitch back a stumbling step. Why, he wondered, were people always grabbing hold of him and babbling about things
he didn't understand? The wizened hand reemerged from
the cloak's folds, a small wad of tissue-thin cloth resting in
its wrinkled palm. "This may mix things up a little. It goes
on the right-hand side, in the third aperture down from the
top. Your reward for suffering the idle chatter of the aged.
I wouldn't advise touching it until it's warmed up a bit."

Hitch held out his own hand. He accepted the object and
pulled back the layers of tissue with his fingers. Something
small and black, like a button or a bead, gleamed inside. He
rolled it into his other palm and dropped it immediately
with a yelp of pain. "Ai-yah!" The object struck the floor
and rolled along the uneven planks, Hitch trotting after it
with a pained scowl. He cornered the thing with the side of
his boot and went down on one knee to gingerly scoop it
up into the folded tissue again. His left palm had the beginnings of an angry blister and the skin felt partially numb,
but whether from searing heat or intense cold he could not
decide.

"What is this thing, and where does it . . ." He straightened up slowly, realizing that his query had been addressed
to the empty air. The table was unoccupied except for his
mug. He looked around the room. The two salvers were

giggling obscenely in their corner; Paddifraw's kin bent to their duties at the serving wall. Hitch moved beneath one of the larger skylights and examined the object carefully. It was a tiny concave oval, black with golden flecks in a net of thin gray striations. He held his fingertips an inch above it, feeling the waves of extreme cold that radiated from its surface. With a shrug, he folded the tissue tightly around the thing and dropped it into his pack next to the copper disk.

He left the refectory with a bemused look, turning the bizarre incident over in his head. Third aperture down from the top? His somnolent friend . . . ? He wandered deep in thought until he realized he was lost again, then stopped a small boy in brown vest and shorts and inquired as to the whereabouts of a path that would lead him back to the green pier. He heard the commotion when he was almost there. Turning a corner, he saw a great crowd of wayfarers pressing through the small door that led to the outside.

He joined the back of the crowd and squeezed out onto the dock. The onlookers made a jostling wall that bore him along as they headed down the pier toward the Turning Folk wagons. Not for the first time, Hitch wished for an additional foot or two of height, as he tried to see around and over the towering backs in front of him.

Snippets of conversation were making their way through the crowd as they neared the end of the pier:

"—guards saw nothing."

"Why all the—"

"—sitting out there like an angry blister for a day and a night and now they're gone—"

"—anything missing?"

"Who else could it have been?"

Hitch tried to make some sense of the snatches of speculation. Then the red-haired man in front of the black-skinned woman directly ahead of Hitch turned back and said quite clearly: "There's been a murder. Someone from the new caravan that docked yesterday morning."

Murder! Hitch's blood jelled and his knees felt shaky. He struggled closer through the press of bodies, beginning to use his fists and fingernails to clear his way.

"Ow!" cried the woman who had been in front of him. "You needn't shove!"

A man whose toe he had trod upon reached out with an oath and tried to catch him by the knot on the back of his skull. Hitch ducked forward, losing Alacrity's stylus and several strands of hair, and scooted between the legs of an enormous salver.

"They say it was some boy who joined the caravan late," a high-pitched voice declared to his right as he pressed forward. "A pack-man called Itch or Twitch or some such foolishness."

His mind vibrated in confusion. Was he being accused of killing someone? Who was the victim?

"It's Hitch," he muttered dazedly as he sidled by a burly man dressed in the ragged, many-layered costume of a Sand Rafter. "A perfectly good mountain name. It's because I was forever getting tangled in things when I was little and they always had to tie me to a fence post or dangle me from a tree limb to keep me out of trouble . . ."

"Well, either way," the unseen woman sniffed, "Hitch or Stitch, he's dead as dirt, and the poor wagon's been turned inside-up."

He was almost at the front of the milling crowd. A cordon of brown- and blue-garbed women and men stood just beyond, forming a barrier with their bodies at the edge of the dock. Hitch stopped in his tracks, feeling as if he were trapped in a familiar nightmare. He was able to see only snatches past the moving thicket of arms and legs in front of him. At the edge of the dock lay a body—or what was left of one, to judge by the scatter of twisted lumps beneath the long green cloak that covered most of it. Welleck was standing over the corpse, a look of great sorrow on his kindly face. Breitling stood nearby wearing an expression of distaste mingled with something like triumph. There was no displeasure to be found in Nury's pinched features; only a self-righteous satisfaction that fairly burned in her narrow face.

The wagoneer was engaged in solemn conference with one of Paddifraw's strong-jawed, blue-clad offspring. Hitch strained forward to catch his words:

"—hadn't enough glint to go back inside this morning, and one of the guards saw him moping about. Aside from the soldiers, he was the only member of our party to be excluded from the ramble house." He lifted his face to the marchmaster and the Hubwoman, mustaches bristling. "Now, because of our parsimonious practices, a good boy will never see manhood!"

Nury muttered something Hitch could not make out, and Welleck stepped forward with arm drawn back as if to strike her. Breitling and one of the ramble-house men intervened and separated the two.

Blood had seeped out around the robe to leave a brownish stain on the faded planks. Hitch stared down at the crumpled form for a long moment. Finally he wormed his way through the onlookers in front of him and stepped out into the open. A woman in a blue smock held her hand up to keep him back.

"It isn't me," he told her quietly. "I'm sorry, but Alacrity gave me his badge and I've been inside the house."

The woman blinked at him. Heads turned nearby in curiosity and confusion.

Breitling saw him first among the Turning Folk on the pier. "Wha . . . ?" The freckle-faced marchmaster took a half step forward, eyes narrowing in disbelief.

After that, it seemed to dawn on half a dozen people all at once.

"Hitch!" exclaimed the wagoneer. "Hitch! Hitch! You're alive!"

Shevoss slapped her lean thigh with the flat of her palm and flashed him a wide grin of relief.

"O Alacrity!" wailed the stout cook, beating his breast with massive fists.

The crowd threatened to close about him like a flood, till Paddifraw's kin drove them back with Welleck's assistance. "Give him air," the wagoneer bawled. "He's just back from the dead!" He looked down at Hitch. "How, lad . . . ?"

Hitch made his way to the porch of the cook's wagon and leaned against the blue wall. He gulped out his story with his eyes fixed on his listeners, unable to look at the crushed body that lay beneath his cloak. Welleck gave a heavy nod at the end of the tale. "Poor scrivener boy," he said, "wrong place, worse time."

At his side, Nury expelled a long, rattling breath from her bony chest. "The dear, dear little one," she moaned, "always so quiet and correct." She shot Hitch an accusatory look. "He'd be alive at this moment if the world turned as right as the Wheel."

"Yes, and I'd be stony dead!" Hitch thrust out his chin belligerently, his eyes bright with moisture. "It wasn't my fault he didn't want to mix with Wander Men, and it wasn't my fault somebody pinched him, so you can stop staring fire-eyes at me."

"We think it was brigands looking to raid our larder," Welleck told him. "Though the guards saw no one and the body was hacked to bits. Another thing—Captain Race-me-for-it and her northern caravan's gone missing." He turned to jab the air toward the spot where their rival had sat through the night and morning waiting for a place to dock.

Hitch had been leaning hunch-shouldered against the car,

staring sightlessly at the faded green planks. Suddenly he raised his head. "Diligence!" he said, looking around wild-eyed at the throng of faces. "Where is she?"

"The Daughter took to her wagon, lad," Welleck told him in a quiet rumble. "She turned white as a new tooth and went all trembly soon as she heard the news." He laid his big hand on the mountain boy's shoulder with a smile. "You know, her mood might benefit considerably from the knowledge that you're more or less alive."

Hitch sprinted around the outskirts of the crowd to Diligence's wagon. He knocked hesitantly at the door, his arms and legs tingling. When there was no response he called out to her: "Diligence? It's Hitch. I'm all right. I need to talk to you."

There was a long moment of silence; then the door flew open and a pale and shaken Diligence rushed out, her cheeks streaked with moisture.

"You're—you're—" She began to hiccup, unable to get any further with the statement.

"I'm all right. I was inside the ramble house. It was poor Alacrity that got killed." He hauled his backsack off his shoulder and rummaged in it till he found the small paper package. "Here, I traded some underwear to get this for you." He took a step back and hugged his shoulders with his hands, his voice sinking to a whisper. "Oh, Diligence, I know they were looking for me. I just don't know why."

She added her arms to his and hugged him hard.

FIFTEEN

AMBUSH

They buried Alacrity's remains in the hilly plot north of the ramble house. One of the yeofolk handlers went up first, two of the great clanking creatures trudging at her side. Ten minutes later she was back. The others carried up the little body, still wrapped in Hitch's green robe, and laid it in the perfectly round pit.

Nury led the brief ceremony that followed. Hitch watched the rhythmic, circling dance with a feeling of hollow numbness in his belly. He found it impossible to muster the good spirits necessary to make fun of the Hubwoman, who resembled nothing so much as a long-limbed marshbird as she wheeled and kicked her stick-thin legs in the sparse grass by the grave.

The small group walked back down to the ramble house.

"We don't have any kites," Diligence said sadly, gazing back over her shoulder at the empty golden sky. "There should have been kites . . ."

Paddifraw allowed them to stay moored overnight at the ramble house for a fraction of the regular tariff. The caravan departed the green pier early the next morning.

Hitch rode with Diligence in her wagon, unable to face the cook, who had taken the scrivener's death as if it had been his own son cut to pieces. They sat in somber silence at opposite ends of the car for well over an hour, Diligence respecting Hitch's disinclination to hash over the events of the previous day yet another time. She sat inspecting the copper artifact Hitch had given her, wondering at its possible connection to the Wheel, and sending sidelong glances toward her downcast companion. At length she came to a decision and carried her mug of peppery tea back to the rear door. She dragged one of the collapsible chairs from its cubby and set it up next to Hitch's. He raised his head with a wan smile, then lowered it to stare at the floorboards once more.

"We need to talk," Diligence began. "What you said yesterday—about you being the one they were trying to kill. Did you mean it?"

He gave a barely perceptible shrug. "I'm pretty sure. It seems to fit the facts."

Diligence raised her blond brows. "Just what facts are these?"

"Well." He lifted his head again with a weary look, as if it were weighted down with a stone collar. "I guess it all started back in the western forest, halfway to Waterside . . ." He proceeded to tell her about the stonecrush's attack on his employers' camp, and his own fortuitous visit to the stream to wash out his breakfast bowl. "After that I found the old woman in her house. I think she was one of Pomponderant's Society members, from what you've told me of their great interest in green moths, or maybe she'd just heard the phrase somewhere. That's where I got my green cloak. I told you about that, didn't I, with the bird and all? No?" He described his experience soaring high above the tiny valley, and the line of dark warriors he had seen marching single-file toward the little house. "I'm pretty sure those were the same figures we spied on the ridge a few days ago, after we left the basin. They were carrying someone on their backs in a box of black wood." He shook his head. "Both times I saw them, it left me with a cold feeling, like a chill playing on my backbone."

"You think they're the ones who killed Alacrity?" Diligence asked. "And that they mistook him for you?" She tried to keep the skepticism out of her voice. "How could they have followed you this far? You said they never saw you leave the little valley. And what about the stonecrush? It's far too heavy to be borne in a litter—and we surely would have noticed if such a hulking beast had been marching among them."

"I didn't say I'd worked it all through yet," Hitch replied. "I just said it seemed to make sense."

"But what about the other attacks? The astilfe only went after you because you stumbled onto it while it was poisoning the yeofolk."

"Did it? Or was it waiting there for me, watching from the yeofolk hole till I walked by?"

Diligence refused to be swayed. "And the first two guards we lost to freezing—poor Huben, poor Tarler? You hadn't joined the caravan at that point. In fact, you were still asleep at the lakeside, not even damp yet from hauling in your hatchling."

"I don't know how every little detail fits together," Hitch said testily. "But I do know that it was supposed to be me moping in the cook's wagon yesterday, not Alacrity. He gave me his badge and it cost him his life."

"But it's foolish to assume whoever did it was after you," she persisted. "Why, only members of our own caravan would have known that you were in the wagon—" Diligence stopped short, her eyes widening. "You know, that's true," she said. "Dark marchers and mountain hobs to the side, if someone in our own party had wanted you killed, they would have known when to do it—or thought they did. But why? Even Breitling, even Nury, can't hate you enough to kill you for it."

"I should hope not," Hitch agreed. "Not just for a few arguments and some less than tactful words. Other than that, I'm not mixed up in your Wheel business at all."

"The inside of the cook's wagon was torn to pieces," Diligence continued in a musing tone. "The bunks pulled out of the walls, food and supplies thrown every which way, but almost nothing actually missing once they got it all back in order. What if—what if they didn't really intend to kill Alacrity, or you for that matter, but he was just unlucky enough to have gotten in their way while they were looking for something else?"

"For what? Cook's recipe for braised treehen? Alacrity's paint trough?" Hitch shook his head in bafflement. "My own pack, with its collection of hob guides and lace underwear?"

Diligence straightened slightly at the mention of the underwear. "I didn't say that it had—"

"The *stick*!" Hitch sat suddenly bolt upright, stamping his boot on the floor with a loud thump. He stared at Diligence, then looked wildly around the narrow cabin. "They must've been after the walking stick! You took it from the cook's car while I was sick. What did you do with it?"

She regarded him blankly for a moment, then swiveled in her seat and pointed to the storage space beneath her bunk. "There. I put it under there."

Hitch raced to the side of the bunk and shinnied underneath. He pushed his way back out seconds later, the length of twisted wood clutched in his hand. He sat on the edge of the bunk and cradled it wonderingly in his palms as Diligence walked back to join him. "I'll bet this is it," he said. "I'll bet this is what they were after."

Diligence looked dubious. "An old piece of stick with a stone on the top? Even if it lights up now and then, it's no better than an ordinary torch of cold fire—worse, since you don't know how to make it shine when you want it to."

"It lights up when important things are happening," Hitch said. He was turning the stick over in his fingers, examining the rough wood intently. "Sky things. Falling eggs, funnels of twisty color. Maybe it does other things we don't know about." He held it up to the light, peering at the nearest window through the cloudy gem caught in the roots of its head. "It explains the stonecrush. I found the stick under some bushes after the beast had left. He must have forgotten it, or maybe it fell out of sight during the massacre. Then he remembered it and came back to try and find it. I heard him, crashing through the wood." He shivered slightly at the memory of the approaching footfalls. "That's when I acquired the walking stick and that's when they started coming after me."

"Do you think so?" Diligence was impressed by his earnestness in spite of herself. She reached out to stroke the bluish stone with her fingertips. "But why attack the wagon camp and kill our guards? We didn't have the stick."

He shook his head. "Maybe they can only track it in a general sense," he conjectured. "Like when you hear a nighthoot clacking off to the east, but you don't know exactly where he's squatting. Maybe they were heading toward me at the lakeshore, and maybe your wagons just happened to be parked in the way, so they figured I must be inside one of them. Maybe they would have destroyed the whole camp if the golden egg hadn't scared them off."

"But who are they? And how would they be afraid of a falling egg if they're powerful enough to make a stonecrush fetch and carry?"

"I don't know. Maybe it wasn't the egg at all. Maybe they ran off when they saw Pomponderant. He cuts a very imposing figure if you don't know him that well—and he's practically a sorcerer."

"Not quite. He's a knowledge gatherer." Diligence

frowned. "We should probably tell someone about this. Warn the others before anyone else gets killed."

"I guess we should . . ." Hitch tapped his fingernails on the shaft of wood with a pained expression. "Only they'll want to confiscate it."

"So? It calls down death on those who're near it. Better it should lie next to Manscythe under Nury's bunk than flash like a beacon beneath my own."

"There's many I'd trust with it before Nury," Hitch said sourly, "though I wouldn't mind if they came searching for it and found her by mistake. But wait—it wasn't your wagon they tore apart yesterday when they came looking for it," Hitch said. "If it truly is like a beacon, but they're only able to track it in a general sense—"

"Then someone must have known you used to have it stowed under your bunk," Diligence continued. "And that same someone must have reported that knowledge to whoever has been trying to find the stick." She paused. "This is too dangerous. I wish my mother were here. I wish we could give it to her."

"So do I. And we shall when we reach the Unseen Wall. But what do we do with it *now*?"

"Well . . . whoever they are, they now know one thing for certain: that the stick is not under your bunk in the cook's wagon." Diligence rubbed her forefinger under her lower lip. "So that's where I think it should go."

Hitch could find no flaw in her logic. They moved the walking stick back to its original resting place near the end of that evening's dinner break, while the sad-eyed cook was off cleaning up his utensils by the fire ring.

Breitling reckoned that their various delays had left them about two days behind schedule. The decision was made to alter course slightly to incorporate a brief shortcut through the barren region once known as the Effulgency, and still home, it was said, to roving bands of candlemen.

About noon the next day they entered the Blasted Lands. Hitch was astonished by the rough emptiness of the landscape. "It makes the Siccative look like a garden plot," he declared as he and Diligence watched from the front window of the guards' wagon. They had decided to ride with the hatchling for a while and attempt to get him to eat something. As was becoming common practice, the silver man first had to be coaxed down off the roof and back inside the car by Hitch. The three of them sat at the forward table and ate dried fruit from a shallow pan. It was an odd scene: the girl's hand alternating in the bowl with two others that dipped and retreated in precisely identical movements.

Shevoss sat nearby polishing her blades. "Amonwelle's shadow stretches far," the guard commented with a nod for the sterile plains that surrounded them. "The tales speak of a great cleansing and scouring that took place following her victory in the Battle of the Stolen Air."

Hitch looked back and forth between the destruction visible through the forward window and Diligence, who had cracked open one of the hob guides and sat with her golden curls bent over a pair of intricate illustrations. The mountain boy gave his head a small shake. It was all beyond him.

The rear door slammed. Hitch turned back to the table to find the hatchling missing. He exchanged a wry grin with Shevoss as faint scrabbling sounds from the roof indicated that the silver man had resumed his perch above.

As the day wore on, the landscape showed signs of devastation more fierce than even those familiar with the countryside had expected. The ground was scored by vast trenches of blackened earth, and an odd, sharp smell hung in the air that did something unpleasant to the back of Hitch's throat. The wan breeze was hazy with tiny particles.

"Always hard to know where you are in the Blasted

Lands. Everything is so ripped and scoured," Welleck commented during midday break. "But I've never seen a stretch as bad as this. Strange thing is, some of it looks recent . . ."

That evening one of the guards thought he glimpsed the line of dark warriors again on the western horizon shortly before the caravan ground to a halt. After a hurried conference with Breitling, Welleck rushed among the wagons, making adjustments to the drive mechanisms and panting out instructions to everyone who would listen. "Should anything happen, should there be an attack," he said to Diligence and Hitch when he crawled out from under the guards' wagon, "Let the car go where it will. I've opened up the steering boxes in all the wagons, so you can find your way around the rocks and steeper ditches, but remember to keep a light hand on the tiller."

As if his preparations were an invitation, the attack came the next morning.

They were rounding a bend caused by a huge upthrust of tortured looking rock in an otherwise empty stretch of land when suddenly an eerie whistling sound throbbed across the plain and hunched black figures were everywhere. Among them rode a different sort of warrior; these were mounted on thick-bodied ponies and wrapped in bloodred armor that completely concealed both body and face. Hitch stood at the rear door of the guards' wagon as the Turning Folk soldiers raced past him, jaws set grimly and weapons hefted high. He peered out and around the car in time to see Diligence appear at her own back door. He waved to her frantically. "Get back inside!" The wagons were beginning to fold into their battle circle as the attackers swarmed around them, the discharge of peculiar weapons on both sides filling the air with strange sounds and smells. Hitch ducked back into the wagon, looking around in sudden horror for the hatchling. When had he had time to slip out onto the roof? He stood swaying in indecision by the rear door, waiting for the heavy sounds that would mean the roof armor had begun to unfold.

Instead a series of blinding flashes and muffled reports issued from hidden points between each wagon and its neighbors. Hitch reeled back from the windows, his eyes swimming with colored patterns. Odd clanking sounds came from somewhere. The yeofolk? He pressed his face back to the window, blinking to clear away the bright after-images. Before his astonished eyes, the wagon train came suddenly apart, dividing like a pop-bug into separate sections. He remembered Welleck's feverish preparations of the night before and squinted down the aisle at the jury-rigged steering apparatus in the forward salon.

Each vehicle had taken off in a different direction, radiating away from the center of the attack like the spokes of an exploded wheel. Hitch moved to a side window, trying to find Diligence's wagon in the confusion. One of the cars was surrounded by a handful of black-clad soldiers, but whether they were guards or attackers he could not be sure from this distance. Abruptly there was a thunderous explosion and the car keeled over onto its side. A door sprang open at the back and a slender figure crawled out. Hitch gasped as her bright hair caught the sunlight. He raced to the rear door and leaped out. He ran as fast and as hard as he could, looking neither right nor left. Diligence was crouching dazed on the near side of the wagon; from the far side came sounds of vicious fighting. Hitch dashed up, grabbed Diligence by the hand, and turned in his tracks, dragging her after him as he sprinted back to his own wagon. Another explosion blew rocks and dust into the air, and Hitch saw the guards' wagon topple half-demolished onto its side. They changed direction and ducked behind a waist-high ridge of churned rock until Diligence pointed ahead of them and to the left where the cook's wagon trundled slowly across the ground, its back door swinging open listlessly. The car seemed to have some difficulty rolling on its own; it was moving noticeably slower than the others. Hitch nodded and they ran for it. Gasping and wide-eyed, they pulled themselves up the rope ladder a minute later and collapsed inside the car. The cook was nowhere to be seen. Hitch yanked the door shut behind them. The wagon lurched on beneath them, gaining speed gradually as if whatever had been slowing it down were working its way out of the mechanism.

Something landed with a heavy thud against the top of the left wall a few moments later; then there was nothing for a long time but the crack and swing of the car's trundling progress over the barren land. They lay together until their breathing had lost its ragged edge. Then Diligence dragged herself up to one of the windows.

"Storm coming up," she croaked. "Dust, wind. They happen often out here. I can't see behind us."

Moments later, there was a clatter of sharp, hard objects against the walls as more than dust was caught up in the fierce winds. Hitch staggered to the front of the car and peered out the window, his hand hovering uncertainly over the makeshift tiller. *Let the car go where it will*, Welleck had said.

He turned around as Diligence made her way to his side. "I think we made it," he said. "I think we actually got away." Then Diligence pushed past him and stumbled forward, her face white.

"Look!" She was staring out the forward window.

The way before them had been clear ground a moment ago. Now a gigantic circular pit yawned directly in front of the wagon.

SIXTEEN

WORMHOLE

"We're going in!"

The cook's wagon tilted forward, hung at an impossible angle for several seconds, and then plunged downward, great wheels spinning madly.

Diligence flailed backward, managing to secure a handhold on one of a pair of ornamental brackets beneath a shelf above the forward table. Hitch was knocked off his feet. The table's legs were permanently affixed to the floor of the vehicle. He grabbed hold of the nearest one as he hit the floor, and held on for dear life. There was a sharp cracking sound a second later and he found himself clinging to the stump of the leg, which had broken neatly in two.

Diligence reached out her hand. "Here!"

Hitch grasped it and slowly pulled himself up. Diligence grimaced as knife blades of agony shot through her shoulder and forearm. Finally Hitch lunged for the opposing bracket and clamped it in his hands, releasing his hold on her. They hung face-to-face and gasped at each other like fish in a net.

Hitch had expected the car to smash momentarily against the rocky bottom of the pit. Instead, the wagon continued to plummet forward at an angle, as if they fell down an extremely steep slope. The sound of their descent was nearly deafening, though lost in it somewhere were noises that made him think the walls of the pit or tunnel through which they hurtled were coated with thick mud. Long seconds passed and still they had not hit bottom. "What's hap-hap-pening?" he yelled over the crashing din, his jaw vibrating madly as the wagon bumped and bounced downward. The light from above was fading rapidly, replaced by a reddish glow that flickered with veins of pink and purple.

"We're in a worm-ho-hole," Diligence shouted back through chattering teeth.

Hitch twisted to stare out through the forward window. The glass was streaming with what looked like sheets of thick rain. He turned his head. A sickening liquid jumble of pink and red and yellow rushed by the side louvers. "Where-where's the worm that du-dug it?" he asked. "Have we cru-crushed it yet?"

"N-no-no." Diligence gave her head an unnecessary shake as the wagon caromed into something semisolid and glanced off. "The wor-orm *is* the ho-hole. They stretch— one pla-place to another—of-often very fa-far. Take in foo-foo-food at one end. What's le-left comes out the oth-other."

"Then we'll co-come out somewh-where?"

"What's *left*, I s-said." She lifted her chin toward the front window. The glass itself seemed to have grown cloudy and pitted. It bulged inward, like thin eggshell still partially stuck together by its contents. "Eats through peop-eople. S-sometimes bo-bones remain. Sometimes n-not."

"Eats ev-every-th-thing? Can it ea-eat through the whole wa-wagon?"

It was difficult to shrug while clinging to the bracket. "Depen-pends how lo-long it is. Sometimes the wh-wheels survive. Sometimes m-more if it's a sh-short worm."

Please let it be a short worm, Hitch prayed silently. His eyes flew open seconds later when a moist, muffled impact shook their bones and the angle of the tunnel changed

abruptly. The wagon teetered to one side, flipped over with
a sloppy crash, and began to coast on its right side as the
tunnel leveled out beneath them. The manner of their
movement changed as well, as their velocity slowed. Rather
than sliding down an angled shaft, they now seemed to be
traveling more or less horizontally in brief jerks of fifteen
or twenty yards, as if a succession of huge hands were
passing them along from one to the other.

It had grown too dark for them to see more than shapes
and outlines in the pulsing reddish glow. Finally even the
outlines were gone and they shook and jerked in absolute
darkness. A horrible stench had slowly permeated the cabin
as they headed downward. Hitch wondered how long he
would be able to retain ownership of his breakfast. Now the
unseen hands tipped the wagon away from the tunnel walls
and rolled it ponderously upright again.

The right-hand window exploded inward with a wet
sound and globs of warm, gelatinous ooze studded with
glass splinters splattered against the walls and ceiling.
Hitch's arm and half his face were coated with the slick
substance. He gagged, amazed to find that the odor inside
the lurching wagon had actually gotten worse.

Time passed unmeasured in the noisome darkness as they
were jostled along. Hitch hung like a side of cured meat
from the ornamental bracket. He could no longer feel his
own hands or fingers. He drowsed in the swaying, stinking
darkness and wondered if Diligence was still hanging there
in front of him, or if she had in fact ever been there at all.

After some time, the cabin began to brighten again with
a faint reddish radiance. Soon the cloudy forward window
was suffused with striations of poisonous-looking pink and
yellow-orange. His stomach churned when the car began to
move more rapidly as the angle of their passage altered.

Up? He was not sure if he had said the word out loud
or merely thought it. "Hoy! We're head-heading up, I

th-think!" he called out. Diligence did not respond. It took him almost a minute to release one of his hands from the bracket's sharp curves. He waved it limply in the darkness, but could find nothing but empty air where she had been hanging.

There was a rumbling noise that had been in the background for some time and a high-pitched whine that he had only just noticed. Both were growing steadily louder. The light outside the car grew slowly brighter, distant daylight blending with the sickening glow. We're almost there, he told himself as he swung crazily at the end of one arm. We're going to make it!

The main stanchions gave way with a deafening crack and the roof began to buckle, shattered interior panels thrusting down to within a few inches of his upturned face. The sharp edges of the wheelwork carving scraped along his skin as he flailed out with his left arm, trying to shield his head. He felt rather than heard the shelf bracket pull free of its fastenings.

"Diligence!" he shouted. Then something else cracked near his head and the brightening red turned to solid black once more.

SEVENTEEN

A BIRD IN THE HAND

It was the smell that woke him up. Hitch pushed up on his elbows, the effort bringing him shooting pains in every bone and joint, rolled over onto his side, and released the contents of his stomach. He lay back panting, belly heaving, too weak to move again. After a while he realized that the worst of the smell was by now lodged inside his own nostrils and mouth, for the odor of the surrounding air had become something quite different: an acrid, smoky tang with a hint of something else he could not define.

It was cold and pitch dark. Could they still be inside the tunnel? The movement of the air made him think that they were not. He wondered how far and for how long they had traveled through the belly of the worm. His eyes closed and he drifted near sleep again. Then he heard a choked, gurgling noise and suddenly remembered hanging by one arm from the shelf bracket while feebly swiping at the black, empty air in front of him with his other hand.

Diligence.

He heard the sound again, followed by a low cough. Twisting over onto his other side, he dragged himself by his elbows in the direction of the sound, pulling himself along through the pain and fatigue like an engine driven by the memory of a vanished sun. During his slow progress he bumped and slid over slime-coated pieces of shattered wood, twisted metal, and other remnants of the wagon's contents. The earth was damp and chill beneath him. At last the back of his left hand nudged against something that felt slightly warmer than the rest of the cold, black world.

"Dil . . . Diligence? C'mon—wake up." The words came out thickly, as if they, too, were coated with chill slime.

No response. He pulled himself alongside the clammy body, curving his legs spoon-fashion against the backs of hers in an attempt to transmit as much heat as possible from his skin to hers. Her heart thudded faintly against his chest when he leaned closer. He draped his nerveless arms along her bare shoulders and willed his hands and fingers to move. They dragged in a limp massage across her skin, covered like his own with gooseflesh and cold jelly.

At some point he heard her groan and felt her move in response to his ministrations. "Hitch . . ." Her own voice was sluggish and leaden. "Are you alive, Hitch?"

"I think so." He laid his head down on the ground at her side, curving his body tightly against hers. "If that's what all this soreness means . . ."

"Oh, good," came the faint reply. "That's very good to hear. Night's hairbrush, what's that *smell* . . . ?"

He chuckled and pressed his face to her slime-streaked shoulder, giving in to total exhaustion.

It seemed only seconds later when he felt a hand brushing his cheek and opened his eyes again. The world was dim and misty, overcast with low billows of gray fog. He was still lying on his right side. Dawn was a wan pink glow somewhere on the other side of his body. The ground felt cold and wet as he stretched out his arm behind him and brushed the warm skin pressing up against his own. At some point they had reversed their positions. "Mm?" he said.

"It *is* you." Diligence's breath was warm against his neck. "I've been lying here—it felt like hours—but I was afraid to move. I thought maybe you were just a log or a dead animal. And the stink made me afraid I'd bring up yesterday's meals if I didn't lie completely still."

"Mm. I already took care of that, the first time I woke up," he said, smacking his lips with distaste. He lowered his head and fell asleep again with her hand stroking his cheek.

The next time he woke the sky had lightened, the pink flush of dawn transmuted into a shifting, pale gray. He rolled cautiously onto his back and stared up at the clouded sky through layers of mist. Diligence was sitting about three feet to his left, watching him as she hugged her bare shoulders and shivered. He saw that her clothes were in tatters, as were his own. At some point she had apparently draped a partially dry blanket over him that must have come through with them in the cook's wagon. Lying by his side was the jewel-headed walking stick.

"I did some exploring," Diligence said as she followed his startled gaze. She pointed to a mound of rubble fifteen or twenty feet away. "That's part of the flooring with one of the bunks still attached. The stick was inside."

"Huh. I don't know if that's good or bad. Where are we?" he asked her, pulling the stiff wool up around his shoulders. "What happened to us?"

"We fell into a wormhole. It's really quite remarkable that we survived." She sniffed and wiped a grimy forefinger below her nostrils. "It doesn't happen that often, and usually people don't live through the experience. We must've reached the end just before the wagon gave way completely. As to where we are . . . could be almost anywhere, but I'd guess some part of the northeastern Madescent. The worm's body makes a long tunnel through the earth. Its two ends are usually very far apart and its stomach travels back and forth as it digests its prey. The openings lie covered under a thin layer of soil or rock when they're not in use. You can sometimes tell when you come across one of them, because you'll find scattered rubble, bones, metal, the remains of everything that's passed through. What you can't tell is where the stomach is at any given time—and, of course, that's what decides if a particular end is dangerous or harmless . . ."

Hitch noticed that she was speaking quite rapidly, her legs drawn up in front of her and her eyes focused on the damp ground. He decided that it was probably a reaction to the experience they had just been through—the same sort of reaction that kept Hitch's hands trembling and his teeth chattering in his jaw, even though he was not particularly cold.

"I heard a tale of a man who was traveling across the Siccative, one of a band of Dry Pirates," she continued. "They were on the tough pull-ponies that they use, dragging behind them a great chest they had taken from a southbound caravan. They thought it was full of glint, but it was securely bound with bands of iron, so they had called an early halt to their season of brigandry in order to bring it home to their lair where they could break it open." She paused for a breath and cautiously cleared her throat. "Well, three days out on the desert, a wormhole opens up under their camp and swallows them. Only the one man escapes because he's away from the camp relieving himself behind a rock. When he sees what's happened he continues on alone on foot, watching the stars and trying to head toward home. And it's weeks later and he's almost there when, what do you think, he stumbles across the other end of the same worm. Here sit bits and pieces of his comrades' belongings, a few bones and some wagon wheels—and there sits the treasure chest, its iron bindings mostly eaten away. Naturally the pirate's filled with a great need to know what lies inside the chest that cost him and his fellows so dearly, so he breaks the bindings open with a sharp rock and he finds that it's filled with teeth."

"Teeth?" Hitch looked skeptical above the rough wool blanket.

"Yes, large ones. The pirate lets out a great howl of frustration and races away from the spot, half-mad with disappointment. Eventually he reaches the nearest ramble house, where he tells everyone of his discovery. Now a Society member happens to be there who knows from the man's description exactly what these teeth are: broodwing's incisors, and each one worth a wagonload of yellow glint anywhere south of the Siccative."

"They're worth something?" Hitch interjected. "Why?"

Diligence shrugged. "Ask a Society member. Anyway, the pirate sets out with a group from the ramble house to recover his fortune, but when he reaches the spot where he'd left the treasure, there's no sign of it at all, the worm no doubt having reswallowed the chest when its next bit of prey happened by. The man goes mad for certain then, and the others are obliged to run a sword through him before he does them harm." She lapsed into silence, her eyes still on the rubble-strewn ground.

"Hm. Cheerful story . . . I'll be back." Reminded by the tale of his own pressing need, Hitch heaved to his feet and stumbled off behind a rock to relieve himself.

When he returned Diligence was holding a loose bundle of leather-wrapped items in her lap.

"Your pack came out of the wormhole about half an hour ago," she told him. "When I went to find where it had landed—"

Hitch clapped a hand to his own bare shoulder. "My backsack! It must have come off during the trip. But you mean it showed up after we did?"

Diligence nodded. "It's not at all uncommon for smaller objects to come through at different rates of speed. They often get left behind the main bulk when a larger container like a wagon or a sand raft ruptures inside the stomach."

Hitch knelt in front of her and inspected the partially digested flaps of leather. He picked up a handful of small objects and stuck them in the torn pocket of his trousers. "My finger knife, those little sharp things . . . I'm amazed this stuff survived! Did you see if—"

She pushed his hands away and covered the remaining contents of the backsack protectively. "*Anyway,* as I was saying—when I tracked it down I found that it had come through the trip pretty much intact, but fallen apart when it hit the ground. Certain kinds of stitchery dissolve long before the leather they're sewn into. So I collected what I could identify as yours—including this." With a tired flourish, she lifted a hoop of thin silver filigree from which dangled a yellowish tooth the size of a ripe rockfruit.

"I forgot I had that," Hitch told her. "It's one of the things I found after the—" He stopped, eyes widening. "Hey, that wouldn't happen to be a—a—"

"Broodwing's incisor? Yes, and quite a fine one. That's what reminded me of the story."

"You did say they were valuable . . ."

"Very. It means you never have to work again, Hitch—at least not as a pack-man, or at anything you don't want to do. In fact, you could be very wealthy, if you find the right buyer. I'm sure Pomponderant would be interested."

"Well." Hitch squatted down next to her in the cold muck, not sure exactly how to take the news. "That's very nice to know. Thank you. And here I've been carrying it with me all along."

She nodded. "You could have bought passage from any caravan you met with this, and still had enough glint left over for a small palace and a wagon train of your own."

"Huh." Hitch rocked back on his heels. "And yet right now I'd trade the thing for a hair comb and a chewing stick, or maybe two cups of tea and a nice warm bath."

He became conscious of a low humming sound that hovered at the edge of audibility. The hum evolved quickly into a rumble that was accompanied by a fluctuating, high-pitched whine. The earth began to shudder.

"Look out!" Diligence leaped to her feet, swayed and almost lost her balance. "It's another afterthought!" Hitch ran toward her just as something erupted from the ground not far from where she had been sitting. A red-brown object shot up out of the muck, arced gracefully through the misty air, and landed with a heavy sound several yards away in the cold mud. The expulsive orifice closed in upon itself and the trembling died down.

Diligence and Hitch approached the object cautiously.

The piece of jetsam lay steaming against the chill mud. Coated with reddish ooze from top to bottom, it was roughly the size and shape of an adult human being. Glimpses of dark blue material were visible where the impact had knocked off patches of the slimy covering. Hitch and Diligence stood dumbfounded.

"The hatchling," he said at last. "But how . . . ?"

Diligence reached for Hitch's blanket. She hunkered down near the inert body and began to swab carefully at the blue garment. "Remember after we got in the cook's wagon," she said, "we heard that great thump against the roof? I remember thinking it was a weapon of some sort, but it must have been him. He must have landed on top of the car somehow."

"But how did he get off the guard's wagon and onto ours? They were nowhere near each other."

Diligence shrugged and leaned back from her work. Slick cobalt gleamed in several large patches through the muck. "Well, I don't know—but here he is."

"Do you think there's any chance he survived?" The blue man was lying facedown, his limbs outstretched at uncomfortable-looking angles, much of his body still covered with putrid reddish slime. Hitch bent down to turn him over and immediately snatched his hand back. "Ai!"

"Don't touch him!" Diligence said. "The digestive ichor will eat right through your flesh when it's still warm like this."

Hitch shook his seared hand with a hiss of pain. "Thanks," he said through his teeth. "I appreciate the warning."

He found a stave from the shattered wagon and used it to lever the hatchling over onto his back.

"Oh, Hitch. Look at his face," Diligence said in a hoarse whisper. She went down on her knees near the hatchling's head. "Oh, it's been melted away."

Beneath the coating of red muck, the hatchling's face was a smooth, featureless ovoid of dark blue. Hitch looked away, feeling his gorge rise.

The motionless body suddenly contracted its four limbs and sprang neatly to its feet. Hitch and Diligence cried out in unison, falling back from the animated corpse and scrambling away in the mud.

The hatchling stood swaying, ropy strands of reddish slime dripping from his body. Blue-clad hands groped at the featureless head. A forefinger traced the rough outline of a face on the front of the head, grasped tightly at the chin and lifted an oval of slick material up and back onto the skull, revealing dry, pale skin beneath. The hatchling stiffened. His familiar, odd-colored eyes blinked mildly out at Diligence and Hitch as the outline of his garment seemed to waver almost imperceptibly. Every speck and blob of reddish slime departed from his body to hang in the air as a faint pink mist before dispersing into the breeze. Hitch was reminded of a pull-pony shaking itself after a bath in the river as he watched the vibrating figure. He raised his brows at Diligence, who returned the glance with a wondering shrug.

They wandered back toward the ejection point, the hatchling following obediently. Diligence halted Hitch with her arm in front of his chest as he started to step out onto the discolored soil. "Better wait awhile. There's no telling if that was the last afterthought or not. If it wasn't, something else could come shooting out at any time. And if it was, and the stomach still lingers at this end—" She broke off, gesturing for him to follow her gaze. A small woodhop had ventured out from behind a nearby tangle of brush at the perimeter of the area fouled by the worm. It sniffed curiously at a pile of cold red ichor, then scampered out into the midst of the muck, its nose twitching next to the ground.

"Hey . . ." Hitch turned to raise an eyebrow at Diligence, and pointed to the area of slime and refuse. "You left my stuff, my—"

"Your *tooth*!" Diligence looked stricken. She started toward the pile of small objects. Hitch caught her arm and pulled her back. A humming rumble grew in the air.

Out in the center of the fouled ground, the woodhop gave a single squeak of terror as a red-black pit suddenly swelled beneath it, swallowing the hapless creature along with two metal wagon wheels, some flaps of partially digested leather, and a yellowish incisor the size of a rockfruit mounted on a hoop of silver filigree. Diligence groaned and turned back to Hitch with a look of stunned horror.

The mountain boy was staring without expression at the rapidly closing hole. "Ah, well," he said with a stifled yawn. "Five minutes wealthy is better than never at all." He offered Diligence his arm and escorted her back to where the blue man waited by a pile of wagon rubble.

Over the next day, the hatchling's garment reprised the entire color change it had previously taken weeks to accomplish, ending up by the following night at the same gray-silver they had seen before the attack of the black-and-red warriors.

"I wonder what happened to the others," Hitch said that night as he lay close to Diligence before the small fire he had managed to start up with his striking stones. The jewel-headed walking stick stuck up from the soil a few feet from where they lay.

Diligence was watching the stars. "I don't know—but it wasn't your fault," she said sleepily.

The next morning they decided to strike out due north. A pale amber sun burned through most of the mist early in the day. A closer inspection of the now deserted worm area yielded more salvageable material from the remains of the cook's wagon: a sealed container of rations and some water along with two more blankets.

They walked for six days without encountering another living being larger than a woodhop. Their rations, which had turned out to be mostly after-meal sweets and dandytarts, had proved of little use in providing them with the stamina they needed to keep up a brisk pace for several hours a day. They had decided to conserve what food they had by dividing it two ways, neglecting to even offer any to the hatchling. The blue man seemed no worse for this portion of his continuing fast; he trotted along behind Hitch's back as they made their way across the grassy hills and dells of the Madescent.

On the seventh day it was necessary to draw lots to decide who would go hunting. Diligence agreed to cook whatever Hitch was able to bring down. Unable to get close enough to the occasional woodhop he sighted in order to effectively employ his fingerblade, Hitch returned to the camp with an armload of promising-looking plants. Diligence dutifully heated the bounty on a thin, flat rock set atop a firepit, mixing them with some water and a small pouch of dried grummidge to make a gummy stew. None of the probable vegetables were very tasty, though Hitch grumbled around his third portion that a proper cook would be able to wring flavor from almost anything. Diligence promised to hold him to his claim on the following day, when they had agreed that their duties would be reversed.

That night he awoke with severe stomach cramps and a dull ache in his head. He slipped out of the blanket and wandered off to relieve himself, his thoughts growing hazy as the mounting discomfort wrung groans of pain from his lips. The next morning he woke up in a dry ravine with a fluctuating fever and a badly smashed foot, but no memory of what had occurred after he left the camp. He was too weak to move and lay watching the gray-brown clouds as he slipped in and out of delirium. At one point he found himself once again on the slope-hulled boat, forging through the storm-tossed waves toward a rocky coast. He scanned the inhospitable shore, sharply aware this time that there was someone very dear to him waiting beyond those rocks, beckoning to him through the madness of the storm.

Skritch, skritch. The noise rasped dryly just beyond the roll of thunder and the heavy toss of waves. Something sharp jabbed at the palm of his hand.

He forced his eyes open and stared into the flatness of a tiny black eye. Half a dozen medium-sized birds were walking stiff-legged around his sprawled body. As he watched, a gray one, slightly smaller than the rest, extended its neck to peck at his hand again.

"Hey!" The bird ignored his protestation, turned its gray head sideward to inspect him for a long moment, and stepped boldly onto his palm. It stood there for a moment, watching him with a curious intensity, then hopped from his palm to a small dead branch lying nearby in the empty river bottom, its claws making a *skritch, skritch* among the dry leaves. It leaped back to his palm with a flutter of wings.

Remember now, he heard her say in her rasping whisper,

gray and not very large, with a band of white just so across the underside of the wings. Her eyes had been cloudy with weariness and pain. *Not many in the south, I judge, but in the east and north she'll know you.*

The brief days spent in the tiny valley had taken on the aura of a dream in his fevered memory. He watched the small gray head dully for a few moments, lay back on the bed of dry grass, and closed his eyes. Wings fluttered nearby, fanning a brief cool breeze against his flushed brow.

And then he was soaring, gloriously free, high above the world. For several minutes he simply flew, exulting in the feeling of strength and freedom before bending his wings to their task. It took about half an hour for him to locate the small campsite and Diligence crouched disconsolately by the cold firepit. She looked up in dull startlement when the gray bird landed on her shoulder.

It took some time before she understood that the small creature expected her to follow it. She had ingested less of the stew than Hitch, but still needed to stop and rest half a dozen times before she reached the narrow ravine where his racked body lay. The bird coaxed her on with small circular flights while Hitch lay against the dry grass, his lips moving slightly and his eyes roving restlessly beneath closed lids.

The fever and the cramps lasted another half a day. Diligence sat by his side until he felt well enough to accept some water; then she helped him limp back to the campsite with agonizing slowness. His foot was an ugly purple hue, badly swollen.

Now that they had left the heated plains of the Siccative, the weather was growing rapidly cooler. They could not afford to wait for his foot to heal completely. Diligence tore the extra blanket into strips and fashioned a makeshift crutch from the jeweled walking stick and another piece of stout wood. With the gray bird's help, Hitch was able to range far without moving, locating berries and leaves he knew were safe to eat, as well as hidden streams to replenish their store of water. A week passed before Hitch was able to stand on the foot again without a wince of pain. They started walking, the cloudy blue jewel swathed in a cushion of wool and tucked up under Hitch's armpit.

They covered a fair amount of ground the first day, neither one voicing the obvious concern that they might not be going in the right direction. Hitch tired easily, though he forced himself to continue on until true exhaustion set in. That evening found them seated side by side at the fire, Hitch with his head resting against Diligence's shoulder. He was enjoying the warmth, dozing peacefully between memory and dream, when he imagined a familiar, pedantic voice cutting through the night.

"Best to find another angle for your head, or you'll have a stiff neck come morning." Hitch allowed his eyes to drift open, smiling faintly at the image of old Pomponderant standing across the fire from them in his purple robes. In fact, he was standing directly *in* the firepit, flames licking harmlessly at his tasseled slippers.

"You're a bit off course," the apparition continued, appearing to survey the campsite with a sniff of disapproval. "You should have crossed that river when you had the opportunity this afternoon. Now you'll have to double back and lose an hour."

"It was too cold on my sore foot," Hitch murmured, snuggling in against Diligence. "You're standing in the fire, you know."

The image looked down at its slippers with a *tsk* and moved slightly to one side. "We have important plans to make—"

"Not now." Hitch raised his palm and made a shooing

motion. "I want to go back on the ship. I like that dream. It's exciting." He gave a groan of protest as Diligence shifted her shoulder beneath his cheek. Suddenly she stiffened, jarring his jaw as she sat up straight.

"Pomponderant!"

"Ow. It's just a stupid dream," Hitch told her, feeling his jaw gingerly.

But Diligence was pushing to her feet. "Pomponderant, what are you doing here? How did you find us?"

"The Dreamwright found you, some little while ago," the apparition told her. Small changes in hue passed over its body in rippling waves. "I have kept you under periodic surveillance as my own schedule permitted, since your first employment of the dowchit."

"You've seen the Dreamwright?" Her tone was rapt. "And my mother? Are they—are they well?"

"Fit subjects for lengthy discussion at some future moment, when our bodies are in actual proximity," the image told her.

"The dow-what?" Hitch squinted up at the wavering apparition from his awkward seat on the ground. It had begun to occur to him that the old tutor's appearance was no dream.

"The dowchit. The gray bird. They are closely allied to members of our Society." The old man knit his brows in a stern expression. "Of course, if you had seen fit to inform me earlier that you had been granted rights to their assistance, I might have helped you much sooner."

Hitch bridled at the notion. "But I had no idea—"

"Precisely. Knowledge concealed is knowledge rendered impotent."

"What?" Hitch reached out for his walking-stick crutch and began to struggle to his feet. He scowled at the apparition. "If I had an eight-spot for each little secret you've kept from *us*—"

"Ut!" The image raised its hand. "Argument for its own sake accomplishes little. Come seat yourselves nearer to the firelight and I will instruct you as to the route you must begin to follow tomorrow . . ."

EIGHTEEN

THE UNSEEN WALL

Despite the unrevealed demands of his own mysterious schedule, Pomponderant managed to appear to the exiles on a fairly regular basis, usually flickering into being by their campfire around sundown to bring them course corrections, weather forecasts, and exhaustive advice on everything from the treatment of insect bites to which form of meditative attitude must be adopted if one wished to scan a complicated landscape without missing a single minute detail. Diligence eagerly awaited each evening's manifestation.

Privately, Hitch soon began to dread the glimmer of colored sparks in the air that signaled the onset of one of the old man's instructional visits—though even he had to admit that there was something greatly comforting in knowing that they were being watched over from afar by a benevolent, if occasionally overly didactic, guardian.

They were both taken aback one evening when a stocky, nearsighted individual in robes of periwinkle blue appeared at their fireside in Pomponderant's stead to discuss the morrow's projected route. For his part, Hitch found the comparatively taciturn and unpretentious Derbelderhed a treat after a week's worth of lectures from Diligence's talkative and opinionated tutor, and the mountain boy was privately disappointed when Pomponderant himself returned the following night.

The Madescent presented a relatively mild landscape,

with few overt dangers to the careful traveler other than the growing cold of approaching winter. Following Pomponderant's meticulous directions, the trio moved swiftly through its woods and dells. Once they came across a village of chest-high, manlike creatures whose naked bodies were protected by a yellowish, segmented covering that seemed both smoother and tougher than conventional human skin. The villagers spoke a simplified form of human speech and greeted the travelers with curiosity and uncomplicated friendship. When Pomponderant was informed of their encounter with the diminutive race, he instructed Diligence and Hitch to barter the tale of their adventures in the Siccative for woven plant fiber that they might use to augment their own badly worn garments. Hitch was intrigued by the villagers' shiny integument and their own disdain for clothing. "The duarbar wear their bones mostly on the outside nowadays, and so have no need of artificial coverings," the old tutor explained with uncharacteristic brevity when Hitch brought the matter to his attention. The duarbar themselves evinced strong interest in the silvery skin of the hatchling during the following morning's bargaining session.

Signs of possible civilization appeared on the horizon late one night in the form of softly glowing lights. The forest thinned and dampened to become a bog, and the next afternoon found them on the doorstep of Penbarb's Balm of Golden Rest, a modest but well-appointed two-story ramble house hard by the salt marsh that marked the Madescent's northernmost border. There the weary wayfarers were both astonished and delighted to be greeted by Welleck, who informed them that he had managed to elude the red-and-black attackers and make his solitary way to the ramble house some weeks ago. There he had been contacted by Pomponderant and told to await the arrival of Hitch and the Daughter. After an emotional reunion—during which he took them out back to the livery and proudly displayed his lone remaining wagon, still in excellent running order despite its long ordeal—the wagoneer further surprised them by telling them what he knew of the ambush's other survivors, most of whom had gone on independently to the Unseen Wall.

"Breitling and Nury were here when I arrived, and so was one of the yeofolk handlers. Only two of the guards pulled through: Cobby and Shevoss, both of whom showed up three days after myself. Cook didn't make it, nor did the alterman, though I'm told a pair of his beasts came trailing in after the yeofolk handler." He shook his head. "In truth, we were lucky—except for the soldiers, that is. Whoever it was attacked us, they seemed to lose their interest in the battle once the wagons flew away from one another and they realized they'd never catch us all. The way Shevoss tells it, the bastards went after our guards purely as a means of venting their great displeasure at having lost what they came for—whatever unknown thing that might have been." He glanced thoughtfully at Diligence. "Until we heard otherwise from your old tutor, we all assumed you two had been cut to bits or carried off along with the egg-man. You may believe it or not, but the Hubwoman seemed quite genuinely beside herself with grief at the prospect . . ."

Under Pomponderant's guidance, the wagoneer had obtained passage for the four of them on board a small water caravan heading north to the land of the Unseen Wall by way of the River Lehr. After a respite at the way station that struck Hitch as all too brief, they departed for the north and the realm of the Dreamwright.

For the mountain boy, this final leg of their perilous journey took on a placid, dreamlike quality. He spent much of their week on the water musing over the railing at the gliding scenery, as the string of compact vessels chugged upriver toward their destination.

A different sort of dream began when the caravan pulled into harbor at the quiet, nameless town for centuries utilized as a stopover by those lucky enough to have been granted an audience with the Dreamwright. The four went to register at the town's lone hostelry—itself quiet and nameless—there to wait for Pomponderant's further instructions. Hitch suspected that they might have found themselves sleeping in a hayloft, had reservations not been made in their names some weeks earlier; the Dreamwright had inexplicably suspended all consultations for a period of several weeks, and the little town was thronged with anxious supplicants.

The remaining survivors of the Turning Folk caravan were there to greet them in the lobby. Hitch found himself generally indifferent to their declarations of relief and felicity, though he was glad when Shevoss came up and clapped him on the arm, her dark eyes bright with tears. Nury seemed to have changed the most since their last meeting; wild-eyed with delight, she flung her skinny arms about a dubious Diligence and, more unexpectedly, a horrified Hitch, thanking the mountain boy fervently for his role in safeguarding the life and person of "our own sweet precious joy, the Daughter."

"Come, come, plenty of hours for reminiscing once we've seen you bathed and properly outfitted," the hostler told them as he ushered Hitch and Diligence away from the others. He cast a curious look at the hatchling's silver-gray covering, shrugged, and turned back to the travel-worn pair with a fastidious sniff. "You've certainly managed to amass an extraordinary collection of *smells* during your peregrinations, haven't you?"

Trimmed and cleaned and draped in freshly laundered garments, Hitch felt one step closer to paradise as he rendezvoused with a radiant Diligence at the entrance to the high-beamed tavern attached to the hostelry. They were shown to a table in a candlelit corner. As they took their seats, Diligence found her eyes drawn to a piece of ancient-looking portraiture hung in a huge frame between two sconces of cold fire on the far wall.

"Who might that woman be?" she asked the tavernmaster, sinking into the overstuffed chair he held at her back. The stout man blinked at her in surprise. "That? Why that's our Great Lady, Miss. That's our Amonwelle, Guardian of the North, Scourge of the Candlemen, Protector of the Unseen Wall. We've another likeness or two in the sitting room, but this is our best. Over two thousand years old, from the days of the First Dispersal."

"I see. Thank you." Diligence lowered her eyes to her menu and began to study it intently as Hitch sat staring at the age-darkened painting. The woman in the golden armor stood straight and tall, her reddish hair caught up in a jeweled net while a helm of gold studded with green gems rested in her arm. "Does it—does it look like her?" he asked softly, once the tavernmaster had departed with their orders.

"I wouldn't know," Diligence replied with a tiny shrug. "It's the first picture of her I've ever seen."

Pomponderant had not appeared to Hitch and Diligence since their arrival at the Balm of Golden Rest, having assured them that they would be contacted shortly after they reached the land of the Unseen Wall. The survivors of the caravan met to discuss the prospects for an audience with the Dreamwright, judging them currently rather dubious, as the ambush by the red-and-black warriors had robbed them of most of the prerequisite gifts.

They spoke for a short while of the attack and its aftermath, with each member called upon to describe his or her own trek through the Madescent. Hitch kept his own counsel, preferring not to reveal his fears that the warriors—or at least the ones in black—had been searching for him when they struck at the caravan. He had traded for a new backsack at the wander house—one that would carry the walking stick in safe concealment.

A day passed, and then another, without word. Hitch went out to explore the little town, finding nothing unremarkable in it save the people who had gathered there. Where, he wondered, was the crystal palace, and where the fabled wall? He put the question to a young vegetable boiler at his stall in the open market and received a snort of amusement in reply.

"First off, the palace is nobody's business but the Dreamwright's," the man said, speaking slowly in his clipped Northern accent as if he addressed a lackwit. "And as for why you can't see the Unseen Wall . . ." He let the statement hang in the air until Hitch felt a warm flush of anger spreading over his cheeks and turned to walk away. He almost knocked over the tiny old woman who was standing behind him. She tugged at his sleeve, drawing his ear down to her stained and wrinkled mouth.

"Once a year, and once only," she said in a harsh, garlicky whisper, "when the moon waxes full as it ever will, the shadow of the Wall appears across the land and Amonwelle's true enemies feel their hearts stop in their breasts." She clawed at the leather purse hanging limply from his double-wound belt. "A two-spot would bring me a hot meal tonight, while a grain or two more means there's some drink at its end . . ." Hitch had to turn the pouch inside out before she believed his protestations of poverty and shuffled off with a muttered oath.

On the afternoon of the third day one of Amonwelle's servants appeared to fetch them.

In testimony to the commonplace of marvels in the sleepy little town, few heads turned when the unusual messenger came striding down the main thoroughfare, his unshod feet of glass striking ringing echoes from the stone cobbles. Still, Hitch thought to notice a tremble in the hostler's chin that hadn't been there before as they filed past him and walked out into the sunshine. The glass man led them on foot to a small depot where half a dozen stubby vehicles sat pointing outward from the town.

The party consisted of Hitch and Diligence, the hatchling—who could not be left behind, Hitch argued, lest he climb onto the roof of the hostelry and disgrace them all—Nury and the marchmaster, Welleck and the two guards. The yeofolk handler had become disconsolate in the absence of her proper charges, who had wandered off during the ambush; she elected to stay behind at the hostelry and see to the two remaining alters. The travelers squeezed into the back of one of the little cars. An engine purred to life beneath their feet as the door clicked shut and the vehicle rolled forward. There was no one in the driver's compartment. Hitch looked around wildly when he realized that the messenger had not joined them, then jerked back in startlement when he peered out the side window and saw the man of glass loping smoothly along at their side.

They traveled for more than an hour along a well-worn dirt road that wound through stretches of forest and past placid lakes, their gleaming companion easily keeping pace with the purring vehicle. Hitch wondered what caused the car to move; he had noticed none of the red-brown tiles on its roof that might render it sensitive to the prodding of the sun.

Small isolated farms and houses could be seen along the winding road, fewer and fewer of them as the afternoon progressed. It was nearing dusk when the car emerged from a patch of forest and mounted a small incline. Below lay a tumbled wall of round gray stone, thickly overgrown with tangles of brush. They began to decelerate as they descended toward the small, nondescript gate set in the middle of the wall. Beyond was a broad meadow that sloped gradually upward, first to a rumple of gentle hillsides, and then to a range of formidable mountains, their blue-and-purple peaks lost in the twilight haze of distance. About a hundred yards out into the field sat a dilapidated-looking shack, barely more than a lean-to with a dried and crumbling sod roof.

The road ended at the gateway.

Hitch eyed the shack with foreboding as their tireless escort sprinted forward and swept open the creaking gate. "Where is the Dreamwright's abode, the fantastical crystal palace?" he whispered to Diligence, who could only shrug in reply.

He felt an odd tingling on the exposed skin of his face and arms as they drove through the little gateway. His eyes smarted for a few seconds, and he rubbed at them with his knuckles.

Suddenly Diligence gripped his arm. He heard her sharp intake of breath and opened his eyes wide.

Everything had changed.

The meadow was gone, in its place an endless plain of black, smooth rock broken by a long curving road of hexagonal gray tiles. At measured intervals, enormous designs of colored stone had been set into the plain. Twisting his head to look at them as they rode past, Hitch had the eerie feeling that their true sense could only be read from very high in the air. He raised his eyes. In the distance, at the end of the curved road . . .

What had been mountains on the other side of the gate had been transformed into the sheer walls of a huge crystalline structure of staggering beauty, its many spires rearing like the points of an icy crown to brush the clouds.

The occupants of the car had remained silent for their first few minutes inside the gate. Now they began to speak in hushed whispers. Hitch felt Diligence's fingers release their pressure on his arm, only to squeeze it again twice as hard. "Look," she said. "Look there!"

It was almost impossible to tear his eyes from the glorious sight before them. Finally he looked away long enough to follow her gaze back through the rear window of the car. His head swam with wonder.

Stretching across the shadowed countryside at their back, the Unseen Wall rose in a curving, towering ribbon of shimmering pearl-colored light. Hitch gulped for air as he tried to encompass the great barrier with his eyes and mind, only to discern that it was part of a much larger structure. Pulsing with dense swirls of silver-gray and rose at its base, the Wall arched up into near invisibility high above their heads, then curved down to create a massive dome whose far wall could be dimly seen a league or more beyond the great palace.

· More cries and hushed exclamations brought his attention back to the scene in front of them. The car's progress along the curving road had brought them a gradually shifting view of the soaring palace. As they circled slowly around toward the western side of the monumental structure, it became apparent that something was wrong. A sense of half-seen damage not visible from the southern vantage was growing with their approach, and they craned their necks to make sense of it. Gradually, a scene of utter devastation came into view.

The western walls of the Dreamwright's palace and most of its interior lay in total ruin, reduced to a slag of melted glass and metal above the black plain—which was itself marred by cracks and craters for half a league around the base of the palace.

The travelers rode in numbed silence the rest of the way. The vehicle halted several yards from a huge spar of fused and melted crystal, the purr of its engine dwindling into stillness. The man of glass opened the door for them. He led the party forward, footsteps ringing hollowly, to an unobtrusive doorway beneath a great sagging arch of splintered golden glass. He pointed their way into the doorway, made a low bow, and collapsed like a sudden shower of bright rain into a pool of smoking liquid.

The travelers moved forward cautiously. Just inside the doorway they found a second entrance, this one to a small-ish room whose glassy walls were striated with irregular streaks of faceted lavender crystal. The round floor was ringed with richly upholstered couches.

Translucent panels slid shut behind them and the room hummed. After a slight jerk of movement, Hitch realized that they were traveling again, downward this time, with the room as their vehicle. Staggering slightly, they made their way to the couches and sat down. They journeyed deeper and deeper beneath the shattered palace, Hitch try-ing hard to avoid thoughts of his other, very different de-scent into the bowels of the earth.

Minutes passed tensely until at last there came a gentle nudge against the soles of their feet. The cloudy panels whispered open and a weary-looking but bright-eyed Pomponderant bustled forward to greet them.

NINETEEN

FOLLOW THE GREEN MOTH

"Out, out! Everybody out." The old tutor waved his arms peremptorily as the passengers stumbled forth into a flood of warm yellow light. "We've a crew needing to go up and they can't get there if you dawdle." He motioned behind him to where a shortish woman with close-cropped auburn hair directed a dozen or so individuals dressed in loose-fitting costumes of dirt-stained green and turquoise. "The car is in your service," Pomponderant announced with a nod of his white head as the last of the Turning Folk stepped through the translucent doors.

The leader of the work crew looked up from the small book she held in her hands. "Good." She appeared to be of middle years, with a thickening waist and a probing blue-green gaze that Diligence found oddly disquieting. The woman stood with hands on hips, surveying the new arrivals for a long moment before turning to usher her workers into the moving room. The doors closed and they heard the beginnings of a distant hum.

"Come along now." Pomponderant turned on his heel with a clap of his hands and began to march briskly off down the long, yellow-lit corridor that stretched away from the strange conveyance. After a small hesitation, the members of the group straggled after him.

"Smartly, smartly!" he admonished over his shoulder. "Time is never a friend to the languorous."

"Pomponderant." Diligence skipped forward to catch up to the old man. She tugged at the sleeve of his purple robe. "Pomponderant, what is—" She looked helplessly at the blank white walls around them. "What is *this*?"

"The palace of the Dreamwright, of course," he replied without slowing his pace. "Have you been so long without my tutelage that you've lost the basic powers of deduction?"

Diligence set her jaw and dropped back a step. "What *I* can't comprehend is how you've refrained from throttling his knobby neck all these years," Hitch muttered at her back.

They reached the end of the corridor and stepped out into a crosswise thoroughfare. This passage was much broader than the first. It was aswarm with figures clad in green and blue work suits, all furiously intent on some urgent purpose as they elbowed past the bewildered travelers. The left-hand wall was blank; the right held a series of archways, with doors beneath them bearing elaborate designs.

"This way, now." Pomponderant stepped out of the flow of traffic and guided them to a panel painted with the image of a firebird in flight, indecipherable phrases in bright green script curling out from beneath its beating, blazing wings. At a touch, the panel slid noiselessly to one side.

The room beyond had floor and walls of rich green marble veined with cobalt. It held a rectangular table and eight chairs that had apparently been carven from a single block of the same stone. Shevoss and Cobby took up posts to either side of the doorway as the others filed to their seats. Pomponderant raised his brows at the soldiers with a snort of disbelief, then ignored them and took his own place at the table's head.

"I am informed that you have not eaten since noon meal was served at the hostelry," he told them. Regrettable, as more precious time must be sacrificed to the needs of your bodies. Still, a brain without nourishment houses a mind disinclined to reason." He reached behind him to a small raised section of the marble wall. At his touch the surface in front of them underwent a remarkable and unexpected metamorphosis, the table's central section suddenly splitting along hitherto unseen divisions, some areas moving apart while others folded downward, only to reappear seconds later in front of each of the newcomers as small pedestals laden with goblets and richly fragrant platters. "One half of one hour only may be allotted to the consumption of these refreshments," Pomponderant told them. He paused as if consulting an invisible timepiece, then lifted his hand. "Begin now!"

Diligence was sitting to Pomponderant's right. Ignoring the tempting victuals that had risen before her, she leaned forward and asked softly: "Is my mother here, Pomponderant? Is she all right? When will I see her?"

"When she is free of other duties and so wills it," the old tutor replied sternly. "Eat! Eat! We are losing time."

Diligence sat back with a sigh of frustration and picked up her fork.

The old man sat in rigid watchfulness at the head of the marvelous table, turning aside all attempts to question him while the travelers drank and ate. The group was visibly more relaxed by the time he again sought the raised panel on the wall at his back. The table immediately reopened its miniature wormholes, reswallowing the goblets and serving plates along with whatever crumbs and residue remained in them.

"Now." Pomponderant surveyed his small audience with little sign of liking what he saw. "Much as I would prefer to rapidly impart to you only those select pieces of information necessary for us to charge forward from this moment to the accomplishment of our mutual goals, I recognize that such a procedure would be not unlike pouring grummidge into a bowl made of cobwebs. Your minds must be prepared for the information they are about to receive or it will not be properly retained. Therefore: a brief lesson in the history of the Green Moth Society."

Welleck rumbled in his marble seat. "Now, what's your old Society got to do with—"

"Ut!" A bony forefinger pointed to the ceiling. "We must establish a single rule: no one questions, no one comments, no one belches without permission."

Breitling made a sound of disgust in his throat. "In that case, let me be the first to ask for—"

"Permission denied," Pomponderant stated flatly. He folded his hands before him on the table and cleared his throat ominously.

"That entity which was later to evolve into the Society as it is known and revered today," began the aged tutor, "came into formal being some eight hundred and seventeen years ago. Before that time there had been various loose associations of wandering gatherers, whose shared purpose was to add in some fashion to the total store of humanity's knowledge. Facts came in piecemeal: a rumor here, a discovery there. Then one scholar whose special interest lay in varieties of insect life happened upon a new species in the forests of the West—a large moth with wings and body of a delicate green hue. Now, this man had at his disposal exhaustive records of every such creature thought to exist, but this was something neither he nor anyone else had ever seen before. Over the course of two years he collected several specimens of this new moth, tracking it eventually to a hidden cave deep in the western mountains.

"Within the cave he found an object like a great oval mirror—but one which reflected an image that was totally unrelated to the dark cavern in which it sat. Thoroughly intrigued, the man brought his supplies into the cave and seated himself before the object. In the weeks that followed, so the story goes, he did nothing but watch the mirror and the world within it. Days passed with the rising and setting of a reddish sun much larger than our own; remarkable flowers opened their buds within the mirror's oval and pale green moths came to drink from them. Now and then tiny insects would come crawling over the mirror's edge and into the cave. Once a small furred creature stuck its nose past the frame, squeaked with fear when it saw the watcher, and turned tail. Occasionally a large green moth floated through and the man was enchanted . . .

"He was able to tear himself away from the entrancing vision before his food supplies were completely exhausted. The insect scholar returned to his colleagues and related his story. Perhaps surprisingly, he was able to convince a handful that he was not mad, and these followed him when he returned to his hidden cave laden with the supplies and implements necessary for a long journey. Before their eyes, he did what he had not had the courage to do when he was alone: stepped through the mirror's portal into the other world."

The room was thick with tension as Pomponderant fell silent. The old tutor stared at his hands for a long moment, examining a split fingernail with a critical frown.

Hitch could bear the silence no longer. "And?" he prompted. "What happened to the insect man?"

"No one knows." Pomponderant blinked blandly. "Those left behind in the cave eventually carted the object away to a safe place, where it has been studied for over eight hundred years to no great benefit—for the mirror became just that directly after the man stepped through, the portal closed forever. Soon winter came to the mountains and the green moths died, one by one. Their like has never been seen again in this world.

"For eight centuries the Society has been driven by its search for another doorway into that distant world. Over the years, the pursuit of the green moth has changed from the literal quest it once was to a metaphor for the search for unknown knowledge." He pushed up from the table and began to pace slowly in front of the blue-veined wall. "In an effort to further our quest, we have long striven to establish reciprocal relationships with those we hoped could be of service to our goal: the Dreamwright, for one, and Amonwelle of the North, as well as a handful of others. In return for the knowledge we have gathered, we have been granted certain privileges by those in a position of power: access to ancient storehouses; the loyalty of various flickers; the service of the gray birds, which we use for observation and communication. These gifts are ours to pass along to those we deem deserving of them." His eyes went briefly to Hitch.

"When Derbelderhed and I discovered the projecting device along with the historical records in the Aulmad, our first thought was to bring it here to the Unseen Wall, in hopes of using it as a bargaining chip for the sharing of information we suspected would prove beneficial to our Society. We arrived shortly after the attack that resulted in the devastation that you witnessed above. Ironically enough, it was our arrival at this time of dire need that played a part in our finally being granted admission to a place we had longed to enter for centuries: the palace of the Dreamwright."

"Who—who attacked them?" Hitch blurted out. "Surely not the warriors in black and red with their slicers and scatterguns." He withered under Pomponderant's glare and closed his mouth.

"Far to the south lies another center of ancient power," the old man told them, "ruled by a being of such ferocity and evil that even we with our boundless curiosity have ever given him a wide berth, and so learned regrettably little of his ways as time has passed. But now there can be no doubt that great forces have begun to stir in the lair of the Shadowsmith." His bright glance flicked to Diligence. "Yes, my pupil, the Shadowsmith is more than a leering footnote in the Fabularies. He lives and works his evil today as he has for uncounted centuries."

"This creature is like my mother, then?" Diligence inquired softly. "Immortal?"

"Pfaugh!" Pomponderant waved the concept away. "Immortality is an illusion. It is true your mother and others of her ilk are extremely long-lived—but like each of us, the great powers are only immortal until they happen to die. Had your mother been with the Dreamwright at the time of the attack that gutted the crystal palace, she, too, would lie dead as a stone."

"The Dreamwright is *dead*?" breathed Diligence. Eyes grew wide around the table.

Pomponderant's expression was sly. "A complex question. For one answer, the Dreamwright escaped largely uninjured. For another, he lost his life during the assault."

He clapped his hands as the travelers gave voice to dismayed consternation. "Come along, now," he said. "I see that we must go to the central chamber if I am to have any hope of communicating further concepts."

He led them from the room. They followed him down the wider corridor till it intersected with another, even broader passageway. At the end of the second thoroughfare was a huge door. It swung open at a rap from the old man's knuckles.

The chamber into which Pomponderant conducted them was the largest enclosed space any of them had ever before glimpsed: a valley of a chamber with a roof of crystal and bright metal for its sky. The travelers stood on a narrow circle of silver mesh suspended midway between floor and ceiling. The walls rising high above their heads and descending far below their feet were covered in a hivework of hexagonal disks that shimmered and flashed continually like cloudy mirrors tilted beneath the sun.

On a green marble dais in the center of the distant floor sat a graceful sculpture comprised of different sorts of metal: gold, silver, blue iron, copper, all cunningly worked into a frozen waterfall of curves and arcs around a central object Diligence could not quite make out.

Pomponderant led them to a break in the silver mesh from which a long ramp of the same material projected downward at a gentle incline toward the central dais. "Follow thusly," the tutor instructed them. He stepped onto the ramp and began to glide slowly downward while his slippers remained firmly planted on the mesh. At first Diligence thought another one of the clever apparitions had been substituted for the old man; then she realized that the surface of the ramp itself was moving, flowing like a shallow stream away from the ring. Gingerly she mounted the strange walkway, flashing Hitch a nervous smile as she was carried away toward the dais below. One by one, the small party mounted the ramp. When they were all safely deposited on the floor of the great hall, Pomponderant led them halfway round the marble platform, to a series of shallow steps that rose into the sculpture itself.

At close range, the sculpture seemed to be divided into four different sections, each one originating at a spot that represented a quarter-turn around the dais, from which it rose to fan out like a burgeoning metal plant and intertwine complexly with its fellows. The arches of its interior were large enough to permit Welleck, the tallest of the group, to enter without stooping. Their inside surfaces were studded with small knobs and protrusions, reminding Diligence of a river squash vine besieged by galls.

Others were there ahead of them, bending like concerned farmers over isolated clusters of the gall-growths. Workers clad in the ubiquitous blue and green uniforms gazed up at the newcomers incuriously before returning to their tasks among the sweeps and curves of many-colored metal. Diligence recognized Derbelderhed in his periwinkle robes, half-hidden behind a span of blue iron, as well as the auburn-haired leader of the work crew they had passed on their arrival beneath the palace.

Pomponderant ushered them ahead of him to the very center of the towering artwork. A low couch of some yielding dark green fabric occupied the midpoint of the dais. Diligence wondered if Amonwelle herself came here from time to time to recline and admire the flash of gold and copper from above.

The old man halted next to the couch and raised his purple sleeves in a dramatic flourish. "Behold," he announced sonorously. "The Dreamwright!"

Diligence tried to follow his sweeping gesture. The other travelers muttered at her back. "Do you mean the sculpture?" she asked. "What do you mean?"

"I mean the device, this beautiful instrument which has functioned flawlessly for millennia, and I also mean its absent heart, so recently slain." He stepped away from the couch. "The undead portion of the Dreamwright gleams before you undamaged," he told his puzzled audience. "A vast marshalling of technological might, wholly subservient to the will of the person who lies in its bright embrace. That person, noble Niirphar, was but the latest to wear the mantle of the worldseer. When the Shadowsmith's attack cracked the Unseen Wall above, only a fraction of the awful energies penetrated to this level. Still, it was enough to take the life of the current Dreamwright."

"I'm adrift in confusion," Welleck said, his booming voice echoing impressively in the huge hall above the metalwork. "Is the Dreamwright a man, who's now dead, or an instrument, apparently untouched?"

"Both," said Pomponderant cheerfully. "What the outside

world knows as its Dreamwright is in reality a dual entity—the perfect marriage of human being and machine. Without the instrument to amplify his own abilities, the human operator would find his powers vastly curtailed. Likewise, without the presence of Niirphar the device itself languishes." He ducked his head and squinted through an arch of gleaming silver. "Perhaps a demonstration might be in order, if Derbelderhed is in the vicinity."

The stocky man in periwinkle robes leaned out from behind the pile of machinery at the sound of his name and waved shyly to Hitch and Diligence.

"Be so good as to activate the first chamber," Pomponderant instructed his colleague. Diligence stepped through the copper overhang to watch as Derbelderhed's fingers played across a section of metal. Tiny lights came and went beneath his hands. She was reminded of the brightly sparking wall-plaque she had seen in the underground chamber of Old Hopshog Impery. Could there be a connection? she wondered to herself.

Then her wonder was all confined to the hall around her: light glimmered here and there about the enormous room in a rising flicker that soon swelled to a multi-hued brilliance, as one by one the hexagonal mirrors lost their cloudy sheen and filled with vibrant color and light. Images formed, moved, changed, vanished and were replaced by others. The travelers stood transfixed, dazzled by the mad dance of images.

"As you can see, without its human component the instrument is reduced to chaos." Pomponderant's pedantic tones penetrated the mesmerizing whirl. "Activation of the machine results in a series of random cycles which yield little if any useful information."

Diligence tore her eyes away from the flashing circle with an effort. "You mean no one is watching? No one is looking over the world?"

The old man shook his head gravely. "A blink, a whisper of color, a flash of meaning. Since the attack, all has been in confusion."

"Then our questions," Nury said tremulously, her eyes wide on the walls of light. "No one can answer our questions about the Wheel and its troubles: why the storms and why the quaking earth."

"On the contrary, you will find your answers here," Pomponderant reassured her. "When Amonwelle has the time—"

"No!" Diligence's voice rang through the great hall in a cascade of echoes. Nearby workers turned to stare. "Not when she has the time. Not when you see fit. Now. I want you to take us to my mother *now*."

The old tutor blinked mildly at his former pupil. "You may take yourself to her," he said. "For there she stands not five feet from your back."

Diligence whirled around.

Still dressed in her stained and rumpled work clothes, the smallish red-haired woman gazed up at them from one of the sparking panels. Her blue-green eyes regarded Diligence impersonally. "Hello, Madawyn," said Amonwelle of the Unseen Wall. "Perhaps it is time I spoke with you and your companions."

TWENTY

AMONWELLE

Hitch eyed the little woman in the work-stained uniform with open skepticism as she faced them across the empty couch. Glancing at Diligence, he marveled at the lack of emotion on the girl's face—though he noticed her skin had gone white as a talking board at the older woman's announcement.

"The problems being faced by your Wheel are being duplicated in isolated regions all over the world," Amonwelle told them without preamble. "Until a successor to the Dreamwright is found, we can only conjecture as to the current magnitude and exact location of the troublings, but we are quite certain as to their cause. The Shadowsmith is attempting to subvert the energies of the Wire to his own uses by establishing a new and separate link to its boundless power."

The Wire. Hitch had heard it mentioned before, in the refectory at Paddifraw's Repose.

Amonwelle scanned the blank faces before her with a sigh. "I see that I must add my own brief history lesson to the one that Pomponderant has already delivered," she said. She settled one knee against the edge of the green couch and wiped grease from her fingertips with a tattered rag. "Humans have been on this world for a long time—yet our earliest traditions tell us that we did not originate here, but were brought as a gift from somewhere else. The Elucidaries state that a vast flower lay floating in the darkness above the worlds at the beginning of Time, releasing small seeds that drifted far on a wind warmed by the stars themselves before they found their new homes." She gave a small smile. "I suspect a much more prosaic tale of colonization falls closer to the mark, but beauty deserves its place in memory. Suffice it to say that when I was born, the world was still ruled by the Guardians, powerful beings claiming descent from the ancient folk who had ferried humankind here, by whatever seed or vessel, from our distant home. The Wire connected us with that home, and leashed us to it, an intangible conduit of incredible power that both nourished and dominated us. During the time of my late youth a war was fought that shook the very roots of the world. At its conclusion, humanity found itself free for the first time to do as it would upon this world—still blessed with the ability to wield the Wire's vast energies, but no longer fettered by its chain of control and obedience to far-off masters.

"New guardians came into being among the rebels. As time flowed by, the power of the Wire allowed the Wielders to alter their minds and their bodies, to lengthen their life spans and bring forth children that were also gifted with marvelous abilities. Instrumentation was developed and put at their disposal that enabled them to harness ever more potent energies. We were idealistic in those days, dedicated to serving others with our power . . ." A shadow fell on the small woman's features as she paused in reflection of a bygone age. "With the passage of time," she continued, "some among the Wielders chose to marry themselves irrevocably to these instruments, becoming from that day forward part machine themselves and no longer fully human. One of these was called Dubiel, and it was ever his way to drink too freely from the Wire's well of might. Once drunk, his thirst was never slaked. And so it happened that not

long after his melding with the machines, he became cor-
rupted.

"In those days the forces of the Wire were available to
all of the Wielders, to be shared equally and employed to
the benefit of all humanity. Dubiel quickly grew dissatisfied
with the portion allotted him. In an attempt to draw more
power to his own being, he mounted a secret war against
the other Wielders, destroying fully half our number
through deceit and treachery before those of us who remained could unite against him and drive him back to his
foul hole in the utter South." Amonwelle's eyes smoldered
with cold fury. "He festered there," she went on after a moment, "wounded but alive, cowed but not beaten. Twice
more the Shadowsmith—as he was now called by the heart-
darkened men and women who were drawn to his service—
made war upon his former comrades, and each time he was
defeated, though at a heavy cost to both sides of the battle.
Ages passed in relative calm. The remaining Wielders grew
apart from one another, each concerned with private goals,
and humanity was left to prosper or wither as it would.
With access to the Wire forbidden him as judgment for his
many crimes, the Shadowsmith's energies began to dwin-
dle, until at last his sinister might had been reduced to the
stuff of children's tales.

"Then this past year fiery winds and heaving ground, as
well as other troubles of the air and earth, were reported—
not only at the Wheel, but scattered far across the land. The
Dreamwright watched and noted and slowly a pattern began
to emerge. Always when the earth trembled or the clouds
rained fire, it was near a place which in the ancient days
had been a repository for the great flow of power from the
Wire. Now in olden times each Guardian had a talisman, an
instrument through which the energies of the Wire were
channeled. But all such instruments were lost long ago, and
without them the building of a new connection has been all

but impossible. Still, the Dreamwright and I began to suspect—hoping always that we were misled by our own fears—that the Shadowsmith had gained some new source of weaponry and strength, and that he was once more striving to establish his own link with the Wire. The recent grievous attack upon the palace of the Dreamwright itself served to confirm our worst apprehensions. The workers you have seen since your arrival have been engaged for weeks in a feverish attempt to fortify the power of the Unseen Wall, in order to prevent the success of another such attack. Indeed, we seek to magnify the scope of the Wall's protective boundary so as to include the town filled with supplicants that wait at our doorstep, lest they be crushed by the blow that is aimed at us."

"And what is this new source of weapons and might?" muttered Welleck the wagoneer, drawn into the discussion in spite of himself.

"An ally," Amonwelle replied bitterly, "of most unexpected origin." She turned to lay her hand upon one of the twinkling panels that leaned in above the green couch. "Little more than a year ago, the Dreamwright recorded an event of unparalleled significance to the inhabitants of our world."

The great walls had continued to flash in a riot of color and mad images; now a grouping of half a dozen disks cleared abruptly, combining to present a dim view of a steamy, swamplike landscape through which dark figures prowled. As they watched, the dark lurkers came upon a pool of shadowed water, where they halted, gesticulating. A cone of dull black metal protruded upright from the steaming muck. It loomed huge in comparison to the human figures who stared up from the floor of the swamp, towering the height of a large hostelry, and its exterior was blazoned with unreadable crimson symbols. Attached to the front of the cone and suspended some twenty feet above the murky surface was a smaller structure, this one a black cylinder perhaps twice the height of a man.

Hitch's eyes and mind strained to make some sense of the odd design. A shelter of some sort, definitely—but to what purpose in those swampy depths? As he watched with the others, the lesser cylinder split evenly down its upward length, the two halves peeling slowly backward to reveal the crouching image of a humanlike figure silhouetted blackly against a blaze of licking flames. The figure stepped forward and gestured sharply with the black staff it clutched in its left hand. Abruptly the image faded from the disks and the wall swirled into madness again.

"The black and red object fell to earth not far from the lair of the Shadowsmith and was met by his agents," Amonwelle said. "That much we know, but little else. Since the events which you have just witnessed, the Dreamwright has remained blind to an ever-growing region of the south, with this swamp as its center."

"Fell to earth," Hitch echoed. "Fell from where?"

Amonwelle's ruddy countenance darkened. "From another sun, or so we must assume, one where human folk also strive—for the object was a vessel for traveling between the worlds, and its occupant wore a form not unlike that of a human being."

Hitch glanced at Welleck, standing close by his side. Both turned to inspect the silver-clad figure posed still as a statue by one of the flaring metal arches.

Amonwelle followed their gaze. "Pomponderant has told me of your hatchling and his golden egg. For some reason still unknown, his own arrival on our world was neither observed nor recorded by the Dreamwright. Though some connection between the two newcomers seems inevitable, we cannot yet say what it may entail. Assuming his unresponsive state is unfeigned, we have no means to judge whether the hatchling be friend or enemy to the thing that now allies its might to the dark goals of the Shadowsmith."

Hitch looked back at the hatchling once more, his expression broadly skeptical. "Anyone can see he's not the sort to promote an evil cause," he murmured to Welleck. "What breed of monster almost expires during his first few minutes on the world he plans to conquer—all because his flying egg falls into the lake and he doesn't know how to swim?"

"I have a question for you." Diligence had been standing off to one side during Amonwelle's impromptu lecture. Now she peered up along one curving leg of the sleek sculpture. "Why are the little lights only shining on the silver portion of the device?" Her voice was cool and flat. "By comparison, the three remaining sections appear lifeless."

"That is because they are," Pomponderant responded. He moved to Diligence's side and pointed upward. "The instrument is divided into four discrete parts—four chambers, if you will, like the human heart. The silver chamber is in use with the activation of the primary Dreamwright function—the retrieval of images anywhere in this world."

"And the others?"

Amonwelle made her way around the end of the empty couch. "This instrument is extremely old and extremely powerful. It is from the time of the original Guardians. The second chamber turns the wall-eyes into portals, similar to the mirror in the cavern of the green moths, but restricted to this planet. By employing this chamber, one may simply step through to whatever location is depicted in the image." She ran her hand along the machine's blue iron flank, moved on. "The third chamber, long unused, brings images of other worlds."

"The fourth?" Diligence breathed.

"The power to visit them, as the ancient Guardians did

freely, and as the insect scholar did eight hundred years ago through his hidden mirror."

"Does it still function?" Hitch asked. "Could you truly walk to other worlds from this room?"

"Once you could have, long ages ago," Amonwelle told him. "Now only the first chamber is operational. The third and fourth chambers were rendered inoperative by consensus of the Wielders shortly after the rebellion against the Guardians. As for the second chamber . . ." She walked out from beneath the twists and curves of metal to regard the distant ceiling. "The attack that devastated the crystal palace represents only the second occasion in two millennia that the enemy has successfully breached the protections of the Unseen Wall. The first time, Dubiel and his creatures actually gained entrance to this room for a brief time and attempted to comandeer the instrument for their own employment. Dubiel was defeated, but that victory was so narrow that it was decided to restrict the functioning of the machine to that of observation post in an attempt to prevent control of its more powerful attributes from ever falling into the hands of the Shadowsmith. Over the centuries the activating node for the second chamber was misplaced or stolen. Now, when its power might prove the deciding factor between our victory or utter defeat, we have reason to fear that the Shadowsmith may have obtained the node, and that he seeks to re-enter the Hall of the Dreamwright so that he may ultimately find the way to spread his black dominion to other worlds. And that is the chief reason why we work night and day to fortify our Wall against the next attack, which we know must come soon . . ."

Amonwelle terminated the consultation on that grim note, commending her guests to accompany Pomponderant to the central dining hall, where they would be served their evening meal. As the travelers filed out beneath the glides and buttresses of the gleaming device, she asked Diligence and Hitch to linger at her side.

"I would be pleased if you would both join me for dinner this evening in my private rooms," said the Protector of the Wall.

TWENTY-ONE

THE DREAMWRIGHT

To Hitch's surprise, the dinner itself was simple fare and plain: crusty loaves redolent of local spices, steamed vegetables submerged in sweetbrine, and oatcakes served with a choice of four lightly flavored broths. They dined in a modest, sparsely furnished apartment located not far from the Hall of the Dreamwright.

Diligence had said little to Amonwelle after the shock of their initial introduction. Now the girl sat with her eyes focused on her plate, while her mother and Hitch traded anecdotes concerning the mountainous region surrounding the Silent Falls, where Amonwelle claimed to have done much solitary hiking two or three centuries past.

At last Hitch's store of pleasantries ran dry. He made an elaborate show of helping himself to more nettle broth, while Diligence toyed with an oatcake and her mother sat brooding silently at the far wall.

Amonwelle had not changed her clothing for dinner. Diligence raised her eyes to the small woman in the rumpled green work suit. "You don't resemble your portrait very much," she observed.

"Portrait?" Amonwelle frowned.

"At the hostelry in town. The tavernmaster said it was from a time called the First Dispersal."

"Ah." The Defender of the North nodded in comprehension. She looked down at her ample midsection with a sardonic smile. "One easily forgets how many dinners may be consumed over the course of twenty centuries. But you're quite right—I shall need to order new armor forged if I'm to cut a proper figure in the coming conflict." Her expression grew serious again as she studied Diligence's face. "You have your father's coloring," she said. "But my eyes. It's good to see you outside the confines of the Dreamwright's wall-eye, Madawyn."

"I'm called Diligence," the girl said quickly. "I mean, that's my name on the Wheel." She paused, her pale cheeks coloring. "My child-name, at least. I'll have another one of my own choosing come next birthday."

Amonwelle gave a thoughtful nod. "Names are transient things at best. Niirphar also preferred the name given him by those who raised him, rather than the one that I bestowed upon him forty years ago at his birth."

"You named him?" Diligence looked puzzled.

"Yes. Niirphar was my son."

This time Diligence's face lost all color. "The Dreamwright was your son?" she said. "The Dreamwright was my brother?"

"Half brother," Amonwelle amended. "His father was a water farmer from the Samsad on the border of the Restless Lands to the far south and east—though he came to dwell here in the village in his later years, unwilling to be parted from his only child. Niirphar served us well as Dreamwright until the enemy cut him down."

"There's been a Dreamwright for a lot longer than forty years," Hitch put in quietly. "Was the one before Niirphar your son, as well?"

"My daughter, Manwen. She served for eighty-three years. Most of the Dreamwrights—all of them, in fact, within the last five hundred years—have been chosen from among my own children." Amonwelle fixed Diligence and Hitch with her piercing blue-green gaze. "The gift is rare, found in no more than two or three individuals in all the world in each generation. Closeness to the instrument breeds the talent, so it seems, though I myself have never shown its spark."

"The successor," Diligence said, her voice suffused with sudden awe. "Is that why you really summoned me here—to become the next Dreamwright?" She thought of the figure stretched out on the narrow couch at the center of the swirl of gleaming machinery, dreaming away his days in the great hall while the world poured in and out of his mind like a tide.

Amonwelle did not respond at once. Then she reached out her hand to touch her daughter's golden curls. "No," she said. "Your talents lie in other strivings. I wanted you here only to protect you from those who might try to strike at me through you." She raised her eyes. "It is in fact why Master Hitch was summoned."

"Hitch?" said Diligence.

"What?" cried Hitch. The mountain boy's face turned comical with surprise, his eyes goggling wide as a spit-frog's. "You can't be serious!" he sputtered. "I've no more skill at dreaming than my hatchling does at conversation. No one summoned me here!"

"Ah? And why then did you climb down out of your western mountains? Can you tell me what drove you away from Jogjaw Pass and out across the level world?"

"You're ringing right I can!" Hitch gave a fierce nod. "I wanted to see the world's things, I wanted to—to have an adventure . . ." As he spoke, he realized that he could not in all honesty recall the events leading up to his decision to depart the Falls—only that the decision itself had been both made and acted upon in great haste.

Amonwelle was watching him calmly. "And have you not had a dream stuck in your head that didn't seem to belong to you these past many weeks?" she asked.

Hitch formed the denial on his lips, then hesitated as the crash of wild waves rose in his memory and he felt again the glorious *rightness* in his approach to the figure that beckoned from the rocky shore.

"I see it storming in your eyes," Amonwelle told him. "The dream was of my son's devising, cast at his mother's behest. Two hundred years ago, I found two paths that would eventually converge and bring forth another with the precious gift, high in the reaches of the Silent Falls. When it seemed some months past that the Shadowsmith's foul plotting might soon touch us, even here behind our Unseen Wall, I instructed Niirphar to send you our summons. The dream has been pulling you northward through all your digressions ever since—until your arrival in the village, when it banished itself from your mind. Had it taken you much longer to reach the crystal palace, you would have found your way through those treacherous shoals and looked upon the face of she who beckoned you. My face."

Now it was Hitch's turn to stare pale-faced at his plate, while Diligence watched him wide-eyed from across the table.

TWENTY-TWO

OPENING DOORS

Several hours later, Diligence stood in the great Hall of the Dreamwright with Hitch and the hatchling. The mountain boy had come tapping at the sleep room set aside for her use, and asked her to accompany him to the vast chamber. "Amonwelle said I can wander around in here all I want," he told her as they made their way to the giant doors. He flashed a tremulous grin. "I guess I have a decision to make, don't I?"

Diligence tugged at the backsack strapped to his shoulders. "Why did you bring this along?" she asked. "Didn't you think it would be safe in your quarters?"

Hitch shrugged, the smile growing smaller and then vanishing altogether. "I thought I might need it, depending on what I decide."

Derbelderhed was in the hall with another worker, their heads bowed over a piece of oddly shaped ceramic material that looked as if it had been hastily bound with black cord to the silver segment on the Dreamwright device. "This is the image projector we came across in the Aulmad. It was the incorporation of this instrument into the Dreamwright device that enabled us to track you after you first utilized the dowchit," he told Hitch with his shy smile. He hesitated, then laid his hand on the mountain boy's arm. "Pandandoleet was my dear friend, and we spent many a happy moment together before her retirement to the little

233

cottage," he said earnestly. "The service you performed for her in the valley before her death must have been of great value for her to grant you the gift of the gray bird."

Hitch looked uncomfortable. "I only stayed with her at the end," he said haltingly. "I only held her hand."

Derbelderhed patted his shoulder and left the dais by way of the sliding ramp, which carried him to one of the lower exits spaced evenly around the hall's midsection.

Hitch and Diligence turned their attention to the Dreamwright device. He strolled around a flaring leg of blue iron, ran his fingers along a gleaming golden flank. He paused before the section Pomponderant had called the second chamber, the one that could transform the wall-eyes into doorways, and frowned. A raised area of metal in the shape of an elongated oval shone from the copper surface several feet above his head. Two vertical rows of small knobs protruded slightly from the plaque. They bore the appearance of polished gemstones, each a different color. One of the stones on the right was missing, a bare shallow socket left in its place.

"What is it?" Diligence stood by his side.

"I'm not sure. Wait a second . . ." He took his pack from his back and rummaged through it on the floor. "There it is." He extracted the bit of tissue paper and gingerly opened it around the black bead. He looked up at the smooth surface. "I wonder . . . If only I were taller." He walked to where the hatchling stood and propelled the other man to the base of the copper leg with his hands on the silver shoulders. "Forgive me for imposing, but—" He bent the hatchling over at the waist like a toy and crawled up onto his back, the silver man staring placidly at the floor while Hitch knelt precariously and extended his arm toward the empty socket.

Diligence watched nervously from the dais. "Hitch, are you sure you should be doing this?"

"No. But then, I'm not that sure of anything these days," he said with a grunt, leaning forward and fitting the stone into the hollow. A low hum filled the air and light began to flash along the bottommost row of disks girdling the floor of the hall.

The worker who had been assisting Derbelderhed dropped a handful of tools and ran over, a horrified look on her dark face. "What have you done?"

Hitch hopped from the hatchling's back with a grimace. "I'm not sure, but I think I've fixed the second chamber."

"Pomponderant must be informed!" The worker watched the play of lights where hazy images had begun to coalesce. "The Lady must be told."

"No, no, no," said an oddly familiar voice from the shadows behind the gleaming instrument. "I think not." Nury the Hubwoman stepped into the light, a peculiar looking device of red porcelain and black metal clasped awkwardly in her gloved fingers. Diligence laid her hand on Hitch's arm. They stepped back warily, leaving the hatchling bent over like a discarded stepstool beneath the restored stone.

Nury came forward and slowly mounted the dais. A great scabbard hung from her waist; it swung ponderously, scraping the marble with each step. As she approached, Diligence saw something strange happen to her face: shadows seemed to flit across her features, though she stood fully in the light. And with each passing shade, her visage changed. Two different faces shared the pinched features, each melting into the next as the false shadows waxed and waned.

The transformed Hubwoman had her eyes on the copper plaque. To one side, the worker reached behind her and came back with a heavy stanchion. She lifted it and took a step toward the woman in gray.

The Nury-thing whirled and fired the odd weapon.

Something black and viscous jabbed in a narrow line from the nose of the weapon. Black splattered on the front of the worker's blue uniform and instantly began to spread, enveloping the woman in a matter of seconds. Gurgling cries came from within the dark cocoon as she struggled madly. Then the shiny black coating began to contract. Diligence looked away as the woman's shape shrank and folded to half its original size to the accompaniment of liquid noises and the muffled crunch of bone.

Hitch and Diligence had started to edge for one of the mesh ramps. The Nury-thing pointed its weapon at them. "Lie down on the floor," commanded a voice which was also two voices, blended together with a rough, throbbing dissonance.

As they obeyed, Diligence noticed the hatchling aping Hitch's movements by clambering down onto the floor across the dais.

Then the Nury-thing began to speak to no one, its face flickering back and forth between the two distorted versions. Diligence watched as the thing paced, muttering, weapon still trained on herself and Hitch. Its restless prowling took it perilously close to the recumbent hatchling, who stared blank-eyed across the room at his model.

The thing was reaching some sort of consensus, the dual faces smiling in grotesque agreement, the two voices concurring. As the gray figure neared the hatchling, Hitch slid his left leg abruptly to one side. The motion caught the attention of the possessed Hubwoman a split-second before the hatchling's leg swept under its own, toppling it forward and sending the black and red weapon flying out of its hand.

"Run for it!" Hitch leaped to his feet and raced past the flashing portals for a ground-level doorway located between two of the disks. Diligence saw the hatchling jump up and imitate his flight, several paces behind him. She joined the group, jerking her head around as a yowl like that of an enraged prowlcat came from behind. The Nury-thing was down on all fours, scrambling for the gun. Diligence reversed direction, swerving behind the golden leg of the Dreamwright device. She calculated. Hitch was a few steps from the small door: he would just make it.

The hatchling would not.

Diligence ducked to reach over the edge of the dais, her fingers closing around the truncheon dropped by the felled worker. "Look out!" She hurled it through the air just as the Nury-thing fired the shadow-stream at the hatchling's back.

Everything seemed to be happening slowly.

Hitch halted, twisted around, and lunged at the silver man, at the same time flicking his small fingerblade at the distorted figure in gray.

Diligence watched as Hitch slammed into the hatchling full force, his momentum carrying them both toward the nearest of the swiftly changing portals. The black beam hit the far wall and splashed harmlessly onto the floor.

The truncheon struck the creature in the shin, causing it to fall forward, just as the fingerblade pierced the mutable cheek. A second bestial howl echoed through the hall.

One of the lower doors slid open and Amonwelle stepped into the room at the head of a battalion of armed green and blue workers. A nimbus of golden-green light came into the room with her.

Diligence realized with a sickening certainty that there was no way for Hitch to stop his forward motion before he and the silver man fell into the wall-eye directly in front of them. She tried desperately to focus on the glimpse of wildly changing landscapes. Then they plunged through the open door.

The creature that had been Nury dropped its black and red device and struggled to pull the golden sword from the scabbard at its side. With unexpected strength, the thin woman-thing hefted the blade high above its head and raced snarling toward Amonwelle.

"Dubiel!" thundered the red-haired woman at the door, her voice somehow magnified a hundredfold in the huge hall. She raised her arms and waves of golden-green radiance pulsed through the space between the two with a noise like a vast whirlwind. The Nury-thing reeled as if struck as the golden tide washed over it, dropped to the marble floor and lay convulsing.

Amonwelle strode across the hall, a trick of the light making the small woman seem like a towering figure. She wrenched the sword from the clawed fingers, a look of contempt on her shimmering face. "You are not fit to touch his blade," she snarled. She stood watching as the shadow-faces flickered and died until only Nury's pinched features remained. Then she continued on to where Diligence crouched at the edge of the dais, the green-golden nimbus gradually shrinking around her until she was a short, round-faced woman again. "Are you all right, Daughter?"

"Hitch—" Diligence pointed at the whirling chaos of the portals. "He went through!"

Hours later, the two sat facing one another at the table in Amonwelle's small apartment. The older woman was using a soft rag to polish the blade called Manscythe.

"The Shadowsmith had darkened the heart of the Hubwoman early on in your journey—most likely the night your guards were frozen. He and his ally found a willing subject upon whom to work their horror. Before Nury died she admitted to using this blade to slay the scrivener boy when he had the audacity to be lying in Master Hitch's bed." Amonwelle frowned down at the golden sword. "It will take much cleansing before Manscythe can be returned to battle."

"The battle will come soon?" asked Diligence.

Amonwelle looked weary. "Too soon—they always do. I have sent out a summons to those Wielders who remain to gather here at the Unseen Wall. But the Shadowsmith grows bolder. I do not know if he will give us time to hold our council before his next attack."

There was a soft rap at the door. Pomponderant entered, his fingers tugging at his chin braid. "We are attempting to trace the destination of the portal utilized by the mountain boy and the hatchling, but it is a lengthy and tedious task at best, an impossible one at worst." The old man poured himself a cup of peppery tea and came to join them at the table.

"I know you can find him," Diligence said fervently to her former tutor. She turned to her mother. "Hitch will come through this, wherever he is. He has his wits and the contents of his pack." She paused, struck by a sudden thought. "He even has the jewel-headed walking stick— though whether that's a good thing or a bad thing . . ."

Amonwelle regarded her daughter with a strange expression. "A walking stick, you say? With a jewel on its head?" She leaned forward. "Tell me of this thing."

Diligence related as much as she could recall of the walking stick and its unusual history. In the end Amonwelle sat back with a weighty sigh, her hands still gripping the golden sword.

"What is it?" Diligence asked. "We meant to give it to you. Is it something important?"

"I believe that what you have described is the Staff of Blue Light, one of a handful of instruments originally used by the Guardians to call down the power of the Wire. With that in his possession, the Shadowsmith could establish his own link to such might as would swiftly bring this world beneath his heel." She turned to Pomponderant. "I share my daughter's faith in you, scholar. Find the boy, and find him before the Shadowsmith does."

The old man drained his tea and got to his feet. "At once, Lady," he said, and left the room.

"Madawyn—Diligence." Amonwelle had set aside the sword and folded her hands on the table before her. "Bad times are coming. I cannot ask you to join me in my battle preparations, though it would please me mightily if you would do so. You are freed of any obligation to remain here with me. If you wish, you may return to your Wheel with an escort of my servants and my best promise of safe passage." She raised her hands in a gesture of finality. "Do as you wish, my daughter. You are my last child, born not as a weapon or a tool, but out of love. The choice is yours to make."

Return to the Wheel . . . Diligence considered the slow, steady turn of the year, the comfort of knowing exactly where the road would lead, from tomorrow to the next day to the end of your life. On the Wheel the Shadowsmith was a tale for children. On the Wheel there were no wormholes, no frozen soldiers, no heart-darkened monsters grasping for dominion. On the wheel there was no Hitch.

"What part do you have for me in these battle preparations?" she asked her mother. "And when do we begin?"

TWENTY-THREE

A NEW ROAD

Hitch came to his senses in the midst of a dark forest. At first he thought it was nighttime, but as he lay on his back and stared up into the darkness he was able to make out small slivers of late afternoon sunlight through the tightly knit lattice of treetops.

He lifted his head slightly and groaned as pain shot through his neck and shoulders. He pushed himself up on his elbows, his eyes adjusting slowly to the darkness. He lay on uneven terrain in a pile of damp leaves at the base of a great humped boulder. Looking at the heavy curve of rock above him, he understood the source of his current crop of aches. When he had stumbled through the portal, he must have come out on top of the boulder, lost his balance immediately on the damp stone and tumbled down into oblivion. He felt gingerly at the base of his skull where an especially strong pain twinged and throbbed.

He surveyed the nearby landscape. A glimmering figure lay facedown several yards to the left. The hatchling did not seem to be moving, but Hitch had enough experience in the silver man's survival skills not to panic at the sight of his apparently lifeless body.

His arms were getting tired from holding him up. He pulled himself up into a sitting position, folding his legs beneath him, and examined the immediate area. Tall, thick-boled trees thrust up in a crowded, inward-leaning maze, their tops tightly twined in a dark vault high above the small opening surrounding the boulder. He saw a ghost of motion near the base of one of the trunks and squinted, turning his head from side to side till he made out the form of a pale blue lizard half the length of his index finger. As Hitch watched, it scurried several feet up the trunk and lifted its diminutive head. A melodic trill filled the dusky gloom.

The Aulmad, Hitch thought with a chill along his backbone. I'm in the Aulmad. He took a deep breath. At least there are no green moths. At least I'm still on the right world.

A dry rustling sound came from somewhere off in the middle distance. The lizard broke off its song abruptly. There was a pale flash and a hovering blue light hung in its place in the air near the rough-barked trunk. It shot off silently through the trees in the direction opposite the rustling noise. Hitch felt a prickling at the nape of his neck.

He got shakily to his feet, shuffled through the leaves to the side of the silver man, and rolled him gently over onto his back. The hatchling's eyes were open, his stare in the dimness so still and empty that Hitch felt his heart catch for a second. He sighed in relief when the odd-colored eyes blinked.

The rustling noise came again, somewhat nearer.

Moving as quietly as he could, Hitch slid his arms under the hatchling's torso and levered him into a sitting position. "Come on," he grunted softly. "We have to get out of here." He raised his head and surveyed the gloom. "Though how far 'here' extends and what we'll find beyond it is an utter mystery," he added.

They began to walk, slipping sometimes sideways in order to fit between the closely packed trees.

After what felt like hours of slowly snaking their way

through the woody labyrinth, they found themselves abruptly at its end. True night had come while they walked: a
meadow sparkling with silver flowers glistened under the
light of the just-rising moon.

The scene before them was completely still and silent.
They stepped out into the field. When they were halfway
across the meadow, Hitch felt a crawling sensation between
his shoulder blades. Looking back, he spied a glimpse of
bright golden hair at the edge of the forest. He stopped in
his tracks, heart tolling in his chest, as a wailing song filled
with grief and desire floated out over the meadow. The
hatchling stirred restlessly at his side, his garment aglint
with its own silver in the spreading light.

Then a shaft of moonlight topped the trees and fell on
the golden-haired creature. Hitch choked at the sight, his
stomach clenching to an icy ball. He stumbled backward,
turned in the damp grass, and began to run blindly across
the field.

Twenty paces later the ground fell out from under him.
Wormholes!

Wormholes everywhere! he thought dazedly before he
landed on the hard rocky floor with bone-jarring impact.
The hatchling's head appeared at the top of the pit. After a
second's hesitation, the silver man hurled himself into the
pit directly over Hitch, who rolled out of the way just before the silver boots came down on his head.

"You stupid, *stupid* . . ." Hitch caught his breath as the
wisp of eerie song floated above the pit. Shimmering blond
locks appeared at the round rim, unspeakable eyes staring
downward. He shrank back against the side of the pit.

He looked around. The roughly circular shaft descended
steep-sided straight into the ground. Its walls were smooth,
unbroken stone rising to the surface some forty feet above.
Hitch sighed. No gray birds inhabited this area of the
Aulmad. Assuming Pomponderant could be persuaded to

look for them with his jury-rigged eye device, it might take centuries for the old scholar to locate them in this dark hole in the ground.

Time passed. The Noose Woman appeared periodically to scrabble claws at the pit's edge and croon down at them, Hitch turning his face away in disgust until the effort became too much. The moon rose slowly to hang like a pale eye, watching with disinterest beyond the hunched shape at the lip of the pit.

Time began to lose meaning for him. Morning came, and then a long empty day followed by another night. When the moon rose the golden-haired creature appeared again. Hitch drifted off to sleep under her gaze. He awoke when something silken brushed against his face, and found himself staring upward at a curling braid of sticky strands. He made a strangling noise in his throat and scooted away from the stuff, pushing back up against the wall several feet around the circumference of the pit. The Noose Woman made a sound like sighing and slowly withdrew the silken threads.

Hitch looked at the hatchling, who had deserted his own spot at the same time as the mountain boy, scuttling around to come to rest once again directly opposite him across the pit. He rubbed his nose and the silver man's arm lifted automatically to duplicate the gesture. Hitch gave a laugh that was part groan.

"Don't you ever get tired of this game?" he murmured, watching as the hatchling's lips writhed in soundless imitation. Hitch shook his head and combed his fingers through his hair, searching for any residue of sticky strands. The hatchling rubbed his gloved hand over his short dark pate.

His hair has never grown, Hitch mused to himself. He doesn't eat, he doesn't drink—except when we trick him into it. He just lies in the sun and lives . . . He yawned, his exhaustion making him feel vaguely amused as the silver man opened his own mouth.

"Remember those times when you talked to me?" Hitch asked sleepily. "First on the beach and then in the wagon?" Closing his eyes, he recalled the rapid-fire voice gabbling about retrieval and revolutions, saw the hands— not silver back then, but a soft leaf green—flickering across the front of the hatchling's suit. He raised his own hand and idly retraced the motions: throat, navel, right shoulder. He frowned. The hatchling had used his right hand, not his left, with the first two fingers pressing stiffly into a small circular area at each location. He tried again, allowing his eyes to drift open as he touched his fingertips to throat, then navel, then left shoulder. Across the pit, the hatchling's silver hand rose from his lap and embarked on the same journey.

Hitch leaned back, feeling a wave of hopelessness. He squeezed his eyes shut as tears stung at their corners.

"That's better," said an oddly accented voice in clear human speech.

Hitch blinked his eyes open.

The hatchling was leaning forward from the wall of the pit, stretching his arms high above his head like a person who has been sitting motionless for a very long time. His suit seemed to be glowing, a clear golden color washing over it in soft waves to replace the tarnished silver. Hitch blinked again. A more important change had occurred in the pale face. It had come to life, he realized, as the hatchling smiled broadly at him. He felt the frown of disbelief on his own lips with trembling fingertips.

"Yes, much better," the hatchling affirmed. "I have to say you took your time about it, but it was probably all for the best."

"My time?" Hitch pressed his back against the smooth

wall behind him, feeling like an insect pinned by the gaze of this new person.

"Allowing me to integrate my memory with the Reference and regain full participatory consciousness. Waking me up." The hatchling's gaze wandered around the pit in leisurely inspection. "The chronometer of the instrument suit suggests that I was actually quite caught up some weeks ago—though I'm sure a little extra recovery time never hurts." He stretched to his feet and moved across the pit, his gait lithe and springy, completely unlike his previous leaden shuffle. He extended a golden hand to Hitch. "This is customary here, correct? To touch the flesh at greeting. Oh—" He looked down at his hand and twitched his golden fingers. Abruptly the smooth, shiny garment melted back to the wrist on both arms. "That's better. I am Jassad Attqua, of Lune, a member of the Arc."

Hitch stared up at the strangely altered face. Finally he took the pale hand and held it limply. "Uh, Hitch," he said haltingly. "My name is Hitch, from Jogjaw Pass at the Silent—"

"I know who *you* are, Savior of Drowning Men, Seeker after Truth, and Staunch Protector of Endangered Comrades and Friends," the hatchling said with a good-humored laugh. "We've been traveling companions for months now." He shook Hitch's hand vigorously and laughed again. "A pleasure to finally make your acquaintance. And now we really should make our return to my ship as soon as possible."

"Ship?" Hitch repeated. "You mean the egg? Did it really fall from the stars, as Pomponderant said?"

"Indeed it did, though it isn't actually an egg at all, no matter how apt the analogy." He rubbed his bare hands together briskly. "And we do need to get to it quickly, if I'm to accomplish what I was sent here to do."

"But we have to find our way back to the Unseen Wall,"

Hitch said slowly. It was hard to think beyond the reality of himself alone in the pit. "I need to make sure Diligence and Amonwelle dealt with Nury, and let them know I'm all right. And I have a decision to make about becoming the next Dreamwright. Then there's the Shadowsmith: he's getting ready for another attack on the Wall, and I think he's trying to take over the whole world, so *he* has to be seen to, as well." His eyes fought to stay open. Talking was making him drowsy.

"A bargain, then," said the hatchling. "First to my ship and then back to your crystal palace."

"Fine. But how?" The mountain boy gestured helplessly to the near-vertical walls and the high rim of the pit where something horrible waited in its shimmer of pale hair. He felt for a moment like a child near tears. "How can we do any of it when we're going to die down here?"

The hatchling surveyed their surroundings for a long moment, lips pursed in a thoughtful expression. He tilted his head back and stared at the moonlit sky with its hunched silhouette. Lifting his right hand toward the rim of the pit, he made an odd drumming motion with his fingers and thumb. A beam of blinding white light shot out from his hand. There was a quick sizzling noise, followed by a shriek of dismay from the top of the shaft. When the bright afterimage had faded from Hitch's eyes, he looked up to see an empty circle of dark night and moonlight.

Jassad Attqua made a fist with his left hand. The reflective surface of the golden suit swirled with translucent layers of rainbow color as he rose two feet directly into the air and hung there like a bright fish in a pond. He gave a matter-of-fact nod and drifted back to earth.

Hitch had pushed to his feet. He stood trembling with wonderment as the hatchling took a step toward him and extended his hand to the mountain boy.

"I think getting out of this unpleasant place would be a good beginning to our new road," the golden man said with a cheerful smile. "Don't you?"

Hitch held out his hand.

The entire world of Might and Magic is at your fingertips. *Don't just read the adventure . . . EXPERIENCE IT!*

Look for these Might and Magic computer games at your local software retailer.

Heroes of Might and Magic
Conquer the Worlds of Might and Magic!
The realms of Might and Magic are expanding. New lands have been discovered and you must rise to the challenge of conquering them. Beware, for three warlords have risen to test your leadership and tactics. You must carefully manage all the resources at your disposal or you will surely be defeated. Now is the time to recruit your heroes, garrison your armies, and lead them to **victory**.

• Exquisite SVGA graphics • Multiple worlds to explore and conquer • Customized computer opponents • Variable skill levels • Unlimited replay • Over two dozen different monster types

Available for IBM & 100% compatible computers, with CD-ROM drives

Might and Magic: World of Xeen
Experience the latest multimedia technology on CD-ROM with Might and Magic: World of Xeen. Jam-packed with adventure, World of Xeen contains 3-D animation, 256-color VGA graphics, 2 introduction sequences, three end games, and much more. World of Xeen contains digitized speech for over 200 characters, plus musical scores and sound effects. The easy-to-use interface allows users to enjoy this imaginative interactive experience without spending hours learning complicated game mechanics.

• Over two hours of digitized speech • Plug & Play directly from CD-ROM drive • Top-notch game design and storyline • Hundreds of challenging quests and puzzles

Available for IBM & 100% compatible computers, and Macintosh computers, with CD-ROM drives

NEW WORLD COMPUTING, INC.®
ENTERTAINMENT SOFTWARE

DEL REY ONLINE!

The Del Rey Internet Newsletter...
A monthly electronic publication, posted on the Internet, GEnie, CompuServe, BIX, various BBSs, and the Panix gopher (gopher.panix.com). It features hype-free descriptions of books that are new in the stores, a list of our upcoming books, special announcements, a signing/reading/convention-attendance schedule for Del Rey authors, "In Depth" essays in which professionals in the field (authors, artists, designers, sales people, etc.) talk about their jobs in science fiction, a question-and-answer section, behind-the-scenes looks at sf publishing, and more!

Online editorial presence: Many of the Del Rey editors are online, on the Internet, GEnie, CompuServe, America Online, and Delphi. There is a Del Rey topic on GEnie and a Del Rey folder on America Online.

Our official e-mail address for Del Rey Books is delrey@randomhouse.com

Internet information source!
A lot of Del Rey material is available to the Internet on a gopher server: all back issues and the current issue of the Del Rey Internet Newsletter, a description of the DRIN and summaries of all the issues' contents, sample chapters of upcoming or current books (readable or downloadable for free), submission requirements, mail-order information, and much more. We will be adding more items of all sorts (mostly new DRINs and sample chapters) regularly. The address of the gopher is gopher.panix.com

Why? We at Del Rey realize that the networks are the medium of the future. That's where you'll find us promoting our books, socializing with others in the sf field, and—most importantly—making contact and sharing information with sf readers.

For more information, e-mail ekh@panix.com